# RAHNUK

*The nations have sunk in the pit which they made;*
*In the net which they hid has their own foot been*
*caught.*

**Psalm 9:15**

i

*ISBN:* 978-0-473-18378-3

# RAHNUK

Stephen Sparrow

## PREFACE

Discontent is the goad for every attempt to construct perfect societies and history is littered with their failures, but the human race is nothing if not optimistic, and following each failure, another batch of social architects waits their opportunity to again have "the house swept and put in order." Utopian dreamers designing nightmares.

Having lived through two world wars, English writer and poet Osbert Sitwell was well qualified to help us peer into the future. Writing in 1948 he used the supremely apt analogy of a chasm, to illustrate the rupture, the place, where one civilization (this one) ends and another emerges. What a future civilization looking back across the chasm would make of us, Sitwell asked. He thought it a good thing that we should never know since, "it is unlikely that we either should see much that would please us or hear much good of ourselves." He also wrote of staring out of the window and "trying to conjure up the metropolises of the future when men have again crept out of the ground into which they will have been forced."

Well, the suicidal Twentieth Century is behind us now but its legacy lingers still, and as for the Twenty First, only time will tell what its epithet or its epitaph will be; but, given the frightening rise in our time of a me first mentality wedded to total reliance on science to conquer every crisis; I doubt many of our descendants will be around to witness the end of it.

v

Rahnuk may be a horror story, but none the less it is a story in which I trust the reader will clearly discern Hope. But it is more than just a story; Rahnuk is a chronicle of events involving some companions I have known for many years. I have walked or ridden often with the people of Riparia; tailing shadows all, prodding me onward whenever I've paused to weigh up which path to take. We've laughed together and argued, worked and taken meals together, escaped danger and at other times stood our ground and fought side by side against enemies both seen and unseen. I know their hearts and they know mine, and the more time I have spent in their company the more I have come to love them; a love I hope I am able to share.

©*Stephen Sparrow*

*Aotearoa - New Zealand.*

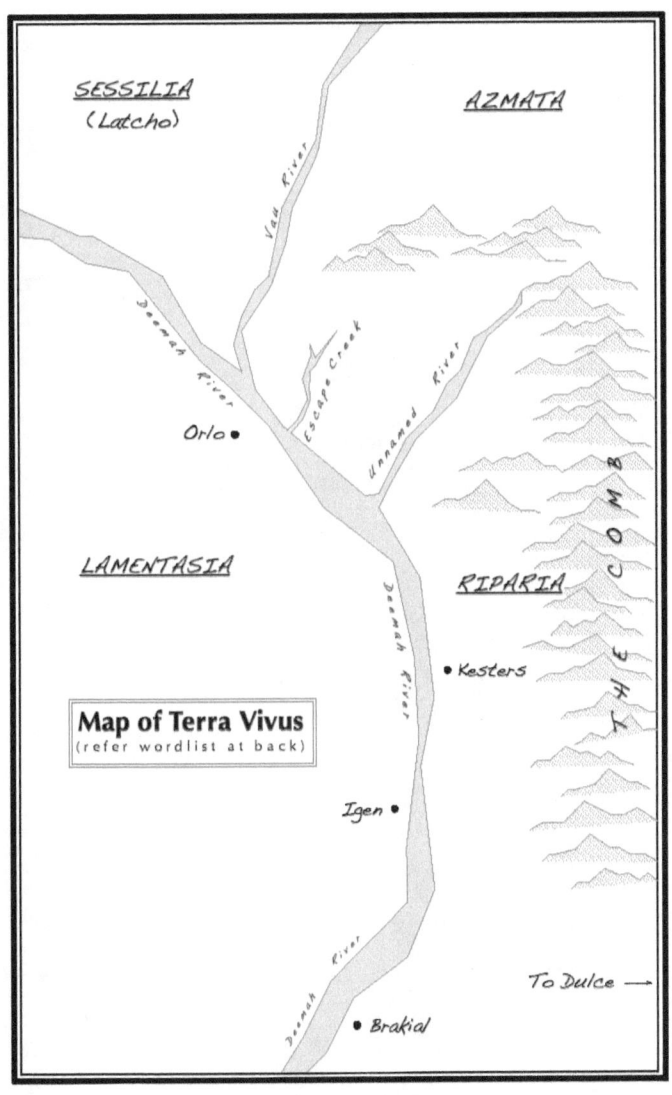

SESSILIA
(Latcho)

AZMATA

Vau River

Escape Creek

Doonah River

Unnamed River

Orlo •

LAMENTASIA

RIPARIA

THE COMB

**Map of Terra Vivus**
(refer wordlist at back)

Doonah River

• Kesters

Igen •

Doonah River

To Dulce →

• Brakial

Word & character list at back of book.

# PART I

## 1.

Malcolm stood near the table and waited. With a kindling stick gripped in his right hand he looked toward the far end of the room, his narrowed eyes following some slow flying thing that made an irritating noise. Unless they were hanging about food blowflies seldom bothered Malcolm, but this one arrived just after the meal table was cleared and its buzzing, bumbling inspection soon got on his nerves. Finally, as it flew within reach; he raised the stick and lunged but missed and the loathsome insect now raced around the room making more noise than ever, and Malcolm, with a furious look on his face tried to follow, lunging at it again and again until with a sudden swerve the terrified creature made its escape through the open door. Pelto, who was seated at the table grinned and said he also hated them, especially inside. The third man present remained silent. Malcolm looked around to make sure it was really gone before dropping the stick on the floor behind his chair, then wiping his hands on the seat of his pants he sat down again at the table.

The early evening sun now began to flare through the three dusty windows filling the room with a soft golden light and where it slanted in under the porch roof through the open doorway, it made a long tapering patch of warmth on the dark hard packed earthen floor. From a nearby sycamore an eager chorus of cicadas chirped and clicked to a pleasant oscillating rhythm and from further away in the distance the faint yells of children playing ball tag could be heard. A sudden clatter of dishes came from behind the heavy drape that screened off the kitchen. Malcolm half turned in his chair and called that he would take care of the cleaning up but a woman's voice answered telling him not to worry, she had time to finish the job. The woman was there to prepare the evening meal and all four had eaten together. The meal was quiet with Pelto the only one making any real effort to keep conversation going and now that it was over and the maddening blowfly gone, they continued sitting, minds seemingly absent, just staring and silent.

In the centre of the table stood a jar of mead together with a plate of figs, a small basket of bread pieces and a wood block with half a dozen unlit candles of varying lengths stuck to it. The men waited saying nothing while the clatter from the kitchen briefly continued. After a pause the grey gowned woman carrying a large basket under one arm, breezed through the room smiling and trilling a farewell. Pelto looked up and called out a thank-you just as she reached the doorway and the sound of her footsteps on the path outside swiftly faded. In the brief silence that followed Pelto began drumming two fingers on the oak tabletop before catching Malcolm's eye and smiling at him. Malcolm looked back at Pelto and then quickly away, his gaze roaming the underside of the roof. Pelto shrugged and mumbled something about the woman being a good cook which Malcolm missed hearing because the other man present noisily scraped his stool back from the table. Malcolm gulped a couple of times and opened his mouth wide in a sort of silent rehearsal before asking Pelto to repeat what he said. It seemed as if he needed to swallow some large invisible thing before the words would come and he often stammered, especially when talking with people he didn't know well. Malcolm was born with a small hole in the roof of his mouth.

"I said she's a good cook." He paused and added;" Don't you think so?"

"Ye- es, sh she, hi izz."

Pelto turned to the young man seated on his left. "Well Leo, that was well cooked food, wasn't it?"

The young man smiled and nodded in agreement while Pelto continued.

"And how long has Stella been widowed?"

Malcolm staring into his lap appeared not to hear. Pelto asked again, this time louder.

"How long has her husband been dead?"

"Sorry Pelto, sorry. What was that? Oh yes, Two years. Joggo's been dead two years."

"And her children, how old are they? Do any still live with her?"

"Oh no no. The youngest Sonya is twenty. She already has two children of her own."

3

"Well now, I wouldn't have thought that. Stella's a fine looking woman. Doesn't look old enough to be a grandmother though." Pelto paused before going on. "Anyway, enough of that. I mustn't prattle. Haven't time, have we? We've other fish to grill, eh Malcolm? What about it eh? We make a start; now?" His voice swept upwards with each question.

Malcolm looked down at the mug cradled in his hands. He drew a long shuddering breath before answering and this time his words seemed to echo in his ears, and his face and bald head reddened as he struggled to speak.

"Yes P-el-toh yes. It's time I sup-ho-hose."

Looking up again he kicked back his chair, half rose to his feet and reached for the mead jar to top up the mugs, but Pelto placed his hand over his and shook his head, and Malcolm, forgetting that he intended to fill his own and Leo's, banged the jar back on the table and sat down once more. With Stella present Malcolm felt protected from Pelto, but now she was gone and there was no escape and Malcolm's heart began to hammer and his gaze to flick quickly around the room. He glanced first at the wood stacked neatly on the right of the open fireplace. From there he looked up to the chimney breast bearing the wood cross with its white painted clay Christ. The dirt streaked squares of glass were next to catch his eye – not for a moment would Rahnuk have put up with dirty windows. He looked again at the tabletop. The table was at the furthest end of

4

the room from the fireplace and as well as the candle block, the mead jar and the finger food in the middle there was a folder of coarse paper lying beside Pelto's elbow.

Malcolm swept his gaze past Pelto to look at Leo. The boy looked back at his father before rising from his stool and moving to sit on the padded bench against the wall. Leo was a stocky young man with a head of dark straight hair. He had turned eighteen only the week before. Each time Malcolm found himself looking at the boy, Rahnuk's dark eyes stared back from the youthful angular face. Malcolm lifted his mug to his lips, drained it and looked back up into the rafters. The roof was more comfortable to look at any day rather than looking at Pelto. He shut his eyes but still saw nothing but that big moon face staring back at him and his head rang with all sorts of imagined questions. But, why couldn't they just leave him alone? Why do they need to know these things anyway? Why should he have to put up with having this old man around the place? Him with his tongue clicking sympathy and sober head nodding; trying to dig around, to find out things. And they don't give up easily either. Nothing was going to stand in the way of old Pelto finding it out and getting it down; the whole lot. He'd want to know every detail. It would go in the Codex so in years to come people in Dulce will be able to read it. He thought of the tutors and their students, wading through it all and asking even more questions. Well, by then they would have to provide their own answers.

Eight weeks earlier Pelto had waited ten days hoping to question him, but Malcolm found plenty to occupy himself with. There was always something to be done and he would often disappear up to one of the horse paddocks to mend or strengthen fences, make sure the troughs had water or check the horse's hooves for worn or missing shoes. Then of course there was the work that took him out of Brakial. So, was it his fault that this meant riding out before sun-up and coming home late – very late? And still Pelto persisted in leaving messages with Leo; him, demanding a meeting. Who did he think he was? At least twice he arrived at sunset, and sat at the table reading and writing long into the night – wasting good candles in Leo's opinion who took himself off to bed much earlier. Funny, those were the only nights Malcolm decided to camp on the job so as to get an early start the next day – and the rest of the time? Well, wasn't he always tired when he got home? But not too tired to go visiting, and over the last two months, he and Leo were frequent mealtime guests at the blacksmith's house.

Lon was a friend of nearly twenty years standing and while Pelto was around, if anyone came knocking and asking for Malcolm, he would bellow through the closed door, that he didn't know where he was, although once Pelto even showed up there and insisted on being admitted. Malcolm was forced to hide behind one of the bed screens, continually pressing the back of a hand to his nose to hold back a sneeze. For a long time afterward when reliving the episode, Lon would fall about laughing; especially considering that for the whole time, his wife was unable to meet the old man's eyes and the blacksmith ordered his youngest daughter to bed for fear she would accidentally let it be known that Malcolm was present. As a result, Pelto filled in his days wandering the lanes of Brakial, playing ball games with children or telling stories.

Malcolm heaved a sigh of relief when he heard Pelto had given up and headed home on the three-day journey to Dulce. He hoped it would be the end of the matter. That there would be no having to sit down and put up with the nosey old Recorder. But then only this morning, and a Sunday morning at that, cunning Pelto again showed up and before realizing it Malcolm found himself trapped inside the church. As he later filed out with the rest of the people, the old man waited outside to confront him and with barely concealed irritation accused Malcolm of avoiding him. Malcolm's face reddened and he looked at the ground about his feet saying nothing but nodding in agreement to Pelto's demand that he submit to being questioned about Rahnuk and the ugly business with Sessilia. Pelto said he would come to the house that evening and if necessary for the rest of the week in order to get the facts written into the record and that the frustration he had so far endured was a gross waste of his time. Now seated around the table both men started speaking together but Pelto stopped as Malcolm struggled with his words.

"H'yime so-so-orry P-pip-elto, I'm sorry." He paused to rub his eyes and began again. "I didn't want this to drag on." His voice trailed off and he looked away eyes misted and vision blurred. "It hurts each time I think about it." He swallowed again and kept wiping his eyes. "We were ha-ha-happy you know."

Pelto nodded and smiled.

"Some folk thought otherwise." Malcolm paused and looked away before again speaking.

"You know how Rahnuk arrived don't you?" He paused again.

Pelto nodded and Malcolm continued.

"Well, that's where it all began. But you already know all that, don't you?

"I know some things, a few things. But there are gaps, many gaps." Pelto smiled and kept on nodding.

"Noh-ohmm-body had any idea; we knew in-in—othing about Sessilia until Rahnuk ki-ame."

"Take your time Malcolm. No need for haste. I know it's not easy. I need only a rough outline. What's happened in the last two years is all I want. But start at the beginning if you like, if you think, I mean, you know, if you think it can help."

Pelto's gravelly voice softened. The Recorder's broad flabby face was set with startlingly blue eyes from the corners of which spread deeply etched crow's

feet. His grey swept back hair ended in a neat pigtail.
He reached down sideways and with a grunt lifted a
heavy leather pouch onto the table and from it drew a
bundle of quills and a clay ink-pot. These he set in front
of him beside the folder of paper. Breathing heavily he
dropped the pouch back down again. After unstopping
the ink-pot he began sorting through the quills, testing
their sharpened ends with one finger all the while
humming and muttering in a singsong voice.

"Time, time, time. It's all on my side."

Having finished sorting the quills, he fumbled in the
pocket of his cape draped over the chair back and drew
from it a little cloth bag that held his precious glass
magnifiers and this he now placed beside the quills.
Pelto remained as in a reverie gazing at the tabled items,
still humming softly before abruptly ceasing and asking.

"Tell me, tell me Malcolm. How are things in
Sessilia now? Have you heard anything? Anything
new?"

"You must know as much as I do." Said Malcolm.

"I doubt it."

"Well I've heard things are bad."

"Yes, yes. I understand that, but what about the
Bitchfolken? Where are they now?"

"I've heard some are left. Not many. Lams are
swarming through there now."

"Yes, yes go on."

"Have you ever watched bees around a dead hive?"

Pelto nodded.

"That's how I think of the Bitchfolk now."

Pelto gave out a long sad sigh and began slowly wagging his head.

"A broken hive and no queen. Munnah saw to that didn't he?" He looked up. "But the Mentor Viat – some of them have gone in haven't they?"

"Ye – es, some went upriver a month ago. F-f-f-forr, all new. I don't think they'll do much good. They're too few. They're too late. The Bitchfolk are done for."

"Yes. I suppose you're right." Pelto paused momentarily. "Well, last time I was here, Dibius mentioned Rahnuk's diary. I never knew it existed." He looked across at Malcolm who looked away. "Is everything she wrote in here?" He leaned sideways and patted the leather pouch now propped against his chair leg. "Is it?"

"No. I've got the last of it."

"Hope I get to see it? At least I have what Dibius collected. Really had to pester him. He's not the man he was, is he?"

"N-n-ohm. He's slipped lately. There's much he could have told you. Rahnuk talked with him often."

"And it was Dibius who persuaded her to write things down?"

"Ye– es. When she arrived it was hard for her, very hard. Most folk were cruel, they didn't understand; couldn't understand. Dibius said keeping a diary would be good for her."

10

"But she had friends besides you?"

"Yes, but after what has happened, most folk here now hate the sound of her name."

"It wasn't always like that was it?"

"No, no of course not. Ailsa and Mado were kind and so was Mali, but she lived upriver, and there was Dibius. But some folk never spoke to her. Not even after twenty years." Malcolm wiped away tears with the heel of his hand.

"Dibius taught her to write Riparian didn't he?"

"Yes. She was raised writing Bitchfolken but no one here could read it. He taught her Riparian script. She wanted to know everything. She held nothing back. Everything was written down. She expected to be taught by return. She was quick at learning."

"Hmm, I've been through some of it – very interesting. Dibius did tell me some things though; I heard that a couple of months after her arrival she waited until there was nobody in Church, went in, tore open the tabernacle and threw its contents onto the floor. Disgusted she couldn't find the Christus hiding inside?"

Malcolm again looked down at his clasped hands. "Yes."

"Amazing woman." Pelto murmured shaking his head. "Yes Mentor Dibius has slipped all right. By the way, how's the new man coming on?"

"Mentor Frankus? Fitting in well. You saw him this morning? Dibius helps him – as best he can."

Their talk stalled, and then before anything more could be said, shrill voices sounded and bare feet thudded in the porch-way as one of the ball-tagging children finding himself cornered, began yelling for mercy. Malcolm's face spread in a grin. He said something about that lot being at it again and Leo stood and headed for the doorway and outside a dog started barking and Malcolm and Pelto listened as Leo told the children to 'go play somewhere else.' Pelto asked if Ailsa's twins were among them and Malcolm nodded saying they were certain to be. Pelto added that with Seth gone they must be a handful for their mother. Leo came back in and sat down and the yells and screams faded as the children ran off toward the river. Malcolm leaned forward in his chair, his folded arms now resting on the table. He looked fixedly at the little basket of bread in the middle and with confidence began his story, his stammer now gone.

## 2.

Malcolm was tall and walked with a slight stoop, his shoulders hunched forward and a worried frown on his face that not even a smile could completely erase. A shag of black hair ringed his balding brown shiny head and a jagged white scar parted his moustache where the healers corrected a hair lip not long after his birth. He was now forty-eight but he started by talking of his youth and those capricious events, which brought him to settle in Brakial. Thinking back, he imagined he must have been like an exhausted sea-bird he once found on a beach after a prolonged patch of stormy weather. He told of being the eldest child in his family but at the age of ten lost both parents and all three of his sisters to the shaking disease. He wondered why he was spared. His mother's sister took him in and raised him with her four children and although he knew he was loved, he still considered himself an outsider: that and his difficulty in speaking caused him to spend more and more time on his own. He mixed readily enough with other children when compelled to but most often preferred his own company. The opinion of neighbours was easily guessed. 'Doesn't fit in well.' 'Typical orphan.' 'Can't put the past behind him.' They meant well but underneath it all he felt a deep hurt. The only bright spot being that about the time his family died, the Tutors in Dulce discovered his liking for study and took him under their wing. Logic and natural history became his loves.

For about a year, Malcolm toyed with the idea of joining the Mentors who were the dedicated religious of Riparia, but at sixteen decided against it. He wanted a change. He wanted to get away from Dulce and all its unhappy memories and being curious about new places he moved to Brakial where he spent a year working at various jobs, such as fishing and cutting timber. He enjoyed the work but restlessness drove him back to Dulce where he lived for a further half year and then finding how much he missed Brakial, he returned and took a job with Caveo who just happened to be looking for more men. By the age of twenty he could no longer recall the faces of his parents and sisters and nobody in Brakial had ever known them. Three years later the Elders granted him a house site and with the help of some friends he built a two-room dwelling out of wood. Later the house was added to but its main room was where the three men were now seated and talking.

Brakial bore the reputation of a frontier settlement. From the river below about two hundred and fifty houses in crooked disjointed lanes could be seen clinging to a sloping terrace above the river Deemah. Most homes were wooden; some others built with stone and a few resembled rounded beehives with roof and walls of thatch and no windows. Some dwellings had outside cooking areas roofed with wood to prevent heavy rain from drowning the fire. On rare windless evenings, a gentle veil of blue smoke lay above the houses, seemingly supported from below by thin spiraling pillars marking where meals were being prepared and homes warmed. The majority of the six hundred or so residents farmed for a living, the next largest group were fishermen and from the remainder came the trades of bee-keeping, charcoal burning, healing and the makers of wheels, pots both metal and clay, chairs, candles, rope and so on. The Church of Christus Risen stood at the downriver end of the town. Built eighty years after the first people settled there it replaced an earlier wooden building destroyed by fire. Some said that Christus himself caused the fire, he being sick and tired of having to live in a temporary cramped house. The new church was built with stone and took nearly fifteen years to complete and about one hundred years afterward a community lodge was added to it.

Upriver of Brakial, a few small hamlets existed, sheltering anything from one to three families; the hamlet names usually being fixed by the name of the founding family. The Deemah, a big wide river separated Riparia from Lamentasia as the land on the other side was known. Riparians called the people who lived there Lamentasites, a name they usually shortened to Lam. The Lams were nomads living in loose tribal groups and they survived on a simple economy based on hunting, gathering and herding. They were superstitious and often violent and unruly with tribal leaders relying on force and sorcery to stay in control.

Three or four days travel upstream from Brakial the Deemah was joined by the river Vau. Riparians named the large triangular region enclosed by the two rivers as Sessilia and its inhabitants as Sessilites. The Sessilites were a community of aggressive, militant, well organized women. A simple religious belief reinforced with continuous ritual held together the social fabric of their lives. Sessilites were knowledgeable in the use of chemicals, especially poisons.

This nearness to Riparia of two cultures one unruly and the other aggressive; compelled it for its own security to establish the Deemah as a boundary and to keep close watch on happenings on the other side of the river. Lams had posed problems in the past but as for Sessilia, the lack of a common border prevented direct contact between the two groups. Riparians were well aware that relations between Lams and Sessilites were often prickly and in any conflict between the two, the warrior women usually came out on top. The Lams used the name Bitchfolken for their Sessilite neighbours and the Riparians also used this name although they shortened it to Bitchfolk. The Lams called Riparians Riverfolken meaning 'to live across the river'. The Sessilites called everyone else Deeves regardless of whether they were Riparian or Lamentasite

A few Riparian missionaries lived among the Lams. They were known as the Mentor Viat and always travelled and lived in pairs. Riparians would shake their heads when speaking of them; especially their lives of discomfort and danger. During the fifty or so years of working with the Lams and trying to teach what Riparians believed; seven of their number suffered violent deaths and others died from disease or other misfortune. Riparians revered these men as blood witnesses to their creed.

Brakial was the base for Riparian security and a small group named Caveo was responsible for it. The usual strength of Caveo was twelve. Four were employed full time and the rest part timers and called on to help only when necessary. At regular intervals the men of Caveo would cross the Deemah to check on the Lams and provide any necessary support for the Mentor Viat. The role of Caveo also included helping the riverside hamlets with security as well as training suitable people in Brakial in the use of weapons and other combat skills, although in the long past nobody on the Deemah could recall any incident serious enough to require a general call to arms.

Malcolm was with Caveo for six years before taking time off to build his house, and as soon as the roof tiles were on and the outside walls complete, he went back to working full time. The head of Caveo, a man named Edgar, held Malcolm in especially high regard. While not saying too much, most people would admit that Malcolm possessed an impressive knowledge of nature and that his field craft skills were superior to most others and they would often ask his advice on matters such as how to keep birds or other pests away from their crops before harvest time.

Through being part of regular patrols into Lamentasia, Malcolm acquired a good understanding of Lam culture, and using tact and demonstrating his skill with arms he gradually gained the confidence of the leadership of those tribes living closest to the Deemah. By the time Malcolm was twenty-five, he was Edgar's first choice to check matters out on the other side of the river and on these occasions Malcolm usually travelled alone. This preference for working solo placed him on the outer with the main stream of Brakial's residents and in contrast with most men of his age, Malcolm at twenty-seven was still a single man, and although nobody disliked him, his shyness and difficulty in speaking, made him feel vulnerable and ill at ease in company and he told of knowing young unmarried women often sniggered among themselves at any attempt he made to get to know them. With the men of Brakial and their wives however there was no such problem, but then none of those with marriageable daughters ever encouraged him to come calling and so little by little Malcolm withdrew even further from such contacts and buried himself more than ever in the work of Caveo.

Brakial enjoyed a high reputation amongst visitors in spite of it being a frontier town. The setting above the river, the careless unfettered layout, natural, smiling almost, gave it a pleasant aspect, and visitors arriving by water often likened it to a mother looking fondly down at her children. Behind the houses the grass covered apron of the grazing common sloped gently to where it met the forest edge and beyond that the tree clad land rose steeply in successively higher folds until it reared to a bare jagged rock barrier known as The Comb which even in late summer, some of winter's snow still lay in a few shaded recesses. Yes, people often said Brakial was a lucky place in which to live. The mild sunny climate, the charm of its setting seemed to rub off on to those who lived there and throughout Riparia the inhabitants of Brakial were regarded as being a friendly lot.

Pelto continued with the interview, taking notes and asking Malcolm to clarify some matters. One of Pelto's loves was old texts, and he loved discussing the past. Any chance he got he would tell the story of the birth of Riparia and the wreck of the culture it grew from. When the word Techno popped into the conversation, the chance was too good to miss. With eyes lit up there was no stopping him. Even though the story was well known, Pelto's version was unique and he loved telling it. Laying down his quill Pelto turned to face Leo asking if he realized that the world they now knew was much smaller than the one that crashed during Tribulation, and without waiting for an answer he launched into how it took only the length of an ordinary lifetime for the frenzy of violence and famine to completely destroy the Technos. Did he know that the Technos rebelled against themselves? That they killed everything of value by trampling down truth and beauty? That they forgot the lessons of the past and ended up like birds that filled their own nests with shit. Malcolm and Leo sat and listened while Pelto went on and on about how the Technos became dazzled by every new thing. How their pride blocked them from knowing they shared kinship with the ancients who rebelled, and how instead, it put them on the broad back of a blind thing called progress. How they then charged over the whole world yelling and cheering and trying to catch up with the future that like a rainbow kept gliding away faster and faster in front. Finally, how they fought among themselves, each trying to make his own lamp glow brightest by dousing everyone else's. Here Pelto always liked to recite his favourite quote from the Wisdom Book. 'The allure of evil shades all good things and the whirlwind of desire corrupts a simple heart.' He said the spell of evil works on men the way fire attracts small children and as fire will cripple and kill, so evil will destroy all who embrace it. He that loves danger always falls into it.

Techno was the name Riparians gave to this dead race and their Codex contained records of at least three earlier civilizations that each followed this same curve from birth to maturity followed by decline and the quickening slide into chaos. But one thing all Riparians were taught was that no other civilization had ever reached such heights or collapsed so rapidly as the Technos.

The languages spoken in the three territories of Riparia, Lamentasia and Sessilia were similar with a shared pronunciation and meaning for many words, highlighting a common heritage at some time in the recent past – although it could be difficult at times for a Riparian to understand a Lam, or for a Lam to understand the speech of one of the Bitchfolk. Only Riparia and Sessilia used written languages and the text characters were quite different from each other. Riparians used the name Terra Vivus for the land occupied by the three cultures and the mountains that bordered it.

Outside of Terra Vivus was a vast virtually unknown region Riparians called Terra Defilia, and it was widely believed that Terra Defilia was uninhabitable. Stories were told and retold of how during The Tribulation, the land was poisoned. In later years wanderers venturing there found great sandy plains and thrusting mountains of craggy rock where no plants grew, rivers and lakes without fish, and other places where sheets of enormously thick ice covered everything. But not all was wasteland. Life had survived in a few safe havens from which trees had spread to clothe and cleanse nearby sick lands and over time merge into large tracts of forest that enveloped and hid abandoned Techno towns and cities. The discoverer of one dead city said it was so large he needed days and days to ride through it – in every direction choking thickets of shrubs and vines smothered piles of rubble, and here and there immense angular towers rose clear of the trees – some, mere skeletal frameworks sighing in the wind while from the crumbling walls of others, row upon row of matching openings stared blindly into space like empty eye sockets. Beneath the trees browsing deer picked their way past the curved bodies of corroding chariots, and from some of the towers at twilight, clouds of bats spiraled upward like fast rising smoke, and after dark wolves could be heard howling.

The death of Techno tools and amenities known from the surviving histories provided Riparian culture with a wide range of sayings and jokes. Somebody in a hurry would be urged 'to fly', or if wanting to talk with another in some distant place, he might be told, to use the 'talking tool'. Always this advice came with laughter.

Brakial was the place where all trade with Lamentasia was managed from and at each full moon trading would commence and last for the next two to three days. Lamentasia provided a range of goods not readily available in Riparia. Dried wild fruits, dried eel fillets, cured hides and furs and in season the collected eggs of plover and duck were keenly sought after and all this in exchange for Riparian made implements, cordage, fabric and especially metal cookware without which the Lams lacked any means to heat water. A rope operated barge capable of carrying up to a dozen men and four horses was used to transfer the trade items and the trading always took place on the Brakial side of the Deemah.

**3.**

Having finished his little lecture, Pelto now picked up his quill again and nodded toward Malcolm who leaned back in his chair and ran both hands across the top of his head and left them clasped behind his neck before starting back on the story. He paused briefly before speaking, casting his mind back to late in the year 396 A.T. (After Tribulation) when a rumour reached Brakial of trouble between Lams and Bitchfolk near where the river Vau joined the Deemah. Two members of the Mentor Viat lived with Lams in the area where a man named Orlo was chief. The rumour was quickly passed onto Edgar the head of Caveo. For many years Riparians had known that the Lams traded in young women and sometimes boys and the Bitchfolk were also suspected of involvement in this hideous trade. With the prospect that the Mentor Viat might be in some danger, Edgar instructed Malcolm to go with two others and investigate and if the Mentors were at risk, they were to be escorted back to Brakial until things cooled down enough to allow their return.

Within a couple of days the patrol was organized and set to start the following morning. Two men, Rolf and Seth were assigned to help Malcolm and not long after sunrise on the day of departure the three assembled at the landing with horses and gear ready to board the barge that would ferry them across the Deemah. In spite of it being early summer the morning air was chilly and a low feeble sun squinted through a thin layer of white cloud. Some large gulls flew lazy circuits above the landing their clipped calls sounding to Malcolm like muted jeers. He shivered and turned his attention back to coaxing his horse onto the barge. When all the horses and gear were loaded and they were getting ready to cast off, the calm of the morning was split by a young woman screaming Seth's name as she ran down through the houses toward the landing. All eyes turned to look at the figure hurrying toward them and next thing a plump teenager arrived, breathless and bosom heaving. Stopping in front of Seth she smiled shyly and handed him a rolled up garment.

"Ailsa." Was all Seth managed to say.

"It's for you." The young woman blurted out. "I've been knitting it for weeks. Mama let me come now. To give it to you. Before you leave."

She was so out of breath that each short sentence was delivered in a spurt with several deep breaths in between. Seth blushed.  He held the garment up to look at what turned out to be a handsome cream and grey knitted wool jerkin.

"Ailsa, is this for me?" Seth sounded confused. "You shouldn't have done this."

"But I wanted to. It's for you."

"Thank you. Thank you, it will be very useful." He bent forward to put a light kiss on Ailsa's cheek but she reached up and threw her arms around him and hugged him tight, her cheek against his. Seth, still red faced pulled free and thanked her again before turning and stepping aboard the barge with Malcolm and Rolf and the bargees all looking on and grinning.  Ailsa stood as if rooted to the ground her eyes following Seth. She looked forlorn, like a puppy that had just been tied up. Seth had known Ailsa from the time she began walking and the two had often played together out in the fields while their parents tended crops nearby. Ailsa was three years younger than Seth and up until the last six or seven months he always treated her like a sister but quite suddenly in that time, things changed. Their meetings become brief, accidental almost and often marked by red faced silences.  Ailsa's eyes would search Seth's face, but for some reason he could not explain, he found himself looking past her and mumbling idiotically.

It took three men to look after the landing winch and already the barge cable was across the other side and threaded through the large fixed wood pulley and was now being rowed back to be connected to the winch on the landing. For safety reasons, two bargees equipped with poles and paddles always travelled on the barge. Malcolm signaled to the winch men that they were ready and the reverse ratchet pin was flicked aside and the two bargees started polling. It seemed like an age for the laden barge to travel the thirty yards to where the Deemah's oily flow fastened its grip and began dragging it across and downriver with the current. The bargees worked a rudder, which helped control the angle of travel, and behind the craft the heavy paying out cable briefly lifted clear of the water before slapping down and under again. Besides the horses belonging to each of the men, a fourth animal owned by Edgar was being taken as a pack horse to carry the necessary supplies for ten days and which included trade goods and weapons plus three carrier pigeons murmuring away in a wicker cage. The barge was fitted with wooden railed stalls for keeping the horses still and quiet during the crossing. Malcolm's little black and white dog Spike was also on the trip and now he stood at the stern of the barge barking at the paying out cable while overhead the jeering gulls still circled.

Seth with thumping heart stood staring into the water with its vague blue green reflections slowly swirling and merging and parting. He felt annoyed. He kept asking himself why he agreed to this trip. Edgar could easily have found somebody else. He glanced

back toward the landing where Ailsa stood and she must
have seen him look up because she started to wave
madly and with a warm feeling he waved back and then
he heard Ailsa's clear soprano voice calling his name.
His eyes began watering and he lowered his head so that
the others wouldn't notice. He felt a hand suddenly clap
on his shoulder and Rolf's voice broke in through his
thoughts.

"You looked as if you were about to fall in."

Seth jerked his head up and gave it a quick shake.

"I've seen it happen." Continued Rolf. "Moving
water. It can do that when you stare into it. It gets to
you."

"Yeah I know. Kind of – makes you dizzy, doesn't
it?"

"You're quite the close mouth, aren't you?"

"Why?"

"Ooh, no need to be so touchy. Ailsa, I mean she's a
nice little girl. You're a lucky young man." Rolf gave
Seth a broad wink and a friendly cuff on the head before
turning and walking to the end of the barge to stand
with Malcolm.

Seth the younger of Malcolm's two companions
was eighteen. His face was thin and serious with a firm
set to his chin and dark prominent eyebrows over blue
eyes. He was slim and lithe and not very tall but he was
strong and regarded by all who knew him as a good
bowman. A favourite trick was to grip the trunk of a
sapling and using only his arms for support, rotate his

rigid body slowly from standing upright through a full circle and back to the standing position he started with. Although Seth was a quiet young man, his curiosity knew few bounds and Malcolm often had to fend off questions on personal matters which he seldom shared with anyone.

Rolf by contrast was a large noisy man, excitable and with a colourful manner of speaking. At thirty-six he was the oldest of the three. He was stocky with a chubby face, piercing brown eyes, prominent forehead, well-receded hairline and a short dark beard. He wore outside leather braces to hold up his pants, which always rode half way up his stomach leaving his pants cuffs well clear of his ankles. Rolf was a curious mix of generosity and boastfulness. A part time member of Caveo his main livelihood was managing Brakial's communally owned cattle herd which also meant keeping and updating the records of animal performance. He was proud of his well-trained horses, especially his favourite, a big chestnut he called Musto. Meeting Rolf for the first time was an experience to be remembered and people would quickly be told that Musto was the best-trained horse in all Riparia. They would have to stand and listen while being told about Musto and how smart he was. How he was gate trained and could cut calves from their mothers and swim the powerful currents of the Deemah with Rolf on his back and could play all sorts of little jokey tricks Rolf taught him and not once was he beaten in any race, even in the most casual of challenges accepted on the spur of the moment, no matter how uneven the ground it was competed over.

Malcolm would have been more than happy to have carried out this patrol on his own but Edgar insisted that it was high time some of the other Caveo people learned from his experience of travelling in Lamentasia. So here he was stuck with these two for maybe the next ten days.

For Malcolm, a journey into Lamentasia never failed to excite. The hint of danger, the slight thrill of the unknown was always present. The Deemah not only marked the border between Riparia and Lamentasia but it clearly marked a change in the physical appearance in the land on either side. The course of the river described a gentle but enormous curve cutting into the foot of the Comb rising behind Brakial. The Comb was the extension of one mountain range from the Azmata Mountains four days travel upstream from Brakial. A half days sail downstream from the town the Deemah entered the sea through a broad estuary backed on the Riparian side by a sprawling confusion of low wooded hills and gorges that marked where the Comb ended.

Flat areas with good soils were rare on the Brakial side and the town and other hamlets were nearly all perched on rocky mounts or escarpments leaving good ground free for raising crops. The Riparian small holders looked with envy across the Deemah at the empty well-grassed dales of Lamentasia. This land with its placid folds and rises like the widely spaced swells in a gentle sea was only partly forested, most of it being more or less open grassland dotted with trees in singles and groves. The open areas were the result of the Lamentasite practice of setting fire to the land during dry weather to grow better grass for their cattle.

Malcolm intended to travel upstream following the Deemah but never straying any further at the most than a half days ride from its bank. In three days he wanted to be at the junction with the Vau River that marked where the border between Lamentasia and Sessilia began. Both the Vau, and downstream of the junction, the Deemah, cut around the foot of the Azmata Mountains. Azmata was a large mountainous plug with rivers radiating out from it like the spokes of a wheel, one third watering Terra Vivus and the rest wandering into Terra Defilia. Forested on its lower flanks and penetrated by rugged gorges, it was a rough, broken, uninhabited chunk of land with many active volcanoes. This and its unpredictable weather meant nobody ever attempted to settle there. The people of Brakial joked that all their bad weather was born in Azmata. The Lamentasite name for Azmata meant "the place of the wailing wind." They believed it was the home of dangerous evil spirits. The few Riparians venturing there related stories of hazards such as vents of scalding steam, boiling lakes and streams and layers of foul smelling gases. On clear days, the Azmata seen from

Brakial were seldom without some sign of steam or smoke and in some years, eruptions lasting months would continually belch out layer upon layer of toppling brown clouds often stabbed through with lightning strikes.

The barge came quickly to the far shore; its bow grounding in the shallows but under the stern the water was waist deep and cold. With much coaxing and bullying the horses were made to jump into the water and still held by their reins the men kept their feet dry as they mounted and rode ashore. Spike leaped in and paddling hard gained the dry land where he trotted a few yards before giving himself a vigorous shake that rattled his floppy ears and made the water spin off all around him and then he raced up to join the men and the horses. The bargees signaled the other shore by raising the return flag and started polling the barge back out into the current. Once on shore the men dismounted to check girth straps for tightness after which they swung back into their saddles and exchanging shouted farewells with the bargees they turned the horses and set off at a good walking pace up river.

The contrast between the order of Riparia and the wildness of Lamentasia was immediate. The fields enclosed with fences of dry stone or post and rail and hedges were here replaced with wide vistas of open yellow grassland studded with clumps of dark trees. Seth's first impression was of a benign pleasant landscape. But the wildness, the savageness soon made itself evident. Early on that first day he gave up counting the carcasses of deer and cattle they rode past. Mostly deposits of bleached bones overgrown with short grass, but sometimes nauseous tawny tents of hide stretched across hooped ribs with eyeless still furred skulls and thin lips shrunk back from yellowing teeth; recently alive, now crawling with maggots. Rolf always commented, especially if it was a big stag or a large bull, or the stench was really powerful. In fact he talked almost non-stop. Nothing seemed to be able to shut him up, not even the worst stinking carcass. Malcolm and Seth would both hold their breaths as they trailed past the foul corpses except if Spike needed growling at to keep him from scavenging. Malcolm told Seth that the Lam bowmen took a heavy toll on the deer and wild cattle. If animals were killed too far from camp only the tongues were taken, the rest of the meat being left to rot. Early that first day Malcolm led his companions a little out of the way to a clear sandy place near a dry creek. A Lam skeleton lay there on its back, half buried in wind-drifted sand: its grinning skull stuck on a stick held upright by a pile of small rocks. There was no sign of any clothing or weapons. Malcolm said it showed how the Lams settled disputes among themselves. The skeleton had lain there for the last four years.

Malcolm's planned route ran parallel with the Deemah but rarely was the river in sight. They threaded wide crescents and ovals of greening grassland edged with groves of oak and thickets of thorny scrub. Like most farmers in Brakial, Rolf was impressed by the grasslands of Lamentasia and any time there he would say how he would love to bring the Brakial cattle there for grazing. Malcolm having heard it all before resisted the temptation to remind him that the Lams regarded any cattle on this side of the Deemah as theirs. But there was also the problem of deer and in some years the animals were so numerous there was not enough winter grass for even the Lam cattle herds, which was why the first thing the Lams did when moving to a new area was to try and get rid of them. From the time of leaving the barge they encountered deer, and as each new vista opened, small groups would cease grazing or resting, and stand, watchful and alert, not tolerating a close approach but wheeling as one and with a bouncing graceful gait vanish under the fringing trees, and Spike with nose to the ground would run after them until called back by Malcolm, and after several chases the little dog lost interest in the timid creatures. Continually in front of the riders small birds with bright yellow heads erupted from the grass and twittering softly flew around in wide half circles before once more going to ground. And every two or three hundred yards in the open meant entering a new territory of nesting plovers. At the approach of the horses the screaming protests would start, the parent birds ordering defenseless little ones to hide while they continued to run and fall over, pretending injury, before lifting into the air and slowly flapping around and landing again and looking totally unconcerned, but staying close to where their precious babies were hidden. Spike found plover chicks irresistible and any he managed to sniff out from their hiding places he immediately pursued and the little birds would with surprising speed dodge one way and another and Malcolm would have to yell and yell at the disobedient little dog to come to heel until Spike would turn and run back to the horses, head and tail down, ashamed, with the parent plovers diving and screaming at him in his retreat. But the hares: Spike was defeated by the hares. Startled from the concealing grass they would streak from sight and Spike knew it was no contest.

That first day was long and uneventful. Occasionally when topping a low rise the soft distant gleam of the Deemah could be glimpsed away to their right. Facing a brisk cool wind meant wearing jackets fastened and scarves tied in place. Apart from one brief halt to dismount and stretch their legs and drink water from a skin bag, they kept on travelling until the middle of the day was past when they stopped for longer near a pool of water from which the horses drank before being allowed to graze while the resting men ate their ration of dried meat and fruit.

Toward evening Malcolm stopped at a favourite camp-site where a slight dry depression encircled with trees offered wind shelter and a supply of firewood from dry fallen branches. The horses were watered at a handy seep before being hobbled for the night after which they moved off a short distance noisily pulling at the short grass and snorting. Seth went in under the trees and returned with an armload of thin branches and twigs and was about to start the fire when Rolf gruffly announced that he was better than anyone at fire-lighting and grabbing the wood from Seth's arms he arranged it inside a small circle of rocks and using the flint from his pocket started a tiny ember and by blowing on it, a cluster of flames was soon leaping and crackling. Malcolm rigged up some branch wood supports over the fire and suspended two pans, one with a mix of meat, chopped carrots and water and the other with water only. He stayed there sitting and watching and occasionally stirring. Rolf joked and clowned a little and then began teasing Seth about Ailsa. 'When would the big day be?' Seth only grunted by way of reply. Rolf kept up the banter, asking questions and answering them himself in a low chuckling voice and still Seth said little, but a red flush now spread from his neck to his ears and he was becoming more and more annoyed until Malcolm came to the rescue and told Rolf to drop the subject and he sat and fiddled with a horse's bridle while the food was cooking and for a while laughed to himself before slowly falling silent.

The sun now slid below the rim of the rolling world and for a short time the western sky held the last of the tilted green light until darkness won and left the men with only their fire and the stars glittering above. The air quickly chilled and from a distant tree came the doleful calls of a grey owl. Malcolm pronounced the food ready and spooned it into three small bowls and they sat around the fire and ate, and drank hot black tea from large mugs. Afterward Rolf put his hand to his mouth and began a duet with the grey-feathered night-watchman, each exchanging soft wavering hoots. Gradually the gap closed between bird and fraudster, the owl's voice now louder, surrounding them almost until a pause heralded the silent shape sweeping in, pitching low past Rolf's shoulder and over the fire to vanish back into the darkness. A large pale cruciform wraith seen for an instant and gone. Laughter followed the bird's brief visit and bedrolls were then laid out and occupied and the men slept until dawn.

The second day began in a cold light drizzle. Seth who lay with his head sheltered by a small bush smiled as he watched Rolf with eyes shut trying to ignore the little spits of rain on his face. Finally unable to stand it any longer he got up and revived the fire, all the while complaining as to why he was the only one awake. A short time later Seth and Malcolm got up and food was heated before being eaten and washed down with hot tea. The horses were found and saddled and the packhorse loaded and the group was soon back on the trail. They kept well muffled against the cold and damp. Apart from Seth who lost no opportunity to ride alongside Malcolm and quiz him about Lamentasia, they talked little. Mid morning the drizzle stopped and a hot sun burned off the remaining cloud and the day warmed and the rain capes and scarves were taken off and tied to saddle horns. At noon they stopped and squatted on the ground and held the horse's reins while they ate bread and dried fruit. Not long after resuming the journey they encountered an old man and three skinny boys tending a mixed flock of sheep and goats. Malcolm wanted to speak with Igen; the leader of the Lamentasite tribe closest to Brakial and the old herder said that if they stayed on their present course they would come to Igen's camp before nightfall. They rode on again but not before Spike tried to settle differences with the herder's dogs and only after Malcolm yelled at him did the plucky little dog scamper away from the bristling growling curs trying to sniff round his tail.

In Riparia, Lamentasite barbarism was the stuff of legends and Seth was fascinated by them. Whenever he rode beside Malcolm, the questions would flow with each answer provoking more questions. But when it came to direct experience with the Lams, there was one episode from the past that Malcolm kept locked in his heart and that was the story of Kamya, and it was to be more than twenty years before he talked openly of the affair and that first evening around the table with Pelto and Leo was to provide the setting. However at the time, Malcolm's peace of mind demanded he unburden himself to someone, and Mentor Dibius was the one he turned to for help. Back then the people of Brakial lived in awe of Dibius who was reputed to know every secret in the town. He was renowned for his irritability, and in fact, it was generally agreed that Dibius's face seemed set in a look of permanent exasperation – he walked around as if expecting to hear nothing but foolishness – but he was the town Mentor and nothing could be done to change that – they were stuck with him and he was stuck with them. At the time of the Kamya affair Dibius was just under fifty years of age and for twenty of those he had served as Brakial's Mentor.

Malcolm said one of his tasks with Caveo was to visit the camp-site of a Chief named Gorah to check on the Mentor Viat who travelled with him. As a result of his visits Malcolm befriended one of Gorah's families. The family was made up of the man as head and his three women and eleven children; the youngest two being only babies in arms and the oldest a boy of about fourteen. Most Lamentasite children were typically quiet and shy and these were no exception, but, after getting to know Malcolm they began more and more to relax in his company and with much laughter and smiles would join in the games he taught them. Malcolm told of how he loved to see their eyes widen at the simple trinkets and gifts he handed out.

The second eldest child was called Kamya and she was strikingly beautiful with long dark hair and a smile that Malcolm said seemed to melt his heart each time she turned it on him. Kamya was about eleven and Malcolm said all he wanted was to protect her. The idea of protecting Kamya grew and grew and took over his mind. He couldn't bear to see such beauty and innocence left to corrupt in Lamentasia. He could think of little else. Her birth mother was dead and the idea took root that he should buy her and take her to Brakial to live until such time as she was inducted into Riparian society and could become his wife. At least this was his dream and whenever he was sent into Lamentasia, he found himself inventing reasons to visit Gorah's camp-site. He told Pelto and Leo that evening that when it came to his feelings for Kamya, he couldn't balance matters of the heart with practical considerations. On hearing this Pelto pushed out his bottom lip and nodded in sympathy. Malcolm said he preferred not to think about wagging tongues back in Brakial – nothing was going to stop him buying Kamya – he would buy her and save her. This meant sitting down with her father and fixing a price and also getting Gorah's permission, which would mean some sort of pay off for him as well. He found reaching agreement with Kamya's father not too difficult. The exchange would take place during Malcolm's next visit.

But jealousy thrived in Gorah's camp and what later happened crushed Malcolm. Near the end of his next patrol, he arrived at Gorah's camp to collect Kamya only to find her missing. On enquiring for her, Kamya's older brother told him the girl was dead. The boy calmly announced that Kamya was with two of the older women collecting gull eggs and was beaten to death for stumbling and dropping a full basket. Malcolm was devastated. Even telling the story after so many years was difficult, but he carried on and told how with the hideous story writhing inside his head and eyes blurred with hot tears he spurred his horse away vowing never to return.

Malcolm did return, the next day. The torment of losing Kamya drove him back. Questions plagued him. Why had he not acted earlier, when the idea first came to him? She would have been safe in Brakial. Sure, people there would have talked a lot, even those he thought of as friends. He would have been able to live with that he had told himself. But why? Why did this have to happen? With eyes puffy and red he went back and demanded to know where the killing took place. Kamya's father without any outward sign of emotion told him he would make the women face Malcolm and tell what happened as long as he paid the agreed price because it was he, Malcolm, who was the cause of him losing what he stood to gain, no matter who in the end Kamya was sold to. Malcolm said nothing. He sat on his horse and cut the goods loose to fall at the man's feet. The man turned and called and the two women came out of a tent and stood in front of him. Both showed signs of bruising on their faces. Malcolm said it was all he could do to restrain himself from leaping down and throttling them. The women stood without sign of remorse and in few words told of the terrible event, and in response to a question, the older one said that Kamya's body was left where it fell. But that was four weeks ago and although Malcolm went and searched thoroughly, there was no sign of any human remains. Carrion eaters made sure nothing of it was left. Even the bones were gone.

For a month afterward Malcolm was inconsolable. Edgar could tell something was wrong but Malcolm kept things bottled up. He was angry, angry with himself, and especially angry with the Christus. This loving Christus who said 'Ask and you shall receive.' And all that happened was this same loving Christus took things. First his family, all dead, and now twelve years later, Kamya. He was confused too. He said that his anger flowed not just from the fact and the manner of her death but was rooted in his anxiety for her soul. It gnawed at him constantly. Finally with his insides becoming more and more tightly knotted and thinking he was going mad, he took himself off to talk to Mentor Dibius.

Dibius ushered Malcolm into the main living room and motioned for the housekeeper to leave. He stood impassive and stroking his beard while listening to the story and when it was finished, Malcolm said he could tell that Dibius realized the discussion might take some time since he gave a deep sigh and pulling out two stools to sit on, asked Malcolm when he was going to start trusting the Christus.

"Why is it?" He asked. "You people always try to do everything yourselves as if Christus cannot help us? You should know he doesn't punish souls for being ignorant. He isn't cruel. Isn't he the crazy owner of the vineyard? The one who never blocks anyone trying to enter? Does he not pay the same wage to all those inside no matter how long they took to come in? Hmm? Malcolm; only stubborn souls are lost. Souls that stay outside the gate peeking in and not moving. Cursing the Christus by doing nothing. They alone deserve to end up forever where all love is absent." He told Malcolm to relax. He said that Kamya's soul was safe beyond all doubt because, not only was she ignorant but that she was almost certainly innocent.

Malcolm said he remembered Dibius leaning forward with arms folded on the table and looking fiercely across at him and then abruptly standing he said he was busy and other things needed his attention. Malcolm said he also stood and made ready to leave but at the last moment thought of something else.

"Mentor Dibius."

"Yes."

"I have a question."

Dibius sighed deeply and looked around the room trying to stop his impatience from becoming too obvious and Pelto began laughing and said that sounded exactly like poor old Dibius, and Malcolm said he then looked Dibius straight in the eye, and asked if it was true, that the souls of the Lams were safe because of their ignorance, why was it that the Mentor Viat meddled with their lives. Why not leave them be, to do their own thing? And wouldn't the Mentor Viat be better off staying in Riparia and helping the people here? Pelto laughed very loud and asked what Dibius said to that and Malcolm said the face of Dibius had reddened with anger and Malcolm thought he was about to be hit, but then Dibius after breathing in deeply asked if what happened to Kamya was a good thing, and Malcolm said that it was his turn to get angry and he shouted at Dibius and called him an old goat and then couldn't get his words out properly and just stood there gaping in rage and Dibius looked worried and said he was sorry and sat down again and told Malcolm to sit down. Pelto was still laughing and said that Malcolm was lucky he got stuck for words or else Dibius might not have felt sorry for him and would have just thrown him out of the house. Malcolm said Dibius then agreed that Kamya's death was certainly not a good thing, that it was a foul and evil deed. Malcolm said he then asked if Christus really cared, why did he allow such things to happen, and at this, Dibius looked up and raising his clenched fists, punched the sides of his head several times before shouting that Christus could do anything except take away their freedom and knowing Christus loved them was all that mattered. Was that love to be kept hidden? Not shared with anyone? Anyone willing to listen? Surely, he said, Malcolm of all people knew the darkness endured by the Lams. They needed to be told what Christus did and why. Why? So their hearts could know the truth. Had he forgotten that Christus was the original Mentor? Had he forgotten that Christus is one with the Caller? That same Caller who before there was even time knew every man and woman and knew each was worth dying for? And why did He do that eh? Was it a mistake? Was it all for nothing? Was Christus a liar? Hmm? Dibius now paused and looked at him sharply before saying.

"Think Malcolm, think. You've been given that power – make full use of it."

There was nothing more to be said and Dibius stood and so did Malcolm, and Dibius put his arm around Malcolm's shoulder and walked him to the door and told him to stop fretting and to get on with living and Malcolm said he remembered Dibius calling to him as he walked away down the path to come back again sometime although he was certain Dibius would be hoping the matter had ended right there and then.

Pelto said he could understand why Malcolm could recall the talk so vividly. Any outburst from Dibius was something to be remembered and he asked what happened after that and Malcolm said that the next day Dibius must have confided with Edgar because Edgar came to him saying he wanted to talk and they agreed that Gorah's territory should be looked after by another member of Caveo. But things did not end there. Malcolm kept dwelling on what Dibius said. Was Christus a liar? Could he have been? That's what Dibius asked and Malcolm couldn't shake the words off. Was Christus a liar? The question kept going around in his head like a buzzard circling above some dying animal. He teased the words out. 'If I haven't got an everlasting soul then why did Christus do that? Why did he allow that to happen? If he was truly the one who called, he could have put a stop to it. And if I do have a soul but it's not in danger, then Christus was a liar and was properly punished by being nailed to a cross.'

A couple of mornings later while at breakfast, Malcolm got up and walked outside to where some timber left over from building the house was stacked. Sorting through the pile he chose two short pieces of square section wood which he first sawed to the lengths he wanted and then again using the saw, and an old paring chisel, he neatly half jointed the two pieces together to make a cross, carefully using the back of an axe head to hammer in two nails to keep the joint secure. Next he went down to the riverbank and filled a large bucket with sticky blue clay. Back at the house he spent until mid morning crudely fashioning the Christus dead with arms outstretched and the chest deeply scored to show where the ancient spear had pierced. Standing back to inspect his handiwork he decided that the wound was too large and he tried to make it less obvious, but his attempts seemed only to worsen it until it struck him that the original wound must have been large enough to take the hand of Tomaso, so he gave up and considering it finished, carried it to the potter's kiln to be fired. Several days later when it was ready, he painted it white, fixed it carefully to the wood cross, took it to Dibius to be blessed and then returned home where he hung it on the wall above the fireplace. All of this helped him relax a little, that and the talk with Dibius. It helped him understand much, but for years afterward he still remembered Kamya's smile and would often pray for her soul and he wondered at times if this was what Dibius meant about not trusting Christus: and until that first night around the table when Malcolm opened up to Pelto and Leo, the only others in on the secret were Dibius and Edgar.

## 4.

While Malcolm was being battered by Seth's curiosity, Rolf astride his big chestnut was doing his turn looking after the packhorse and often Malcolm and Seth would hear an outburst from him as the animal trailed the wrong side of a sapling. Malcolm remembered telling Seth that each Lam tribe was headed by a Chief who made final decisions such as when the camp would shift, but the Chief also took responsibility for settling any disputes that could not be resolved between individuals or families. As well as a Chief, all Lam tribes boasted a Shaman who was a sort of high priest. The men of Caveo scornfully referred to the Shamans as Gusts and sometimes they used the same name playfully when talking about Mentor Dibius back in Brakial. The Lam Chiefs always leaned on the Shaman for advice and Malcolm was of the opinion that the usual way the Shaman came up with answers was to look at the shape of various bones or twigs or cloud formations and then try and guess which piece of advice would most please the Chief.

Malcolm told Seth that all Lam camp-sites were dirty and untidy and stank from poor sanitation. Even when the site was newly occupied the stink was often present. It always made him want to breathe only through his mouth but he knew that the reek would still be there, inside him, it could never be shut out. He said that after three or four months in the same place even the Lams could stand it no longer. They became moody and tempers would fray and there would be more and more violence and thievery and the herds of goats and cattle would have to be driven further and further to find good grass. Finally things would come to a head and the Chief and his Gust would get together and decide to move. That was the Lam way of dealing with problems. They never changed their ways. They just moved from place to place, always doing the same things, always on the move, nothing permanent, always looking for something or somewhere better. First they sent out scouts to report on where to go next, where the best grazing could be found – although familiarity with their patch generally decided the issue, but then something else also needed attention – various rituals must be observed, the strange deities of Lamentasia needed to be appeased. The Shaman or gust as Malcolm called him would officiate. Most of the camp would attend and there would be much chanting and dancing. Some Mentor Viat told of being present when evil spirits were summoned and had heard strange wailing and sobbing. Others witnessed the sacrifice of small children. Malcolm told Seth that afterward, things happened swiftly with people immediately packing for the move – tents would be struck and belongings put on carts or carried by the women, and animals rounded up and within a couple of days the entire tribe would move off and travel for anything from three to seven days before settling down at the new site. During this time anyone unable to travel through sickness or for any reason would be left behind to catch up later, if they could, and often those left behind seemed to just vanish and were never heard of or seen again. Malcolm reckoned that was one of the ways the Lams got rid of the unwanted and unfit. They just left them, to starve or freeze.

Malcolm said that the Lams knew the value of clean water and reliable springs were the property of particular tribes and in this way the various tribal boundaries were settled although it still did not prevent tribe from fighting tribe and the fights could be bloody, but they were not all that common since each side knew it depended on a reasonable strength of numbers to stay in control of its territory and fighting could make the tribe too weak to survive. However from time to time cattle and women brought them together for trade purposes, especially if there was a surplus of either, and one thing was certain, the Lams valued their cattle above their women.

## 5.

The men travelled at a leisurely pace but in spite of it and earlier than expected they saw smoke rising ahead and a little later Seth smelt his first Lamentasite camp. The stench filled the air as they rode into the main compound surrounded by dirty awnings and tents gently flapping in the light breeze. Five surly looking men armed with short throwing spears quickly appeared and confronted them. A group of curious women and children and some older men formed up behind but the usual smiles and banter that Malcolm expected was absent. Malcolm stayed seated on his horse and in greeting them he enquired also about Igen. The Lams stood their ground and made no attempt to answer. Malcolm repeated his greeting and again there was no response. The two groups just looked at each other and Malcolm again spoke up saying there were two Riverfolken named Alexis and Paulus in their camp and that he wanted to meet with them, but his words of greeting were still met with stony silence. Malcolm suddenly urged his horse forward to go round the group and on into the lines of tents but one of the armed men with his spear raised leaped forward and yelled at Malcolm to stop which he immediately did. The man slowly lowered his spear and in cold tones informed Malcolm that he was not allowed to enter and that Igen was not in camp and had left instructions that no strangers were permitted entry. Malcolm pointed out that they were not strangers and that both he and Rolf were known to Igen but the Lam spokesman continued to stand there shaking his head and repeating the warning. Malcolm asked again after the Mentor Viat and the man said that they were under Igen's protection but that Malcolm and his companions must leave immediately.

"Now go. Now. Now." He shouted.

The meeting was plainly over. The Lamentasite spokesman displayed coolness verging on hostility. Malcolm was expecting an invitation to join the camp for the night, but none came. The change in attitude puzzled Malcolm. They were obviously not welcome. Malcolm asked the spokesman to give the greetings of all Riparians in friendship to Igen when he returned and reining his horse around he led the others through a band of thorn scrub, and the stink, the smoke and the dirty tents were left behind. Rolf now spurred his horse alongside Malcolm and with a pleased look on his face said.

"Well, what was all that about?"

Malcolm wagged his head. "I don't know."

"Did you see them?"

Malcolm turned and gave him a queer look.

"You mean you didn't see them?"

"What are you on about? I saw what you saw."

"You mean you missed them?"

"Out with it Rolf, what did you see?"

"Okay, okay, so you didn't see the Bitchfolk?"

"You saw Bitchfolk? Back there?"

"Yes."

"You sure?"

"Sure I'm sure. Had a real good look at them. Two of them. While you were talking they came out of one of those side tents, took a quick look at us and went back inside."

"What were they wearing?"

"Oh you know. Tunics and kilts. Nothing like the Lams. They sure looked like women except for the cropped hair. They were short to. You know, kind of stocky. Shorter than Lams."

Malcolm's face stiffened.

"I'll bet Igen wasn't away. There must have been more than two Bitchfolk there. He's not that easy to push around."

Seth holding the packhorse tether kicked his mount forward and asked.

"Rolf, did, did you see Bitchfolk? Did you?"

"Yep."

"Were they those two odd looking women?"

"That's right. That's what you saw."

"But, but, why would Bitchfolk be here Mal?"

"Don't know, don't know at all. They do get around though." Observed Malcolm half turning in his saddle.

"What about Alexis and Paulus?" Asked Rolf.

"I'm sure Igen wouldn't let them come to any harm. They're too useful."

Malcolm said he knew a lot about the Lams but about the Bitchfolk his knowledge was shaky.

"I reckon they know a lot more about us than we know of them." And he reminded the others of the gossip in Brakial about the odd looking people who turned up at times during the trading days and how these strangers tended to stand apart, surly and silent and watching everything and that on those occasions the Lam traders seemed morose and fearful, and that there were also reports from some of the riverside hamlets of sightings of people who were neither Riparian or Lam. The sightings were not common and were mostly fleeting glimpses of furtive figures fading into cover or sometimes just strange sandaled footprints in soft riverside silts. Since nothing much else ever happened, Caveo saw no reason to follow things up.

After leaving Igen's camp, Malcolm led the way back toward the Deemah and then keeping the Comb on their right they straightened course and continued traveling up river. Malcolm was feeling more than a little uneasy but kept it to himself. The hair on the back of his neck felt bristly and he kept imagining they were being followed. Each thicket of scrub they neared acquired menace and it was with relief that any hollow of dead ground could be scanned when its rim was gained. Finally Malcolm called a halt and told the others what was bothering him and was relieved to learn that they also felt worried and when they restarted they observed a strict regime of dividing the immediate and changing prospect in front into three sectors that they shared among themselves to watch. A little later their nervousness became heightened by a noisy outburst from some nearby plovers. The three riders immediately turned and halted, facing in the direction of the racket, but then from over the tree tops sailed a hunting hawk with the two plovers in pursuit and taking turns to dive down and hurry the large predator out of their territory.

Malcolm reckoned there was still a quarter of the day's good light remaining, and by nightfall he wanted to have as much distance as possible between themselves and Igen's camp-site. Ahead was an extensive stand of tall trees which Malcolm said would take a while to travel through and he wanted to be well clear of the trees before making camp. It would be possible to outflank the woods by bending their route away from the river but this would make it easy for anyone following to catch up, and the presence of Bitchfolk at Igen's camp continued to worry him. Malcolm always favoured where possible traveling in a straight line – the flight of an arrow was his maxim.

Once under the trees the going was if anything easier than in the open, with the ground bare except for infrequent clumps of waist high fern. The air was still and pleasantly cool, heavy with the smell of decaying leaves and dampness. The leaf mould muffled the noise of the horse's hooves except for an odd clink when iron horse shoe met the occasional stone. Dapples of sunlight escaped through the tree canopy making spangled shawls of twig and branch shadows that slid over horses and men alike, momentarily confusing Seth into thinking Malcolm was some complete and silent stranger, but then the reverie ended with a head shaken return to alertness, and with eyes now hand shielded against the flickering shafts of sunlight he stared around, trying to see past the serried ranks of rough tree trunks and into the enormous dark caves of distant shade. He saw nothing of interest and gave up looking and now focused instead on the shiny brown rump of Malcolm's plodding mount in front and allowed himself to be carried along almost without thinking. After a futile attempt to ride alongside Malcolm and get him talking again, Seth dropped back and lapsed into silence. Rolf was the only one to say anything at all and invariably it was abuse hurled at the packhorse he was leading for mindlessly trailing around the wrong side of a tree. Spike skipped along often glancing sideways but always staying just clear of the heavy thudding hooves and the only other sounds were the bell like calls from unseen birds.

# 6.

Seth was impressed with Malcolm's local knowledge and apart from occasionally veering to bypass wind thrown trees, it was as Malcolm predicted, their course was straight until the trees ceased abruptly at the edge of a steep bank.

Below them a wet sedgy bog speckled with sprays of small orange flowers stretched for two hundred yards before another bank scarred with clay and loose stones signaled the trail climbing out of the bog and again entering more open country. On the other side, groves of trees confined the view at ground level but above the trees the base of the Azmata Mountains dominated, their rugged summits lopped off by a wreath of dark cloud. Rolf now handed the packhorse back for Seth to lead and Malcolm led the way down the bank to the bog and after a short period of sloshing through its knee-deep water and sucking mud floor they were soon lurching up the opposite bank onto firm ground and welcoming grass. Malcolm stopped and turning in his saddle said they were half the distance from Igen's camp to where he knew there was a good place to spend the night and they could reach it in daylight but only if they kept moving at their current pace. No sooner had he finished speaking when from close at hand came shrill cries and uncouth laughter which stopped almost as suddenly as it began only to be replaced by a rhythmic chanting. All three admitted later that the sound was both frightening and hideous and Seth said it made him feel as if the back of his neck jumped in an instant to the top of his head. The noise was deep and seemed to be dragged from the chanter's stomachs with a definite emphasis on the beginning of each chord and then a clear sibilant intake of breath and more booming chords all uttered in unison and in the same key. About one hundred yards away seven figures stepped clear of the trees and started swiftly walking toward them. Rolf began yelling.

"Look, look. Bitchfolk, Bitchfolk."

Malcolm and Seth knew instantly who they were; no need for Rolf to tell them. The horses were nervous, restless and crabbing sideways but Rolf quickly brought Musto under control and the other mounts were also steadied as the men turned to face the advancing figures. Four of the seven headed straight for them. Except for a narrow growth of hair worn down the centre, their heads were shaved and their cheeks daubed vertically in bands of orange and white paint. They wore sandals, leggings, short kilts but nothing else. Behind them the other three wore shaven heads. They seemed to be larger and more muscular than the front four and carried large loads on their backs. They wore both jerkins as well as kilts but their faces were unpainted. The chanting commenced again and the front four advanced with bows ready and arrows fitted. The pack horse now shied and pulling back hard snapped the line at the knot tethering it to

Seth's saddle and his horse took fright and reared high and began stepping backwards and Malcolm wheeled on his mount and quickly grabbed the pack animal's rein before it could bolt. Rolf on Musto also wheeled and they all moved another forty yards back before turning to face the advancing Bitchfolk. Behind the horses little Spike stood, stiff legged and ears erect, alert but puzzled looking. Malcolm and Rolf quickly glanced behind to make sure they were not surrounded and Malcolm hissed for them to stand their ground. The packhorse and Seth's mount were still nervous, snorting and stamping hooves but both Seth and Rolf managed to get their bows ready. The front four Bitchfolk now silent, stopped some sixty yards away. There was a sudden movement and an arrow flew toward them and stuck into a saddlebag on Musto. The horse stood steady.

Malcolm still held the packhorse tether and he looked across at Seth and nodded.

"Go on Seth, give 'em a good fright."

Seth aimed and was about to let fly when a shriek from one of the Bitchfolk caused his horse to again rear and his arrow went wild and struck the ground a short distance in front. Derisive hoots came from the Bitchfolk and another arrow flew by, sailing close over Malcolm's shoulder. Rolf cursed and took aim.

Malcolm called to only frighten them but Rolf's arrow skewered the leading attacker who was thrown back on the ground and lay still except for one leg that kept jerking upward at the knee. Malcolm, spluttering with rage looked at Rolf, who yelled back that the Bitchfolk were trying to kill them and then Malcolm got his words out and roared that he deliberately shot the woman.

"I didn't. I didn't. Stupid bitch. Jumped the wrong way."

"Fool."

"They're trying to kill us." Yelled Rolf.

The horses were nervous, whinnying and snorting, trying to step backward. The six remaining Bitchfolk came together and two of them inspected the one lying on the ground and said something to the others and the three front ones now turned and shot arrows which came uncomfortably close.

Malcolm quickly tied the packhorse's rein to his saddle and fitting an arrow let fly telling Rolf and Seth to also shoot, but only to frighten the Bitchfolk who realizing their bows were well out ranged by the more powerful Riparian weapons, backed away still making loud cries before taking cover under the trees. Malcolm keeping a safe distance led the others forward in a fast trot to outflank where they were sheltering, forcing a further retreat and with more shrieks and loping fast the Bitchfolk broke cover and headed toward the next line of trees some two hundred yards away and Malcolm led the parallel chase, but then, without warning, the Bitchfolk regrouped in the middle to stand and fight until an arrow from Malcolm whistling low over their heads sent them on their way again and still shrieking they ran under the trees and vanished. Malcolm continued to watch the place where they disappeared and then wheeling his horse led the way back to where the fight started so they could retrieve their arrows. Rolf made no attempt to take his from the dead woman but Spike was very taken with the body, running around it and sniffing at it until Malcolm growled at him. Then Rolf remembered the arrow stuck in his saddle bag and pulled it out and looked at the point before passing it to Malcolm with the comment that judging from the purple gum smeared on its head it looked like it carried poison. Malcolm looked at it, held it to his nose looked at it again and then with a grunt tossed it on the ground. He was still furious with Rolf for killing the woman. He looked across at Seth whose face appeared drained of all colour.

"You okay?"

Seth nodded.

"Well, what now? Where to now?" Asked Rolf.

"We go on." Grunted Malcolm.

"Is that a good idea?"

"I said we go on." Snapped Malcolm.

"But, but. What about all this?" Rolf waved his hand around where the fight started.

"Yeah. Thanks Rolf. All we needed. Stirred up Bitchfolk."

"They could have killed us."

Malcolm ignored the remark and giving the packhorse tether a jerk he turned his horse and urged both animals on. His pounding heart felt like it was stuck inside his Adam's apple. He clenched his teeth, squared his shoulders and rode on staying in front of the others and determined not to look behind but still close enough to hear them talking. He hoped they wouldn't see how shaken he was. Seth rode up beside Rolf and asked in a lowered voice.

"Is this wise?"

Rolf looked at him, shrugged and stared ahead.

"I mean going on like this."

Rolf continued looking straight ahead.

"We should be going back, shouldn't we?"

"Well why don't you say something – to him?" Rolf nodded toward Malcolm.

Seth looked at the lone figure riding a few lengths ahead.

"That was the scariest thing I've ever seen. Never want to go through that again. Ever."

For Malcolm, the frightening event wouldn't go away either. The chants, the laughter and shrieking, the dead woman - her knee jerking in spasm. He'd never seen anything like it. And here he was keeping on going when any sensible person would turn and run for the safety of Brakial. Malcolm's head felt like it was on a frozen stalk and he wanted to look neither behind him nor to either side. This wasn't courage – he was caught in a paralyzing fear that made him afraid of either going on or turning back. Turning back was what he dreaded most of all – the dread of what Rolf might say. But he was also afraid of an unseen enemy hidden ahead and waiting. He shook his head and took a deep breath. The numbing fear subsided somewhat enabling him to sneak a quick look behind. He needed reassurance – to make sure that the other two were still following. They were – in single file – horses plodding along – keeping the same pace he was. Malcolm breathed out in relief and now that his head was clearing he turned his attention to the fear of what may be waiting ahead – that they could still be in danger – and he began making sure their route avoided going close to dense cover.

The sky clouded over again and Seth was sure he could smell rain and looking out to his right toward where he guessed the Deemah flowed he could no longer see any part of the Azmata mountains – hidden now behind a dense low lying cloud bank that was rolling down the river, and it wasn't long before he felt the first light spots on his face and soon they were riding into a thickening drizzle. Rolf was the only one to have his rain cape tied to his saddle and he now pulled it over himself but Malcolm and Seth just rode on getting wet. Gradually the light dimmed and Seth lost all track of time and then before he realized it, it was dark and he was left relying on the keen night vision of his horse and wondering when Malcolm was going to stop for the night. His eyes began to close as he lurched along and then he would come suddenly awake as his mount brushed against wet scrub and the water-laden twigs at the slightest nudge unloaded onto the wet and chilled riders and even though he was wearing a rain cape, Rolf's voice would in protest rumble out of the dark.  At least twice, Seth just managed to stop himself dozing and falling out of the saddle.  It was a long day even before the fight at the bog and he was now past caring when without warning he rode his mount straight into the rump of the pack animal and was jolted wide awake.

Malcolm had stopped next to the trunk of a large tree and announced in a tired voice that here was where they would spend the night.  They creaked off their mounts and set about unsaddling and unloading gear but instead of hoppling, the animals were tethered to some tall sturdy scrub trunks. The horses, free of saddles and girth straps stood snorting and shivering their hides and the air was filled with a strong stink of horse urine as bladders were emptied with the loud sounds of water pouring on turf.  The men stood together under the tree chewing on straps of dried meat and handfuls of dried fruit, and then the bedrolls were laid out and covered with rain ponchos.

"Aren't we going to set a watch?" Asked Seth.

"N'yo, no." Said Malcolm.

"But what if the Bitchfolk come?"

"And what if they do? And what could we do? They can't see us and we can't see them. Don't worry. They couldn't have kept up with us. They'll be resting somewhere warm and dry by now.  Just you lie down and get some sleep." And as an afterthought added.

"And try not to think about them." He whistled to Spike and made him lie down beside him.

Malcolm was woken next morning by Seth sneezing violently and then Spike started to growl and then bark but he stopped when Malcolm yelled at him. First light arrived and a brisk cool wind was blowing but at least the drizzle had stopped. Through a gap in the trees the Azmata stood in sharp relief against a pale green sky and as the darkness retreated nearby trees assumed first shape and then colour. They were all up now and Rolf filled the nose-bags with chaff and hung them over the horse's heads. Malcolm pointed in the direction of a spring behind the trees and Rolf and Seth untied the horses and led them away to be watered. They were gone a short time. Malcolm seemed more cheerful than the previous evening and Rolf decided it was time to try getting on side with him again.

"How did you know there would be water through there?" He asked, but Malcolm said nothing and Rolf shook his head and muttered something to the effect that Malcolm must have known where they were all along.

They busied themselves getting ready to move out, saddling horses and trying to eat and drink at the same time – dry rations washed down with cold water. When ready and before mounting, the three at Seth's insistence, came together and hand in hand called on Christus and his virgin mother for guidance and protection for the day ahead.

"What happens today Mal?" Asked Rolf.

"We can't stay here. We've left an easy trail to follow. Too many hoof marks."

"We're going back?" Asked Seth.

"He just can't wait to meet up with those women again, that right eh Seth?"

"No." Malcolm replied. "We're sticking to the plan. Safest thing."

"We're heading for Orlo's?" Asked Seth.

Malcolm nodded.

"How far off is it?"

"From what Edgar said. Little more than a day at the most I'd say."

"But what about the Bitchfolk?"

Rolf started to laugh and Malcolm said.

"Well I don't know their plans for today, but up ahead the country's more open, lots of hard ground. We won't leave much of a trail."

"What say there's Bitchfolk at Orlo's?"

"What if there are? Unlikely they'll know what happened yesterday. Anyway we've got to check on the two Gusts. That's what we've come for."

"I don't like it."

"Me neither." Cut in Rolf.

Malcolm swung into his saddle and turned to the others who were already mounted.

"Even without checking on Justin and Andre, it's still the safest option. We can wait at Orlo's for a couple of days and then head home."

64

Malcolm said they were close to where the Deemah curved left before being joined by the Vau. He explained that downstream from the junction, the Deemah cut hard in against the cliff bound Azmata and then at a point known as The Gullet, the river entered a long section of thundering rapids where the water dropped one hundred yards over a six hundred yard stretch before being joined from the other side by an unnamed stream and at that point the Comb stretched out and away from its Azmata mother and the Deemah began its wide gentle curve all the way to Brakial and beyond to the sea.

As Malcolm had told them, the country they now rode through was more open and trees scarce and the worry of a surprise attack lessened. The horses ambled and the tension from yesterday eased and the only worry they all shared but none spoke of was the certainty that within the next few days they would be returning home using much the same route. At the first stop of the day Malcolm said he was surprised they had not come across any of the herds belonging to Orlo's people. There was an abundance of new grass here and although it was a big expanse of land he was expecting by now to have run into a few Lam herdsmen, but then sometimes he said you could travel for a couple of days without seeing anyone, even in the best country.

The day before leaving Brakial, Edgar and Malcolm discussed the probable whereabouts of Orlo's latest encampment and now Malcolm said that in view of what happened the previous day they must be very careful. He didn't want to arrive at Orlo's after the middle of the day and in case they were being followed, he planned for an early and false camp in daylight from which they would move as soon as it was dark.

In late afternoon they stopped and unpacked in a grassy hollow. The horses were tethered to small scrub bushes and they stood patiently, ears flicking forward and back and tails swishing at annoying flies. No fire was lit so it would be the second evening meal in a row of dry rations. The weather was sunny and warm and the men made the most of it spreading out damp clothes to dry while they rested. Seth spent some time playing with Spike throwing a short stick he'd found which the little dog would race after and retrieve and drop at Seth's feet and look up at him begging for the game to continue and when Seth eventually tired of it Spike showed his displeasure by barking until Malcolm ordered him to be quiet and when that failed he caught Spike and with a rope to his collar, tied him to the saddle pile from where he gave imploring looks and whined and whimpered before giving up and lying down with closed eyes, but every so often he would come to and snap furiously at a fly. Seth lay on his back in the sun with one arm across his forehead to shield his eyes. Close to his head small orange butterflies visited tiny nodding blue flowers and from all round came the slight songs of hidden insects and the sweet smell of the warm grass soothed him and he drifted asleep.

As soon as it was dark the horses were saddled and the gear loaded and tied on and for some time they rode in silence until a low rise loomed out of the darkness and Malcolm halted his horse and Rolf and Seth also reined in their mounts.

"What's this place?" Asked Rolf.

"Lark Hill."

"We're stopping here?"

"Yes."

The rest of the night was divided into three shifts with each taking a turn to keep watch while the others slept with hand weapons in easy reach. Seth kept the first shift and wondered to himself why they bothered since Malcolm thought there was no need for a watch the previous night, or was it because they were too tired to stay awake. As far as he was concerned, it hardly seemed to matter now as he strained to see through the blanket of night and listen to the faint sounds the wind made through stalks of dried grass and imagine how an approaching footfall might sound. The only footfalls he heard came from the hobbled horses as they clomped around grazing the short grass.

# 7.

The sound Seth woke to next morning was a lark circling in the air above. It was still dark and no one spoke as the unseen bird poured out its medley of trills and runs. The first rays of the sun caught the tops of the Azmata but the campsite was still in shade and a cool faint breeze drifted through as they packed up and prepared to leave. Seth looked up as the first lark was quickly joined by two others.

They got on with shaking and packing bedrolls and Seth leaped in fright as a large spider fell out of his when he picked it up. Breakfast was again dry rations. The horses were rounded up and nose-bags of oats hung around their necks. Spike gulped down his ration of dried meat and Seth gave the pigeons fresh grain and water. Before riding out the men came together in brief prayer, their heads bowed and hands holding reins, and behind the horses waited Spike, rapidly panting with his pink tongue hanging out. After mounting to ride out Malcolm led the way to the spring which bubbled from the base of the hill's far side and the horses were allowed a long drink before the journey to find Orlo's encampment recommenced.

Mid morning they halted. The sun was high and the air calm. Both riders and horses were hot and jackets and scarves were removed and tied to saddles. The Deemah hadn't been sighted for nearly two days and they were now well upstream from the Gullet, but everywhere on their right and at no great distance, the gaunt cliffs of the Azmata rose out of the hidden river like a great rough wall and the top of the cliff barred the view beyond. Rolf pointed in the distance to where several columns of smoke could be seen which Malcolm said must be from Orlo's compound. A short time later, they rode through a loose herd of humpbacked cows; some were grazing and others lying down. Most had small calves and the standing animals stopped and stared and the four Lam herders keeping watch waved and called out and Malcolm returned their greetings. They kept moving and not long afterward encountered the first shabby tents of Orlo's encampment.

Several lean raw-boned camp dogs circled and closed in on Spike until Malcolm with a raised arm shied at them and they skulked off and circled now beyond a stone's throw. Malcolm thought that the number of tents looked smaller than usual and was surprised at how few people were to be seen but they kept on riding all the while looking around to see where Orlo's compound might be. A short man appeared walking briskly and as he came closer, Malcolm recognized him as one of Orlo's sons. The man stopped in front of them and bowing in a grand manner said that his father's compound was out of sight on top of a small rise behind him. With a wave of his arm he pointed out the direction.

Malcolm had known Orlo's son for some time now and always thought of him as creepy because of his habit of staring at some imaginary spot above the head of whoever he was talking to giving his eyes the appearance of being under slung, mostly white with hardly any pupil showing. He grinned widely and talked in a flattering manner of his friendship with Malcolm. He said his father already knew he was coming and was looking forward to meeting him again and if they followed he would take them to Orlo's tent which he again waved his arm in the direction of. With Orlo's son leading they rode a little further passing through a gap in some small trees before stopping at a place where a clay path disappeared into the scrub.

Malcolm told Seth to wait behind and mind the horses while he and Rolf would go with the guide. The fact that Orlo knew in advance of their arrival worried Malcolm a little and although their guide protested, both Malcolm and Rolf carried bows and full quivers and Rolf wore his short sword. Orlo's son looked hurt and said it was unnecessary to carry weapons. 'Didn't they know they were among friends?' But Malcolm still felt uneasy.

There was something about the oily nature of their welcome and he cheerfully brushed aside the man's concerns and told him he felt naked when unarmed and besides he wanted to show Orlo the new style bows they carried. Before leaving Seth, Malcolm leaned up to him and whispered to keep a good lookout and to not trust anyone here and that most Lams given half a chance would steal anything not tied down, then slapping Seth on the thigh, he winked, turned, motioned to Rolf and the pair started following their guide up the short steep path through the scrub.

Malcolm and Rolf quickly arrived at the top of the rise. The ground here was level and dotted with low trees. A much larger collection of tents was randomly spread over this area, many taking advantage of the trees for support, and here and there among the tents, unattended cooking fires smoldered. A few small children in shabby clothes and with dirty faces stood around, fingers in their mouths and at the approach of the three men they ran in behind the tents and hid. Malcolm could hear laughter and shrill voices but there were no grown-ups to be seen which he thought unusual. Walking behind their guide they passed through a screen of thin shrubs and came on a sight that would long stay in the memory of both men. To their right and barely thirty yards off the clay track lay two bodies. Malcolm stopped and took a few steps closer to look, Rolf did the same. The bodies appeared to be women and numerous bloody slash marks testified to the violence of their deaths. A small sullen boy crouched near one corpse. Rolf said something about not liking things and that they should return to the horses. Orlo's son also stopped and beckoned vigorously and turning continued to stride on. Malcolm grunted they would keep going and as he did, the boy picked up stones and began flinging them with such accuracy they were forced to duck and hurry out of range to catch up with their guide who having walked another hundred yards was now standing and waiting. Behind him and hooked around in a rough half circle were a collection of tents, some small and several much larger ones. A half dead fire puffed out smoke and close by was a firewood heap and two partly filled hayricks. The guide told Malcolm and Rolf to wait. He walked to the most imposing of the smoke stained dwellings and pushing the flap aside entered. Malcolm thought it most likely that Orlo was probably still lying around with some of his women.

"He won't come out until he's got on his most elaborate robe. He's a poser. Always keeps people waiting."

Rolf asked about the two bodies but Malcolm shrugged and said he'd seen similar things before, but not women as victims. Black flies crowded around and both men rubbed the biting insects off the backs of their necks and ears before being driven a short distance to the fire where they hoped the smoke would discourage them. They waited with growing impatience, and still no short portly grinning figure pushed out of the tent to greet them.

The sound of the distant voices stilled and it was quiet the way birds fall silent when a hawk circles overhead. Rolf was looking at an unusual piece of firewood and bent down to examine it and as he did so an arrow cut the air above him and clattered against a tree trunk behind. Malcolm noticed the tent flap drop where the arrow come from and he yelled an oath as they scrambled for the cover of the wood heap and more arrows sliced the air. The rest was all blur and confusion. Malcolm remembered bits and pieces of the fight. He remembered Rolf cursing as they sheltered in the gap between the wood heap and one of the hayricks and how they fitted arrows while trying to work out where their attackers were hiding, and then came the chanting and they knew who they were up against.

Malcolm jumped up and yelled, trying to warn Seth.

Rolf picked a tent entrance at random and shot into it and then they both ducked again as arrows whirred in from several directions. There was a short lull while they each carefully peered around and then Malcolm caught Rolf's eye and gave a puzzled shrug. Nothing seemed to be happening until suddenly high pitched whistling sounds announced more arrows coming, this time raining straight down. Rolf was cursing as they both made themselves as small as possible. Both men knew that unless they could escape, all their attackers needed to do was wait and keep sending up arrows to rain down until one or both were hit. The whistling arrows came more thickly, some thudding into the ground close to where they crouched while others clanged and bounced off the wood heap. They crawled under the hayrick but then had difficulty seeing. Rolf pressed for going back to the horses but Malcolm told him to stay put while he took another look. He crawled out; half stood and quickly looked around before shooting at the tent where the first arrow flew from. Immediately returning arrows seemed to come from all directions and he ducked back down and told Rolf they were cut off. Rolf yelled that he wasn't going to wait around and get killed and Malcolm said neither was he but going back would see them dead before they'd gone fifty paces. Rolf now crawled out and stuck his head up and looked around and the same thing happened to him. Malcolm now grabbed his arm and told him to help push the hayrick onto its side and they put their shoulders to it and heaved it up but not completely over and while Rolf supported it Malcolm grabbed some sticks of firewood and wedged it so their overhead shelter now provided headroom. This move was greeted with yells and screams from the Bitchfolk who were now forced to expose themselves to shoot and Malcolm and Rolf took full advantage of the situation, taking it in turn to let fly at anything that moved. Malcolm still targeted the same tent having shot six arrows toward it. Several times a head, arm and shoulder had appeared through the entrance slit, let fly and then withdrawn. Malcolm crouched and waited, and by some freakish intuition, shot just as the head reappeared, and immediately two arms flailed clutching at the tent flap before a body collapsed through the entrance. Rolf looking and shooting the other way was demanding to know where Seth was and why hadn't he turned up with the horses until Malcolm yelled at him to shut up and then elbowing him in the back said.

"Rolf."

"What?"

"See the tent?"

"Which one?"

"Over there. There. That one. The one with the body." Rolf crouching rested a hand on Malcolm's shoulder and turned to look where he was pointing.

"I'm going for it."

"What about the horses. Why don't we go back for them?"

"No. No way."

"Why not?"

"No." Malcolm cursed angrily and slammed the heel of his fist into the dust. "We're going there. Okay?"

"Okay, okay."

"Now; you ready?"

"Okay."

Malcolm took off doubled over with Rolf's screams of 'go go go' urging him on although he reckoned it gave advance warning to the Bitchfolk, which was something he could have done without. He arrived at the tent and hurdled the corpse in the entrance and then stepped over another just inside it only to be immediately attacked by a large man with a shaven head and wielding a wooden stave. Malcolm caught a glimpse of somebody tied up and propped against the back wall of the tent. The large man went for Malcolm and tried to club him and Malcolm managed to dodge the blow but in doing so tripped over a body and lost his balance and the next blow smashed into his shoulder and knocked him flat. He tried to stand but his attacker dropped the stave and grabbed him around the neck with both hands and began strangling him. With one arm now useless Malcolm tried with his other hand to loosen the throttling fingers but his head and eyes felt like they were going to burst as both blood and breath were choked off and all he could see were little points of sparkling light against a black wall before he passed out.

The next thing Malcolm saw was a blurry image of a round face. Rolf was staring closely into his eyes, holding him up by the front of his jacket and slapping his cheeks with his free hand. Malcolm's neck hurt and when he tried to sit up his left shoulder ached and he couldn't lean on his hand. Beside him on the floor of the tent sprawled the large man lying face down and a small show of dark blood oozed from his side. Thin smoke was drifting through the tent and Malcolm could hear a dull medley of yells and screams as Rolf helped him roughly to his feet, thrust his bow into his good hand and then strode to the back of the tent and using his sword slit the wall from top to bottom. He glanced down at the bound figure at his feet, "Woman eh!" before he peered through the slit and then turning and grabbing Malcolm he pushed him through the opening.

Outside was thirty yards of bare ground and visible through the smoke, a rough screen of small trees and low bushes. "Wait for me" grunted Rolf and Malcolm doubled over, ran for the cover of the trees with each thumping footfall making him wince from the pain in his shoulder. He reached the shelter of the outer scrub and turned and crouched just in side of it and waited.

Rolf, now ready with an arrow fitted waited, watching carefully to see where Malcolm went and then relaxing his bow he stepped back inside the tent where he stood over the bound woman who looked up at him impassively. He drew his bloodied sword and bending down, cut the cords around her wrists and ankles. The woman instantly leaped to her feet, grabbed up a bundle beside her and fled through the tent wall ahead of Rolf who now dashed across to join Malcolm. The billowing blue smoke thickened making it harder to see and Malcolm anxiously watched as Rolf ran toward where he was hiding and he stood and beckoned to show where he was. From the direction of the fires he could hear men and women yelling at each other. It looked as if not only were the hayricks on fire but at least two of the tents as well.

Everything happened so quickly that later Malcolm reckoned the time from the first arrow flying until Rolf joined him in the scrub would have enabled a man to tack two shoes on a quiet horse, and the whole while they were trapped behind the wood heap, arrows whistled around and over them. So far they had escaped being hit but probably their greatest stroke of good fortune was Rolf's curiosity that made him bend down to pick up that piece of firewood, which meant the first arrow missed its intended target, a warning that enabled them to take cover and defend themselves.

## 8.

After Malcolm and Rolf were led away, Seth sat on his horse trying to keep the other three animals calm, not an easy task in the hot sun with those annoying flies, and the horses became irritable and restless and swished their tails and stamped their hooves and bumped each other like mischievous boys. Spike was also restless. He was tied by a long string to the packhorse's saddle and was being watched warily by some five or six slinking mangy dogs. The hot sun brought out the rancid stink of horse sweat and Seth felt dozy but he remembered Malcolm's parting reminder about light-fingered Lams and so he shook himself alert again. A small group of children stood watching him. He wasn't sure how much time had gone but it was certainly not long when he heard someone yelling and he recognized Malcolm's voice.

Almost immediately another sound broke in on him and looking back to the path they used to enter the camp he saw five Bitchfolk loping toward him and chanting in that same horrible manner of two days ago. They carried bows at the ready and came on fast and when less than eighty yards away Seth put up his bow and got a hurried shot away and although it missed it made the Bitchfolk stop and crouch. Seth looked toward where Malcolm and Rolf had gone with their guide, and then at the belt of scrub fringing the base of the rise and then back to where the Bitchfolk were crouching and shrieking. The path up the rise wasn't meant for horses and the scrub along its foot looked too thick and dense to get one horse through let alone four animals and one of them a laden pack animal. His heart began rapidly thudding. The children were gone. Malcolm and Rolf were in trouble that was certain. The Bitchfolk were advancing again, spread out now with bows armed. Seth fitted another arrow and urged his horse a few yards closer and taking careful aim let fly and his arrow struck one in the thigh and with a scream she fell clutching at her leg. He fitted and aimed again but the other four dropped back to a safe distance and watched, quiet now, while out in front the wounded one sat up and called for help. Seth wheeled and trotted back to the other horses and leaning across to the pack animal he grabbed some pouches and full quivers. He leaped out of the saddle, untied Spike and clutching the food and the arrows and his bow took off at a fast run toward where the scrub poured off the rise and occupied the flat ground in front of some large trees. Spike pranced along at his heels. Seth reached the scrub edge and forced his way through the tough outer hedge of wiry twigs and then once under cover he stopped and looked back to where the Bitchfolk were.

Seth could see the horses but not the Bitchfolk, and then he remembered Ailsa's gift. He looked again but still could see no sign of his attackers. He decided to risk going back for the jerkin and dropping what he was carrying he tied Spike to a handy thin branch and keeping crouched over, scuttled the fifty yards back to the horses. Nearby he could hear voices and peering under the horse's bellies he could see three Bitchfolk helping the wounded one toward him. One was talking loudly and pointing to where he had run to. Seth's horse was standing untethered away from the others and with ears back was watching the approaching Bitchfolk.

Seth crawled on hands and knees and stood up beside it, stroked the animal's neck and pulled the jerkin out of a saddlebag and then crawled back to the other horses before standing up and making ready to dash back to where Spike was tied. He was just about to go when he heard a guttural cooing sound coming from the back of the pack animal. He ducked under the bellies of Musto and Malcolm's mount and untied them, gently stroking their flanks as he did so and then with his knife cut the packhorse's tether before reaching up to the wicker cage which fortunately was facing him and he cut the leather catch and lifted the hinged lid. Nothing happened so Seth gave the wicker basket a shake and with clattering wings one after the other the three birds climbed into the air and flew off. He yelled and gave Musto a hard whack on the rump, which frightened the animal and sent it and the other horses running off in the direction of the Bitchfolk and with Ailsa's jerkin tucked under his arm he raced back to the cover of the scrub followed by a renewed outburst of screams and yells.

Safely out of sight, he untied Spike and grabbed up the gear and looked about him. To his left the ground sloped steeply upward. Somewhere up there Malcolm and Rolf were in trouble. He looked back again toward the Bitchfolk and saw two of them approaching cautiously with bows armed. That settled it. His neck throbbed madly and felt strangely stiff. His mouth was dry and there was a pounding noise in his ears. He turned and set off rapidly threading his way through the tangle of thin naked tree stems that soon gave way to much larger trees. Spike with tongue out panting, bounced along at his side. Seth kept the rising ground on his left. Underfoot the going was soft and spongy but frequent drifts of large dead leaves crackled with every step and wrecked any chance of his flight being quiet. After about three hundred yards of walking and half running, Seth stopped to catch his breath and listen for sounds of any chase. He leaned back against a tree trunk but could hear nothing over the sound of his own rapid breathing. He thought maybe the Bitchfolk were distracted by the horses and the goods they carried. He raised his eyes and prayed. At his feet sat Spike looking up at him and panting. The little dog looked eager as if he was all set to see the race start up again.

Seth began to feel better, his breathing was slower but now he was sure he could hear the distant sounds of dry leaves being scrunched so bending down he gave Spike a quick pat, picked up the gear and started swiftly walking but with more care than before and he tried to avoid walking through the drifts of crackling leaves and the slower pace gave him time to think. Should he keep going in one direction? For the time being yes – it was roughly parallel with where he thought Malcolm and Rolf were. What other option was there? To his left the ground still rose but under the trees he was unsure if his flight was either straight or veered unintentionally left. He needed to keep moving, to keep ahead of any chasing Bitchfolk, but he also thought they would be careful not to come too close, after all, he had already put one out of action and if that slowed them a bit, he might be able to stay ahead, maybe even shake them off altogether, work out exactly where he was and if possible find Malcolm and Rolf – if they were still alive.

Seth walked fast, hips swinging with a good even rhythm. Sometimes he leaped small depressions or clusters of surface snaking tree roots and now he found he could cross the drifts of dry crackling leaves with less noise if he waded them rather than just crashing his way across. Spike trotted alongside panting and every now and again looking up at him. The trees here were of a different sort; big spreading oaks that blocked the sky and made everything at ground level gloomy, and now on his left the ground no longer rose. Again he stopped to rest and to see if there was any chance of getting some bearings.

All around him the ground was flat with thick clumps of leafy laurels stopping him seeing any more than thirty yards in any direction, but at least the laurels offered good cover. There was no wind and no sound at all except for Spike's rapid panting. Seth crouched down, sat back on his heels and waited. He looked around trying to work out his next move when in front of him in the distance came the noise of an indistinct crash. Seth stiffened in fright and his heart started thumping again. There was another crash, faint, and then another, louder this time and off to his left. He moved back behind a screen of laurel and grabbed hold of Spike by the loose skin of his neck and held him against his leg. More crashes came, giant footsteps, each one becoming louder. Images raced through his mind like running acrobats. It was some animal, a deer perhaps or a stray cattle beast. No, no, deer never crashed around slowly like that and as for cattle, well it didn't sound quite right. It must be Bitchfolk trying to cut off his escape. The noises stopped and then after a short pause started again with some muffled thumps.

Seth let Spike go and fitted an arrow and readied himself. If there was to be a fight, he was determined he would not die easily. 'Christus please. Please help me now,' he whispered.

Seth looked around to see where Spike was but the little dog was nowhere to be seen. He drew back his bowstring and aimed in the direction of the last noise. Whatever it was now broke a dry stick with a sharp crack. He could see a shadowy figure lumbering toward him. His heart was thumping and he could hardly hold the bow steady and now he heard a male voice, a familiar voice call out ' Spike, its Spike, come here Spike, here boy.' He laid his bow aside, his knees felt strangely weak as Spike calmly trotted back into view and behind the little dog the shadowy figure now turned into Malcolm walking toward him – holding his arm, and behind him came Rolf carrying two bows and the three came together and hugged and slapped each other's backs.

Seth asked what happened and Malcolm quickly told of the ambush and their escape and Seth said he also was attacked and now Rolf cut in and said they could talk about all this later, and he turned and grabbed Seth by the shoulders and looked into his eyes.

"Right. Where are the horses?"

Seth pointed back the way he had come.

"OK. Let's go find them." He said letting go of Seth.

"We can't."

"What do you mean?"

"They've been taken."

"Taken?"

"Yes. I, I had to leave them." He was stammering now. "I, I, I had no choice."

"You mean. The Bitchfolk have got Musto?" Rolf looked around at Malcolm. "They've got our horses." And then turning he looked fiercely at Seth. "Well let's go and take them back."

"We can't. We can't. Listen will ya listen." Seth cupped a hand to one ear. The faint sound of dogs baying reached them. "That's them. They're after us. We can't go back."

Rolf glared at Seth. "Christus and Maria, why didn't you come for us? With the horses we could be half way home by now."

The noise of the dogs sounded a little louder and Malcolm broke in.

"Come on Rolf, leave it. We gotta go."

"But, but, I could have galloped Musto up that hill: and you, you left him behind, left him to the Bitchfolk. The best horse, the best I've ever owned. And you – you left him. I don't believe this." He gave his head a shake.

"Come on Rolf, drop it, do ya hear, drop it. There's no time." Malcolm's voice died with a hollow groan and the rest of the things he tried to say refused to come. "Which, which?" Was all that came out as he closed his eyes and shook his head as if trying to shake the words free. Seth with a puzzled expression looked from Malcolm to Rolf and back to Malcolm again, but Rolf just cut straight in.

"So you came from that direction, right?" He said pointing.

Seth looked and nodded. Rolf looked at Malcolm who looked like he was gulping something and then he stopped and the words came easily and he waved his arm and said.

"Right, right. This way. Let's go."

Another burst of baying came from the dogs and Seth looked at Rolf and muttered something about being sorry. Rolf didn't bother looking up or saying anything as they stooped to grab the gear from the ground and share it for carrying and turning they followed Malcolm who was stalking off holding a bow and his injured arm and beside him trotted the little dog.

After covering maybe only three hundred yards, the big trees started to thin out and then stopped altogether and the land in front was covered in short yellow grass and dotted with scraggy dark tohmu trees. The ground now began to slope away into a gentle hollow leading away out of their sight. Malcolm continued walking but with each jolting step he winced with pain and he tried to lessen it by holding his useless arm with his good arm but it didn't seem to make much difference and he clenched his teeth and tried to ignore it. The tohmus stood silent witness to their flight and looking about him Malcolm shivered at the sight of the gaunt furrowed boughs lifting leafless thorn clad crowns to the sky, and still behind came the noise of the dogs, each baying outburst louder than the last.

Malcolm started praying, harsh whispers and broken phrases bursting from his lips, words he kept repeating over and over. And then for some reason which he could never explain he slowed and half running sideways he looked at the others and it was then that he noticed the woman. The others also slowed and turned to see what he was looking at and Malcolm groaned and muttered that that was the last thing they needed and he turned and led off again with a good loping stride, still holding his left arm and the noise of the dogs coming louder and louder, and following fifty yards behind came the woman holding a bundle in one arm and her robe above her knees in the other. Malcolm heard Rolf grunt his name twice and he turned to hear Rolf say that if they didn't do something quick, the woman would lead the Bitchfolk right to them and Malcolm asked what he had in mind and Rolf said to watch, and dropping the gear he carried he fitted an arrow and aimed at the woman who stopped, her face empty of expression.

"Don't." Said Malcolm, but Rolf continued to take aim and would have let fly had Malcolm not jumped to his side and grabbing his arm said

"Didn't you hear me?"

Rolf glared at Malcolm but put down the bow and gathered up the rest of the gear and turned to follow and Malcolm between deep breaths grunted.

"Wasn't she in that tent?''

"Yeah."

"How did she get loose? Did you...?"

"Yeah."

"Why?"

"Thought it might help. You know, muck things up. For the Bitchfolk."

Malcolm could think of nothing to say and he cursed softly under his breath and turned to take another look at the strange young woman and in doing so almost tripped over Spike running in front of his feet and his shoulder gave an extra spasm of pain and he cursed the little dog. Malcolm reckoned the chasing dogs and handlers were only about three or four hundred yards behind and gaining. He was vaguely familiar with the area they were hurrying through and remembered that ahead was a stream with high banks which might give shelter or at least a place where they could stand and fight and as if on cue a slow shallow stream came into view and curved out of sight to the right and the ground on its other bank sloped steeply upwards and was covered with thick head high tohmu scrub.

Malcolm reached the stream bank and looked around. Rolf and Seth were keeping up but the woman was obviously tiring and falling well behind and her hurrying stride was broken with stumbles and staggering steps and she was gasping for air. Malcolm waded into the water. It was barely knee deep and he hurriedly crossed and reached its other side where muddy silt sloped up to meet the scrub. Walking carefully he left deep footprints to the scrub edge and then walked backwards to the water placing his feet in the same prints and Rolf and Seth did the same with theirs. Malcolm bent down and with his good arm scooped up Spike and holding the little dog waded down the middle of the stream.

The chasing dogs sounded almost on top of them and they could clearly hear the high-pitched encouragement coming from the handlers. Malcolm looked around to see where the woman was. She was staggering directly toward where they were in the water and Malcolm found himself muttering "Come on, come on, hurry it up." and Seth with one arm beckoned, urging her on. If she was seen and captured Malcolm felt certain they would be killed or captured soon after, but now reaching the water's edge she waded in and started following. Fifty yards on, the stream curved right and flowed between steep banks and Malcolm led them there to where they were out of sight of the ford. The water deepened here to waist level and it was cold. Once out of sight and sheltered by the bank they stopped and Rolf and Seth found a dry sandy place just above the water to put down the gear so that they could stand with bows armed and ready.

The only sound now was the slight rippling noise of the water but then from the woman's bundle came a noise like a cat's meow followed by another and the men realized with horror that the bundle the woman carried concealed a baby, and it was hungry, and now they could hear the howling baying dogs arrive at the ford and they listened while handlers and dogs noisily crossed the stream to try and pick up the trail on the other side. Malcolm exchanged glances with Rolf and Seth who with bows at the ready stood in the waist deep water scanning the edge of the bank above in case one of the Bitchfolk should decide to come downstream and search, and then looking back to the woman he saw she was breast feeding the baby which was sucking away and making quiet contented little sounds. From where they stood they could tell that the dogs and their handlers had twice crossed the stream and come back to where they started, trying to work out what to do next and there was much loud argument until a single voice rose and the others fell silent and they listened to the measured speech of someone in authority giving orders and looking at the woman Malcolm noticed the terrified look on her face. The voice now stopped and again came the sound of splashing as the handlers dragged their dogs back through the water to the other side and then with huge relief they heard the baying and barking start again as the chase moved into the scrub and the sounds of it became less and gradually died. Rolf looked at Malcolm and said something about going and taking a look-see. Holding his bow at the ready he waded quietly to the bend and disappeared around it. Almost immediately he returned to say the ford was deserted. Malcolm nodded and grinned.

"Good, good. Those dogs are onto something else. There were deer tracks back there."

"But they'll come back won't they?" Said Seth.

"Yeah, and we're not going to be here." Said Rolf.

Malcolm turned and started wading downstream with a restless Spike under his good arm but a harsh insistent whisper broke from Seth.

"Mal, Mal, Malcolm. Where are we going?"

"This way." Malcolm kept on walking down the middle of the stream.

"But where? Where to?"

"To the river."

"The Deemah?"

"Yes."

"And then what?"

Malcolm turned around to face him. The water was less than knee deep and Malcolm let go of Spike who flopped into it before splashing his way to the bank.

"Now what's the problem?" He asked. "Didn't you hear me say what we're doing? Hmm? We're going to cross the river. Okay?" Malcolm turned as if to walk off.

"How?" Bleated Seth.

"We're going to walk on the water aren't we, eh Mal?"

Malcolm turned around and looked at Rolf through narrowed eyes. "We'll try to find a boat." He whistled out to Spike and started walking down the stream again. Seth grabbed Malcolm by the arm and at once let it go. "Sorry. Sorry. I didn't mean. I mean what if we can't find one?"

Malcolm turned, his face twisted in pain from where Seth grabbed him.

"Can't find a what?" He asked in exasperation.

"A boat."

Malcolm pursed his lips, turned and walked off.

"We'll be stuck here won't we? Until the Bitchfolk come to finish us off. You should have thought of that when you left without the horses. We could be on our way home now. Up here for thinking." Rolf tapped the side of his head.

"But we'll be caught if we can't get across?"

"Yeah. So why doncha use one of those Techno things and talk to Edgar and tell him that we're stuck here and ask him to come and get us. And tell him to be quick."

Malcolm heard the last exchange and turned around again and angrily told Rolf to shut up and that he wasn't looking after the horses and if he'd been in Seth's shoes he might have done exactly the same. Rolf started to say something but stopped. Malcolm was in no mood to listen anyway, but he was curious about the woman's whereabouts. Maybe she was still feeding the baby back at their last stop and had no plans to follow any further.

After another hundred yards the high bank on their right sloped down to a small sandy beach but they continued wading to avoid leaving footprints and then Spike spoiled it all by leaving the water and giving himself a good shake he scampered over the soft sand marking it with paw prints and Malcolm muttered under his breath about useless dogs and softly called Spike to come to heel, but he refused and calmly trotted beside them on the dry sandy bank. Malcolm gave up on him and led the others through the shallow stream water that began now to slow and widen until it was only ankle deep and Spike abandoned the dry ground and splashed across to them. A short distance ahead the stream petered out completely losing its identity in a wide area of marsh with scattered clumps of tall sabre reeds and plume grass and in the distance the reed clumps became larger and more numerous and then joined forces to form a continuous palisade marking the edge of the swamp proper, and above that and beyond the reeds, the cliffs guarding the Azmata reared out of the unseen river.

The men walked on without talking and sloshed through the shallow muddy water toward the forest of reeds and alongside trotted little Spike making small pattering splashes and then before realizing it the cover of the reeds was reached and the long sword like leaves arched and met over their heads. Brown stagnant water oozed at every squelching step and the air was heavy with the fetid smell of broken reed leaves mixed with the stink of mud. Malcolm nursing his sore shoulder asked Rolf to take the lead in forcing a way through the dense tangle and he now took over walking in front and pushing the reeds out of the way or treading them down. Malcolm quipped that it looked like they were building a road, and it was true that their path through the reeds was broad and paved with the flattened and squashed leaves of sabre reeds.

The resident marsh hens resented the intrusion and continually marked their clumsy passage with grating screeches and the men seemed to take it in turn to curse the jittery birds. After some time of squelching progress Malcolm called a halt. He reckoned the river was only a short distance away and didn't want to risk breaking suddenly out into the open river bank and being seen, even by Lam fishermen who would probably tip off the Bitchfolk. They were about to move off again when a rustling in the reeds announced the arrival of the woman. Malcolm hoped she might have given up following but now she was close behind although barely in sight and judging from the mewing sounds issuing from the bundle she carried, her baby was still hungry. Malcolm craned his neck to look at her. He thought she looked young, maybe only fourteen years old, certainly not more than eighteen. She didn't really look like a Lam although she was dressed like one. There was something different about her. Her skin was dark, darker than a deep tan, her hair short and curly and in the middle of her forehead was a small tattoo of some sort. She looked almost like one of the Bitchfolk, with the same build, but no, that was hardly likely although she was definitely shorter than the normal run of Lam women. Her likeness to the Bitchfolk was based mainly on what he remembered of the ones who attacked them two days earlier. He thought it wasn't all that important but he did know she was tied up in the tent and for some odd reason Rolf cut her loose. The woman ended up following and almost got them caught and killed. That was a close call at the ford: but why all the fuss? Why were they attacked? What did the Bitchfolk have against them? Unless it was because of what that idiot Rolf did by killing one of them, but then it was the Bitchfolk who attacked and, without provocation. In fact, the first attack was an ambush and happened well before Rolf freed the strange woman.

## 9

Malcolm shook his head. Nothing made sense. He turned back to the others and in the confined space in the reeds he squeezed past Rolf and pushed his way carefully and quietly for another thirty yards and then suddenly and as expected, the forest of reeds ended on the shore of the Deemah. The others peered past him through the last thin screen of reeds. The river they looked out on was wide, very wide. Two hundred yards separated them from the other side where a shingle beach spilled from the foot of a craggy cliff and from a slot in the cliff tumbled a rapid stream and from where they hid its noisy rush across the stones swelled and faded in the slight upriver breeze.

The men squatted down for a council of war. The woman was nowhere in sight. Seth said she was feeding the baby again. Malcolm winced with pain as he shifted his left arm. Rolf asked him how it was and Malcolm said it ached and he could hardly lift his arm. Rolf turned to the nearest reed clump and cut several wide leaves and roughly twisted a plait that he hung around Malcolm's neck to form a sling for his arm. Malcolm grunted his thanks and the three looked at each other in silence before Seth spoke up and asked what was going to happen next. Malcolm nodded his head in the direction of the river and said they needed to cross it and that meant finding a boat, and it was likely that a careful search would uncover a Lam fishing dugout hidden nearby and close to the water.

"How long have we got?"' Asked Seth.

"What? Before the Bitchfolk catch up with us?" Seth nodded.

"Don't know. Not long. Certainly before dark though. So let's look for a boat eh?"

"Will we use it to get away? Down river?"

"No, no. Too risky. They'll be watching the river like hawks."

"So where do we go?"

"Over there." Malcolm pointed across the river. "If we can get across we'll try and find a place up that creek. Wait until the dust settles and then come back and see how the land lies. But first we need a boat or we won't be going anywhere. Now Rolf you look upriver, Seth you go that way. Take care – don't be seen."

Rolf stepped over the pouches and bows and arrows he had been carrying and disappeared into the reeds walking upstream. Seth headed off in the opposite direction and for a short time Malcolm could hear them as they made their way through the chafing leaves: and then there was silence and he was alone with only Spike for company. He tried to doze but the warm air brought out midges and they crawled around his neck and face biting as they went and Malcolm used his good arm to slap and brush them away. A single bent sabre leaf started to gently sway in some unfelt breath of air, each slow sway ending with a sudden quick flick back to its start and another sway and another flick and Malcolm watched as the errant little wind passed on and the long leaf once more hung still, and beside him on the firm damp mud lay Spike panting and snapping at an occasional blowfly. The image of the dead Bitchfolk and her twitching leg came back. Rolf; he couldn't help himself could he. Couldn't pass up the chance to show how tough he was. How good with the bow he was, especially in front of Seth. He should have stood up to Edgar. Why did he allow himself to be talked into having Rolf along? He'd been a pain in the neck from day one. Always wanting to have things done his way. What happened to Seth could easily have happened to Rolf. But then Rolf owned Musto. The best horse in all Riparia, according to him. Christus almighty, he would have been much better doing this whole job on his own. Instead he found himself stuck with these two, and, part timers at that.

A short time later the sound of something pushing through the reeds jerked Malcolm fully alert but it was only Seth returning with the news that he had found a cracked and rotten dugout without paddles. It looked abandoned. He said he explored as far downstream as the reeds grew and there was no sign of any launching runway. Malcolm pursed his lips and said nothing and Seth sat down. More time passed and there was no sign of Rolf and Malcolm began to feel uneasy in case in case he'd been spotted by the Bitchfolk but he said nothing to Seth who seemed to thrive on anxiety but almost before Malcolm finished thinking about it Seth spoke up wondering when Rolf was going to return. Malcolm told him not to worry and that Rolf was big and ugly enough to look after himself and probably was searching a larger area. Seth sat there his elbows resting on his drawn up knees and his forehead resting on his clasped hands so that his face was hidden from Malcolm who guessed that he was probably muttering frantic pleas to the Mother of Christus. Malcolm and Seth both jumped up again when more rustling in the reeds came from behind and Seth stood and walked a few paces and peered through the sabre leaves. He turned and told Malcolm that it was the woman who was now sitting down resting a short distance away. The two men looked at each other and Malcolm said there was nothing they could do now except wait and if Rolf was in trouble, he was sure they would have heard something by now. A sudden rustle of reeds announced Rolf's return. Malcolm looked at him.

"Anything?"

Rolf shrugged and held out his hands palms upwards. "Nothing." He looked at Seth. "I thought he would have found something."

"He found something old." Said Malcolm. "We'll have to try and use it."

"What did he find?" Rolf asked as if Seth was not even present.

"Ask him yourself."

Rolf turned to look at Seth who described the finding of the derelict dugout without paddles.

"It's close to the water, is it?"

"Yes but it's cracked. It's rotten."

Rolf looked back at Malcolm who said.

"We'll have to use it – got no choice. Can you give him a hand to get it here? Oh by the way." He jerked his thumb in the direction of the woman. Rolf gave a puzzled look before he took several strides and parted the reeds. The others heard him curse softly and he returned and his eyes narrowed as he looked at Seth.

"I still think we'd be better off to go and have a crack at getting the horses back."

"Forget it Rolf. Maybe in a day or two. I want the river between us and the Bitchfolk, and soon, Okay! Otherwise." His voice trailed off.

"Right, right. You're the boss." Rolf cut in with the singsong tone he used whenever he wanted to show that he disagreed with something. It made Malcolm's blood boil.

"Right Seth. Show us where this thing is."

Seth moved off followed by Rolf and they both disappeared into the reeds. They arrived back in what seemed no time at all and without the dugout.

"Where is it?" Asked Malcolm.

"It's useless." Said Rolf

"I'll be the judge of that. I need to see it."

"Why don't we go back for the horses eh?"

Malcolm's face began to screw up and pucker but he looked away and gritted his teeth before turning to Rolf again.

"When, when are you going to get it into your head? We are not going back for the horses. We're going over there. If you hadn't been so stupid, we wouldn't be in this fix."

"What do you mean?"

"If you hadn't killed the Bitchwoman." He stopped gaping and mouthing silently.

"We could have turned back." Rolf snapped.

"There was a job needed doing"

"Yeah, but we didn't do it."

"That's because you had to be the big boy."

"They started it. They tried to kill us."

"Well they're really stirred up now."

Malcolm turned to Seth. "Show me where this thing is?"

"Calm down Mal. We'll go get it." Said Rolf. "You'll see how bad it is."

They disappeared into the reeds once more but not before Seth turned and looked at Malcolm with a helpless expression and gave a shrug. They were gone much longer this time and then the first Malcolm knew of their return was the crunch he heard as the dugout rammed into the muddy bank and peering through the screen of reeds he saw Rolf and Seth step out of it and lift it up before tipping it sideways to empty out the water. Malcolm walked out to look at it. The dugout was narrow and big cracks showed in its sides.

"I see what you mean."

"It hasn't been used in ages. There's no paddles Mal and it leaks. The water just pours in." Seth looked worried.

"But it floats doesn't it?" Said Malcolm.

"Yeah. Just. We'll have to paddle with our hands, and we'll have to use something to bail with." Said Rolf. "You'll have to use my hat. Can you do that Mal? I mean bail water one handed?"

"I'll have to."

Rolf handed over his hat.

"Well, before we load our gear lets stuff some of those cracks with something. Reeds, reeds. Use some leaves."

"Good idea." Grunted Rolf who used his knife to cut some of the long sabre leaves and Seth scrunched them up with a handful of damp soil and packed the largest cracks."

"That's better, now the gear can go in. Do you think you were seen?" Asked Malcolm.

"We saw nobody." Grunted Rolf as he bent down to pick up the gear.

Seth and Rolf loaded in the food pouches, bows, arrows and spare clothing and then Rolf kneeled in the bow. Malcolm whistled up Spike who scampered into the middle of the dugout and stood panting and wagging his tail until Malcolm ordered him to sit and the little dog tried to find a place out of the way of the men and ended up climbing on top of their gear sitting there whimpering and looking worried.

"We'll tip over if he stays up there." Muttered Rolf.

Malcolm got in and kneeled in the middle and one handed hauled Spike down from his perch and dragged him awkwardly behind him while Seth pushed them out from the bank and scrambled into the stern and they shot off from the shore, Rolf and Seth paddling madly with their hands and Malcolm waiting in the middle with the hat flattened in the bottom ready to gather up the water. There was hardly any freeboard and whenever the little craft rocked or one of the occupants shifted their weight, water slopped in and it also began to seep through the filled cracks and before fifty yards were gone, Malcolm was bailing furiously and his injured shoulder ached as he used both hands to slosh the water filled hat over the side. Rolf was busy talking out loud to himself about how lucky they were going to be not to sink in the middle of the river and all get drowned and everything he said started with Christus and Maria.

Malcolm now noticed pale stones showing on the river bottom and then quite suddenly their little craft grounded and they stepped out and towed it through the shallows to the shore. Spike leaped out and began jumping and splashing through the water and once ashore gave himself a good shake. Seth continued pushing the dugout through the shallows while Malcolm and Rolf walked the hundred yards up to where the noisy stream entered the river. The shore on this side was stony in contrast to where they set out from. They looked about for a place to hide the dugout and were just about to drag it to where a large dead tree lay stranded when Malcolm looked back and cursed. The woman was standing knee deep in the water exactly where they paddled from. She was standing looking at them. Malcolm hadn't wanted to think about her. She was her own problem and it was different from theirs. Her being there was the result of another of Rolf's idiotic impulses. Why couldn't she have just stayed hidden in the reeds? Out of sight, out of mind. But now, she was standing in the open, a sign pointing in their direction. He looked away, determined to forget the woman but couldn't stop sneaking looks back at her. Standing there like that was her sentence of death. Starvation or the Bitchfolk would do it; take your pick.

If she's going to stand there like that, we might just as well leave the Bitchfolk a written message saying where we're going to hide. If we go back for her it won't be for her sake. He wondered what she must be thinking. Looking at them, safe on this side, safe for the time being anyway. Rolf and Seth also stood looking and saying nothing. Standing close to the noisy rush of the creek Malcolm shouted.

"She hasn't a chance."

Rolf looked at him through narrowed eyes.

"Forget her. Just forget her."

"No we won't. We can't."

"We sure can."

"She'll give us away."

"How?"

"The Bitchfolk'll get her. She'll talk."

"Well you go get her. I'm not."

"You cut her loose."

"She's not coming."

"She has to. We can't leave her there. Like that."

Seth looked embarrassed as Malcolm and Rolf quarreled.

"She's not coming. She'll be a drag." Said Rolf. "And what about this thing? Wasn't fit for one trip."

Malcolm turned to Seth and pointed to the dugout.

"Get in. You and me. We'll get her."

Seth obediently grabbed hold of the dugout and began to pull it back into the water. Rolf screwed his eyes and shaking his head said.

"You're mad. Do ya hear? Mad. You'll never make it. Your arm's had it."

Seth dragged the dugout back into the water and Malcolm stepped in and sat down and motioned to Seth to push it out from the shore.

Rolf standing on the shore with hands on hips suddenly yelled.

"Stop, stop. Get out. I'll go. Seth and me, we'll go."

Malcolm awkwardly put one leg over the side and stood up and waded ashore while Rolf took his place in the dugout.

"You better start praying man. You know I can't swim."

Seth put one foot in the dugout and pushed off with the other and the little craft rocked and shot back out into the current. Spike started to bark at the departing boat and Malcolm cursed him into silence before turning again to watch. Both men hand paddled furiously but twice on the way Seth stopped and bailed out the water. The return crossing seemed to take an age and when they reached the other side they waded along the shoreline, pushing the dugout to where the woman stood. Malcolm could see both Rolf and Seth beckoning to her. The woman remained immobile. The men beckoned again and Seth threw out more water and still the woman stood in the river's edge like a dark post. And then slowly she moved and with relief Malcolm watched as she waded to where they held the dugout and she stepped into it and sat down at one end and then he saw Rolf waving an arm at her and she appeared to move on her knees into the middle and all the while Rolf and Seth held the dugout steady. Rolf now took his place in the boat and again Seth pushed off and got in and they were on their way back.

They nearly never made it. With the extra weight and only Rolf and Seth paddling and bailing, the cranky craft looked like it was going to sink at the half way mark. Malcolm could see it slowing and settling deeper in the water.

Coming back with the woman took three times as long as their second trip and when the dugout eventually grounded it was half filled with water and the current carried it a hundred yards further downstream from their first landfall. Malcolm was waiting and tried to help pull the boat ashore but Rolf pushed him away. The woman, her clothes drenched from the waist down stepped out holding the baby close to her and unseen in its wrapping.

Once more Seth pushed the dugout through the shallows toward where the creek entered, the others slowly walking over the dry stones beside him and then Rolf helped drag it from the water and across to where the flood stranded tree lay and they dumped it behind the trunk where it was hidden from sight on the river side. Seth ran back to the water's edge to retrieve the gear Malcolm was unable to carry and the group wearily plodded over the soft gravel toward where the creek poured out of the cleft. Half way there Spike stopped suddenly and looked back across the water and Malcolm also stopped to see what the dog was looking at, and then faintly over the noise of the creek came the sound of a another dog barking and across the river they saw two dogs running and circling at the place they had left from and then quite suddenly and with a chill they watched as a figure short and stocky and holding a spear, stepped clear of the reeds and looked across the water. Rolf turned and looked at Malcolm and shook his head. The woman looked as well and then holding the baby more closely lowered her head and followed Malcolm, but Seth looked wildly about and started to call out to Malcolm who did not answer and Seth caught up with him and grabbed his sore arm again making him pull a face.

"They've seen us. We've been seen."

Malcolm said nothing.

"What'll we do? Can we hide up here? Can we? Can we?"

"I don't know."

"What if it's a dead end?"

"We'll know soon enough."

With the sound of feet crunching through gravel, the little group trudged across the stones toward where the stream had sawed its course through the cliff.

# 10.

The creek was not so little and its swift cold flow squeezing between rock walls needed to be waded in the shallows for a short distance before opening out to a large, deep and slowly eddying pool enclosed by more walls of the same smooth stone. The water was crystal clear and looking into it gave Seth the impression that the large rocks paving the bottom could easily be picked out by hand. They walked beside the water on a wide strip of dry sand pocked with deer hoof prints. Seth wondered out loud how they were going to get up past the cliff and Malcolm pointed to the hoof prints and said that if deer could do it then so could they.

The Deemah was now out of sight and ahead the deep pool in front curved slightly to where it was fed by water dropping with a rush over a short steep fall. The strip of sand narrowed to nearly nothing where the water shot with a roar into the pool and beside the fall was a series of moss covered stone ledges from which hung stunted myrtle shrubs. A cold wind from the falling water blasted fine drifting spray as Malcolm and Rolf stood trying to work out the safest and easiest way to climb the rock face. The roar from the falling water made speech impossible but with head-shakes, nods and waving arms the two men quickly agreed about where to make a start. Rolf turned to Seth and motioned for him to go first and Seth dropped the gear he was carrying and lithely sprang up and using a gnarled myrtle branch for a hold deftly swung himself onto a narrow ledge above the others and turned to reach down to help Malcolm who was next, and with only one good arm, he needed to be boosted from below by Rolf before he was able to reach Seth's outstretched hand and half scrambling and in danger of falling he pulled himself onto the ledge and for a moment he stood there unsteadily before moving beyond Seth to where the slope eased. Next Rolf picked up the bows and gear and tossed them up one by one to Seth who caught each item and passed it behind him to Malcolm. Spike was now leaping around and barking and anxious to join Malcolm but he dodged away each time Rolf leaned down to grab him. Malcolm was whistling at him and finally the little dog edged closer to Rolf with his rear end wagging absurdly and his head lowered and Rolf grabbed him and with one swing sent him sailing through the air to land at Seth's feet who nearly overbalanced and the dog looked as if he was about to fall back with his short legs scrambling for a hold and in a despairing lunge Seth caught him by one ear and the little dog was hauled yelping up the face and set down in front of Malcolm who grabbed him by the neck and pushed him further up the now easier rock  slope and Spike scampered up and turning around looked down with a pleased look on his face and panting madly.

Rolf now turned to where the woman waited and motioned for her to come forward. She made no move and Rolf again beckoned and still she stood as if rooted to the ground. Rolf walked over to her and went to take her arm but she angrily shook him away. Rolf looked up at Malcolm and raised his arms in a gesture of helplessness. Malcolm opened his mouth and yelled something but the roar from the falling water drowned the sound. The drifting spray drenched Rolf's face and hair and the woman closed her robe over the baby sheltering it from the cold and wet. Rolf made another attempt to grab her arm but quick as a cat she pulled loose and struck him, her nails scoring red streaks across his face and turning she stumbled back toward the fall. Rolf put a hand to his cheek, looked at the blood on it and then glared at her. The woman looked at him and then slowly and giving him a wide berth she edged her way toward where the others had climbed up but not once did she take her eyes off Rolf.

Malcolm, looking at the little scene from above thought there was no way she was going to be able to make it while holding the baby and he motioned for Seth to go down as far as he could to help her. Seth slid down a little and then holding onto a myrtle branch reached out with his hand. The woman appeared to stand on tiptoe and reached up with her free hand but there was no possibility of grabbing hold of Seth while she still held onto the baby. She looked down and then stepped a little closer but it was still hopeless; hopeless that is until she was suddenly lifted bodily from behind by Rolf who took her by surprise and when her hand made contact with Seth's, Rolf with one mighty shove against her buttocks pushed her to where Seth could put an arm behind her and help her back up to where Malcolm was standing, and she, still clutching the baby inside her robe made her way up and past him and into a small thicket of myrtles where she immediately sat down and opened her robe to check on the child.

Now it was Rolf's turn, and looking around he spotted some large rocks at the water's edge and two of them he dragged over the sand to where he formed a step that by standing on, enabled him to reach the outstretched hand of Seth, who helped him make it up the rock face. Breathing heavily from the effort Rolf paused before shaking his head and then he bent down and picked up some of the gear and carried it further up the sloping stone and past where Malcolm was sitting. Malcolm grinned and asked what had happened to his cheek. Rolf gave him a fierce look and continued walking.

After briefly resting Malcolm said it was time to move and he asked Rolf to take the lead and to keep a look out for a place to camp. Above the rock face the slope leveled. Underfoot was a pad of spongy soil with the roots of the myrtles snaking through it and the scrub became thicker which meant forcing their way through with heads bent to stop faces and eyes being scratched, and then taller trees took over and the scrub stopped and they were able to walk upright without much trouble and a little way on their left the stream made a peculiar howling noise from the deep rocky groove it raced through.

They walked with the stream on their left, the woman only a few paces behind Seth and in front of him was Malcolm with Rolf leading. A short time later the stream cut into the cliff face on their side but an old rock-slide spilled right across the gully floor and the stream flowed underground and out of sight, making a hollow roaring sound. Trees and shrubs assumed grotesque twisting shapes growing through the rocks toward the light and the rocks themselves were green with a covering of thin dry moss. Progress slowed as Rolf tried to find the easiest way through the slide and sometimes they crawled through narrow fissures and tunnels under the tilted sloping slabs and quite soon came out on the other side and again began walking up a gentle slope under straight growing trees. At Malcolm's suggestion they headed toward the valley wall, climbing again as the ground became steeper and all the time looking for somewhere to spend the night.

Rolf led to where their side of the valley floor met its enclosing cliff and for some time they followed this uneven skirting of stone until Rolf stopped and they all stopped and Rolf looked at Malcolm and they both nodded and pouches and weapons were dropped on the ground. The chosen spot was an almost level bench sheltered from above by a massive smooth rock overhang. The floor was carpeted with dry sandy soil and small rocks and Rolf and Seth after stacking their weapons and pouches on one side set about clearing some of the stones to make it more comfortable for sitting and sleeping. Malcolm gathered small twigs and branches and reaching into a pouch for a flint began building a fire and Rolf carried the canvas water bucket down through the trees to the creek while the woman moved to the back of the shelter and sitting down opened her robe and offered her breast to the baby. Seth made several trips to bring in armfuls of dry fern fronds to use as bedding and then sitting down, took off his wet boots and shook them out before putting them back on again. Malcolm, and Rolf who was back from collecting water, also sat down and did the same.

The rock bulge they sheltered under was part of the base of an escarpment that capped their side of the narrow valley. A similar formation rimmed the opposite side and looking downstream over the tree tops they could see through a narrow gateway part of the Deemah and beyond the river a long sweep of Lamentasia and its yellow rolling grasslands. Malcolm sorted through the pouches and mentally reckoned up their food supplies of dried meat straps and dried fruit. He said he thought there was enough for two days, perhaps a little more if they were careful. Rolf asked if that was taking the woman into account and Malcolm said it was but that he thought they should go easy for a start in case they were stuck there for longer. Rolf agreed and added they should be able to kill a deer somewhere nearby and Malcolm said yes but until that happened he wanted to be cautious, and so far it looked as if they were blessed with what Seth managed to grab from the horses.

The fire was smoking strongly but at least it was giving out heat. Mountain thrushes were calling four note fugues like tolling bells, the small bell-ringers unseen in the surrounding trees. The sun lay hidden behind a cloud. Malcolm set out four portions of food and taking a strap of meat to chew turned to look down valley. A puff of warm air blew in. He looked through the gap at the valley entrance and out to the distant reaches of Lamentasia. A storm was gathering with curtains of dark cloud moving parallel with the Deemah, and above them the sky was clear except for the solitary dark cloud shaped like a giant fish with its mouth wide open. The cloud's outline was sharply defined and the fish's belly glowed with a gold edge all the way from its enormous under slung jaw down to its pathetic tail and as he watched, the sun popped out of the fish's mouth and its light flooded the camp-site and coloured the upper part of the rock escarpment orange before beginning its slow dive behind the frowning clouds of Lamentasia. He turned back to the fire where Rolf was heating a meat strap wrapped around a stick.

Malcolm looked to see where the woman was. She was still sitting away from the fire at the back of the overhang. The baby was finished feeding and lay drowsing in her arms. Malcolm picked up the woman's food portion and carried it back to where she sat. She pulled her robe across in front of her and stared up at him. Malcolm held out a strap of meat. After a pause she reached out and took it, put one end in her mouth and began slowly chewing. Malcolm placed the rest of the food on the ground in front of her. He wondered if she was thirsty and went back and retrieved the water bag and handed it to her. She lay the baby down and putting the water bag to her mouth gulped noisily.

"Hey, that's all we've got." Called Rolf. "It's tricky getting to the creek."

"Don't worry. There's plenty left."

The woman finished drinking. Her eyes briefly caught Malcolm's and held them as she put down the water bag before she picked up the baby and cuddled its downy head to her cheek. Malcolm carried the water bag back and set it down beside the rest of their supplies. He crouched down with the other two. Seth sat close to the fire warming a strap of meat on a stick. Malcolm jerking his head in the direction of the woman asked.

"Has she said anything?"

Rolf looked at Seth and then shrugging his shoulders looked at Malcolm who remained crouching.

"Not to me. Apart from that." He stopped and gently patted his red streaked cheek. "What about you Seth. She said anything?"

Seth shook his head and Malcolm looking across the top of the fire at the far valley side asked.

"Wonder what her name is?"

"Do you think she's got one?" Asked Rolf.

"Course she will. Do you know anyone without a name? We should find it out."

"Why? Is it that important?"

"Yeah, I reckon."

"Well. Go ask her. I say the hell with her. She's been nothing but trouble so far."

Malcolm gave a sly grin. "You set her loose."

Rolf turned back to the fire. "Ask what you like."

Malcolm stood up and with his good arm rubbed the fronts and backs of his thighs before moving back to where the woman sat cradling the baby. He stood in front of her, looking down at her. Her robe was off her left shoulder exposing her upper arm and Malcolm noticed it was ringed with a tattooed amulet. He looked at her face and now noticed that the tattoo on her forehead was in the shape of a small crab with one outsize pincer. The woman looked back at him, her dark eyes meeting and holding Malcolm's. She continued to stare, her eyes traveling over him, up and down slowly and then back to his eyes where they remained fixed as if seeing right through him. Malcolm gave a shiver. Never before had he been inspected like this, and certainly not by a woman. He opened his mouth to speak but the words stalled. He closed his mouth and swallowed deeply twice before attempting to speak again and this time the words consented to come. He pointed to himself and blurted his name.

"Malcolm." He said pointing to himself. "Malcolm, Malcolm. My name is Malcolm." He pointed his forefinger at the woman and slowly said. "Your name. What is your name?" She said nothing and he asked her again. The woman continued to stare at him her head tilted slightly on one side as if she could not see properly. Again Malcolm tried, pointing to himself and repeating his name and asking for her's and still she sat there, eyeing him. Malcolm shrugged, turned and walked the few yards back to the fire, shaking his head as he went. Rolf chuckled. Malcolm sat down and then a female voice from behind called out loud and clear.

"Rahnuk. I am Rahnuk."

Malcolm half turned and raised his hand to signal he heard.

"Well, well, well." Said Rolf. "You got through after all. Rahnuk. I wonder what that means."

Malcolm hooked his arms around his knees and gave out a long sigh. "Yeah. I wonder. She knows our talk."

The daylight rapidly faded and cold air started flowing down their narrow valley and in silence Rolf fed the fire with wood while Seth dragged a large twiggy fallen branch close to it and wet garments were draped over it to dry. They sat down again arms clasped around knees and staring into the fire and then Rolf looked up and asked.

"Okay. So what do you think this is all about? What makes eagles hunt flies, eh Mal?"

Nobody said anything until Rolf again spoke.

"Now Seth. Come clean. What's with those crazy women? What have they got against you?"

Seth started to say something and then sighed and shook his head.

"Come on. You must have done something to stir them up."

"You did. You started it. You killed one of them."

"Now come on. We're not going into that again." Said Malcolm.

"Maybe, they're trying to recruit us for something." Said Rolf.

"Sure. Recruit dead men? Ha. Ha."

There was more silence and then Rolf jerking his thumb in Rahnuk's direction said.

"Hey. Do you think she's got something to do with it?"

"Maybe, but why did they have two go's at us before we even saw her?"

"She looks like one."

"When will we go back for the horses?" Asked Seth.

"Good question." Countered Rolf. "You lost them. You lost Musto as well as your own and Malcolm's. And Edgar. Edgar'll be mighty peeved if we come back without his." He started idly poking the fire with a stick.

"I see you brought your nice new jerkin. You didn't bring anything much for Mal and me? Didja free the pigeons?"

"Yes."

"Well that's something. At least Edgar'll know we're in strife by now."

Seth said nothing and hugging his knees he stared into the fire.

"We'll try for the horses in a day or two." Said Malcolm.

"Tomorrow?" Asked Seth.

"Maybe. Depends on the Bitchfolk. How long they hang around for."

"Won't they take the horses?"

Malcolm shook his head. "Don't know if they use horses. They were good mounts."

"Musto was the best." Cut in Rolf.

Malcolm gave a little laugh.

"Edgar's pack horse, it's got a real mean streak. Like as not it'll kick the head off anyone it's not used to." He laughed again.

"What about Justin and Andre?" Asked Rolf.

"Don't know'. Hope they're all right."

"What exactly happened today?" Malcolm said looking at Seth.

Seth told of how he was attacked while guarding the horses and that he'd escaped after wounding one of the Bitchfolk, and then Malcolm and Rolf told Seth the story of their ordeal and afterward all three shook their heads and laughed at their lucky escape. Malcolm was still nagged by the worry that Seth may not have released the pigeons after all and he was trying for reassurance without suggesting Seth was being less than truthful.

"Anyway, the pigeons have gone?"

"Yeah. They didn't want to go. Had to shake the basket to make them fly. The noise they made, taking off. The Bitchfolk almost got me again because of that."

"Been cooped up too long. Don't like moving sometimes."

"What will Edgar do?" Asked Seth.

"Nothing. What can he do? 'Cept get Dibius and his friends to pray." Said Rolf.

"By the way Rolf. Where did all that smoke come from?"

"What smoke?"

"You know. In the tents. Orlo's tents. When I came to; there was smoke everywhere."

"Oh that. I just pulled some sticks out of the fire and tossed them around and things went up in flames. Then I arrived just in time to stop your throat being cut. The rest you know."

"Anyone got any blatto?" Asked Seth.

Malcolm and Rolf looked at each other and laughed. Seth loved chewing the sweet gum blatto and all his supplies were with his horse. He looked crestfallen. Rolf got up to put more wood on the fire. There was a noise from the back of the shelter. The woman was obviously feeling the cold, the lower part of her robe was still damp and she approached the fire to one side of the men and sat down as close to it as she could, holding the baby inside her robe and avoiding looking at them. Malcolm said he was dog tired and gathered some of the dried ferns to lie down on. Rolf and Seth agreed to take turns at keeping the fire going while first Malcolm and then Rahnuk lay down to sleep.

## 11.

It was still dark when the first thrushes marked dawn with their fluting calls, and then Rahnuk sat up to feed her crying baby. Twice during the night she woke to the infant's crying and fed it and each time Rolf put more wood on the fire. Malcolm and Seth dozed on and off all night long but now both were awake and Seth made a start on getting the fire going again while Rolf began wrapping meat straps around a stick before heating them over the flames. Malcolm stood and massaged his sore shoulder and all the while little sucking and mewing sounds came from the baby as it greedily pulled away at Rahnuk's breast.

The clothes hung overnight near the fire were surprisingly dry but further away the air was cold and now in the growing light trees were turning from grey to green. Rahnuk finished feeding the baby and leaving the others began clambering down to the creek to clean the infant. She returned a short time later and ate the food Rolf put aside for her. The men finished eating. The sun was already catching the tops of trees on the opposite side of the valley and Seth picked up his bow and several arrows and announced he was going upstream to try for a deer. With a few light bounds he disappeared into the trees, an eager Spike skipping at his heels. Rolf took the canvas bag to get more water.

Malcolm stood at the front of the shelter staring through the gap and across the Deemah, taking in the view of the now sunlit grasslands of Lamentasia and thinking – thinking again back to the events of the previous days and their chaotic flight. Why, why were they the target of Bitchfolk hostility? A recurring thought nagged him. The woman Rahnuk was maybe mixed up with it? But why? How could she be important unless the baby had a bearing on things? No, no. That didn't make sense. No matter they would just have to wait where they were for a couple of days and then one of them would sneak back to near Orlo's and see about retrieving the horses. They might have to buy them back. That would take some doing. All their trade goods were with the horses.

Malcolm continued to stare, almost in a daze, looking through the gap, across to the river when quite suddenly his little window onto the Deemah was entered by a small dark object that speedily skimmed into view and then disappeared behind the sloping rock spur marking the entrance to their valley. Then another appeared followed immediately by two more. The breath caught in Malcolm's throat. Dugouts – why were dugouts crossing to their side of the Deemah? He watched and counted as eight of the little craft each ferrying three or four people crossed his line of vision. The air was still and then by some freak condition, faint but unmistakable came a brief snatch of sound from yelping and howling dogs. Malcolm's knees went weak. He turned to see if the woman had heard. She was standing, staring back at him, her mouth open and face drained of colour. In that instant it was clear to each of them that the woman warriors from Sessilia had not given up.

Rolf was clambering back from the creek with the water when he heard Malcolm's bellow recalling Seth. Malcolm started to show the woman how to make a sling to carry the baby on her back when Rolf arrived and asked what the matter was and without turning around Malcolm told him about the dugouts, and that there was no time to lose if they were to escape being killed. Rolf dropped the water bag and pulled Malcolm away from the woman and with a fierce look in his eyes demanded.

"She's not coming. She's not. Mal. Is She? Is she coming?"

Malcolm looked at him.

"Mal. Is she?" He kept jerking Malcolm's arm forgetting it was the sore one."

"She'll hear you."

"I don't care who hears me." He shouted. "She's not coming."

"Why?"

"She'll slow us down. Do you know what you're doing?"

Malcolm pulled himself free and turned back to the woman and Rolf with a loud sigh and a look of resignation bent down, picked up a pouch and started to load food and clothing into it just as Seth and Spike came bounding back into the shelter. Without looking at Seth, Malcolm continued helping the woman fold the sling for the baby and said.

"They're onto us. The Bitchfolk. They're after us again."

"What."

"You heard. I've just counted eight dugouts crossing the Deemah. Dogs and all. We've heard them. It didn't take us long to get here. They'll be quicker."

"Where. Where can we go?"

Rolf straightened up from packing the pouches and said.

"If we stay here we're dead. We've got to run for it. Up this valley. And Mal says she's coming."

"But this takes us into the Azmata."

"That's right."

"But. We can't go there."

"Got a better idea?"

"We're like flies in a bottle." Wailed Seth.

Malcolm finished helping the woman and turned to them.

"Now listen." His eyes blazed. "There's at least twenty, maybe thirty Bitchfolk coming after us. If they catch us in these trees we don't stand a chance. But, but if we can make it into open ground and find a place to make a stand we might. There's got to be open country further on. I can't shoot but you two can. We've got about thirty arrows. That's all. And not much food either. Now let's get going."

He turned and looked at the woman.

"There won't be many rests. When we stop, feed your baby."

She made no response but Malcolm continued to look at her before turning and motioning for Rolf to lead the way. Somehow, Christus alone knew how, the woman was wearing a coarse poncho style robe that fastened in front with wood toggles. She also wore stout leather lace up boots and over her shoulder was a strap to a light leather bag, which must be what she used to carry the cloths to keep her baby clean. Apart from her footwear Malcolm thought her whole get-up looked Lamentasite in style. They would have to move rapidly to have any chance of keeping ahead of the Bitchfolk and in rough country good footwear was vital.

Rolf and Seth shouldered the pouches and weapons. Seth quickly cut two walking staffs – one for Malcolm and the other for the woman Rahnuk. They left the shelter behind, the abandoned cooking fire puffing out light grey smoke. Rolf led the way followed by Malcolm then the woman and Seth brought up the rear while Spike with his tongue hanging out trotted along at Malcolm's heels.

The air was cool and still and the going good with little undergrowth beneath the trees and the valley floor rose gently except where occasional rock benches rose in front of them and up the face of these they toiled grabbing for support at whatever they could, small sapling trunks or rocks until at the top, the valley floor would again resume its easy gradient. The trees were tall and varied in type but the clear pale sky was often visible through small gaps. The valley was a narrow gorge and their route lay close to the stream that roared out from its sunken rock bed. Nobody talked. At the top of the second rock bench Malcolm red faced and perspiring called a rest and they leaned against trees or sat on rocks or mossy logs and the woman pulled the sling around to her front and offered a breast to the baby. When she finished, Malcolm signaled for Rolf to start walking again. Small noisy side creeks rushing across their way appeared more frequently and the approach was always mossy and damp and required care in crossing to avoid a slip and this slowed their progress each time.

After leaving their overnight shelter, they stopped three times to take brief rests, and now they noticed a change in the character of the valley. Gone was the narrow gorge; gone the bench like rises, now the stream frisked along beside them tumbling over and around the smooth boulders of its bed. The trees were much shorter and all of one sort and thick moss carpeted the ground and tree trunks and the outermost twigs trailed drooping filaments of another sort of moss, the whole producing an effect of tranquility and enchantment which Seth commented on and Malcolm agreed it was very pretty but reminded him that behind and certainly gaining were fierce women warriors with dogs. He called for another rest and they halted, longer this time as handfuls of dried fruit were eaten and water drunk from a small creek.

They rested in silence while the woman gave the baby a satisfying feed. Malcolm stared into the hurrying creek water, his eye caught by several small orange narrow pointed leaves that were stuck in an eddy, circling each other like tiny boats going nowhere. He reached down and caught one of them up – ironwood leaves – he crushed it and sniffed up the pleasant fragrance that back in Brakial was a favourite seasoning for many meat dishes. The black flies started biting and Malcolm wiping them off the back of his neck stood and said it was time to get going again.

Sunlight dappled the mossy ground. The stream was now both slower and deeper and unlike its down valley rush, its course ahead curved in wide lazy loops. Not long after the last rest stop, the valley hooked left around a long wooded spur and the stream cut close to its toe and Rolf lead the way, climbing for a short time over the spur and down to meet the water again which now flowed through a series of open clearings. They walked on in a warming sun until the trees ceased completely in an uneven line, and each side of them the forest clad slopes steepened into formidable bare cliffs. Ahead a rushing white cataract showed the stream cutting its course down a steep bench covered in a mix of large rocks and thick scrub. The easiest route up lay beside the swift water and they laboured their way to the top with the roar of the water preventing any talk.

At the top the stream issued from a small tear drop shaped lake fed by narrow waterfalls spilling from the heights that enclosed it on three sides. Ahead could be seen drifts of old snow mingled with rocky ground that angled down to the lake from the base of the precipice ahead, and above it, cloud or fog continually drifted slowly upward before vanishing. Standing up beyond the fog the outline of distant snow covered domes lay etched against a clear sky. The cliff on the right hand side of the lake dropped sheer into the water, but on the opposite shore the foot of the cliff merged with a short gentle slope covered in stunted yellow grass and occasional small shrubs. Malcolm led the way toward that side and they walked close to the lake edge where the slope was least and before long found a narrow deer trail winding its way through the grass and myrtle bushes that when brushed against gave off a warm pleasant fragrance, while a few yards to their right the ruffled lake water constantly crunched the gravel of its little beach.

When half way around the lake, Malcolm called a halt and squinted in the sun to inspect what appeared to be the dead end beyond the lake, and as they stood scanning the way forward, two things happened. A light breeze in their faces brought a stink like addled eggs and at almost the same instant, from behind came a medley of barking and yelping. They turned to look and there at the lake edge where they so recently arrived stood a group of Bitchfolk pointing and gesticulating. Malcolm counted seventeen warriors all painted, armed and with a team of dogs. Without saying anything he turned and led off at a fast trot and after covering barely fifty yards, an outbreak of hideous chanting reached their ears.

Malcolm kept turning to check how close the warriors were. The frontrunners were already on their side of the lake and he yelled that they must run as fast as they could. It was not long before the woman Rahnuk began to tire and Malcolm and Seth dropped back to help and plead with her to hand over the baby and this she did after seeing the fast gaining Bitchfolk. Seth handed his bow and one pouch to Malcolm and with two good arms was entrusted to carry the wrapped up child. They made better time now and taking another quick look Malcolm saw the Bitchfolk were no longer gaining so fast. The rearing rock wall in front loomed closer and the men kept snatching looks to see where best to either take a stand or find some way up and over it.

At first sight the fretted stone appeared impassable and the rocky ground at its base seemed to offer the best place to stand and fight, but on getting closer Malcolm saw that as well as the waterfalls, the face was seamed with numerous jagged old water channels and several slanted in such a way as to offer possible ways of gaining the top. Out of the bottom of one spilled a slew of rock slabs forming what resembled a careless set of stone steps and Malcolm decided to make for it. On their side of the lake head the yellow grass ended at a cluster of house sized angular rocks which Malcolm soon found a way through. From there to the cleft he was making for, the rocks were smaller and mixed with old snow and over this rough ground they now carefully picked their way.

Rolf closely followed Malcolm with Spike in between. Trailing behind and hidden among the house sized rocks, was Seth carrying the baby and the woman Rahnuk. The chasing dogs were unleashed and running free with the leading Bitchfolk who were now almost at the field of giant boulders. Malcolm worried that Seth and the woman might be overtaken before reaching any kind of safety at the foot of the cliff. Both he and Rolf now waited, gasping for breath beside a large rock close to a waterfall, and drifting cold spray caused them to shiver as they waited anxiously for Seth and Rahnuk to arrive.

Barely one hundred yards away the angled cleft entrance faced them and pointing to it Rolf said it looked good. Malcolm smiled weakly and nodded before looking back and trying to yell encouragement to the others above the noise of the falling water. At first he couldn't see them, but then suddenly, out of the boulder field appeared Seth with one arm holding the baby and the other trying to drag the woman by the hand. They were two hundred yards away and making slow progress across the rocks and snow. The Bitchfolk were out of sight in the boulders and even their yelping dogs could hardly be heard. It seemed an age before Seth and the woman arrived and she immediately grabbed Seth by the shoulder to make him stop so she could check the baby. Rahnuk was gasping, open mouthed, out of breath and now with her hands on her thighs she doubled over and groaned with fatigue. At Malcolm's urging, Rolf and Seth headed for the cleft and the woman, still gasping for breath, stood upright and staggered after them.

Malcolm glanced back just as the first Bitchfolk came into view leaping lightly across the rough ground and rapidly coming within bow-shot. Rolf led the way toward the cleft over the rocky uneven ground. More icy spray from another waterfall blew over them as they ran the short distance to where the leaning pile of rock slabs spewed from the cleft. Malcolm from behind yelled "Up there, up there" and first Rolf and then Seth reached the opening and then as the woman entered, Seth handed her the baby and waved his arm for her to go on up. Malcolm arrived last just ahead of the chasing dogs and suddenly Spike was in the middle of a whirling, snarling melee of lunging yellow fangs. Malcolm handed Seth back his bow and quiver and followed the woman up the slot, crashing and stumbling on the loose shale of its floor. Rolf yelled at Seth to follow Malcolm. He did, but went only a short distance before stopping and taking cover where he carefully laid out some arrows and waited.

Rolf with bow armed and ready stayed hidden, crouched behind a lone rock just out from the cleft entrance. Rahnuk turned and groaned to Malcolm that she couldn't go further and flopped down. Malcolm tried to tell her they were not yet safe and to make his point the first arrows began clattering off the rocks around them and then the chanting began and looking down Malcolm saw the main body of Bitchfolk gathered in the open and launching arrows at them. Muttering under his breath he cursed softly at Rolf hiding just out from the cleft entrance. Rahnuk lurched to her feet again and holding the baby in her left arm started scrambling further up with Malcolm close behind.

Three Bitchfolk now detached themselves from the main body to pick their way through the rocks to where the dogs were fighting. When the first one stepped clear of cover, Rolf was waiting with an arrow fitted. Grinning with anticipation he stood and took aim. The Bitchfolk stopped – stiffened in fear. But then the unthinkable happened. With a dull twang Rolf's bowstring came loose. Behind him was a thirty yard stretch of open going, no cover and difficult footing. Rolf's belly turned to water as the three Bitchfolk, cackling at his plight, once more began advancing. Rolf was there for the taking. One of the Bitchfolk stopped with a spear ready to hurl while the second fitted an arrow and stepping to one side took aim. The third lounged back, holding her bow loosely and laughing and a little further back, the other Bitchfolk were also laughing, waiting for the inevitable. Rolf stood rooted to the spot, not even breathing. Nearby Spike was backed against a rock with three Bitchfolk dogs slowly stalking back and forth growling and glaring out the corner of their eyes at him.

Rolf drew his short sword and waited. No way was he going down without a fight. He would take at least one with him. The spear carrier still cackling softly now made as if to advance past the Bitchfolk archer. Rolf focused on the spear carrier trying to judge when to make a rush and was just about to when suddenly both front Bitchfolk went down. Silenced by what happened the third turned and scrambled back to where the others waited. Spike growling now lunged at one of the three dogs but ended up being grabbed by the neck and held down by the other two.

Arrows now whistled around Rolf as he ducked behind his rock and bolted over the loose stones toward the cleft. A yell made him look up and he caught a glimpse of Seth standing and waving a triumphant fist before he also took cover as arrows bounced off the rock behind him. Rolf crashed up to where Seth crouched and as he passed, gave him a friendly shove on the shoulder and yelled something about a lucky shot, and Seth grabbing his arrows, jumped up and followed him to where Malcolm and Rahnuk were resting.

Malcolm reckoned they were out of range for the moment even though they were in clear view of the Bitchfolk gathered below who now began to scream abuse at them, most of it directed at Rahnuk and especially at the baby she carried and what they intended to do when they got their hands on them which they predicted would happen very soon. Rahnuk looked terrified and in the midst of everything tried to get her baby to feed but it refused and started to cry. She stopped and bundled him up and tried to pacify the infant with her cheek against its head. Malcolm asked where Spike was and Rolf said he was in the middle of a big fight with the Bitchfolk dogs. Malcolm whistled several times but there was no response except that the Bitchfolk now began their grim chanting and then in a body they made their way toward the slot entrance.

"Let's move."

"Where?" Asked Seth.

Malcolm pointed and said, "Up there. Now move."

"We'll cover you and the woman." Grunted Rolf as he retied his bow string.

"Okay. No heroics. Right? Keep an eye out for Spike?"

Malcolm turned and motioned to Rahnuk to start moving again. Above them the chute steepened with gorgy shoulder height rock on most of the outside. Rahnuk turned and pushed herself off the rock floor and for a moment stood still before moving up unsteadily with Malcolm close behind. Their move provoked another outburst of shrieks and abuse but Rahnuk showed no sign of either hearing or listening. They trudged up the loose rock floor of the slot confident they could not be overtaken, especially with Rolf and Seth covering them from below. When Malcolm judged them to be about half way up he called another rest stop. He felt hungry and thought Rahnuk would also be. They hadn't eaten for a good while, not since the handful of dried fruit shared out while they were still walking under the trees. He scooped out more dried fruit and handed it up to Rahnuk who crammed it into her mouth and started chewing. Where they stopped was screened from the foot of the cliff and so they were spared the taunts and abuse from the Bitchfolk below.

Malcolm was sitting and wondering what the terrain would be like at the top when out of the corner of his eye he noticed a movement. He turned and saw with horror a small band of Bitchfolk climbing up the chute nearest on the right and only a hundred yards away. It was a fluke he noticed because at only one place could it be seen into and that from where they were sitting. The five Bitchfolk were nearly level with them and moving fast enough to cut off their escape. Malcolm

stood and bellowed out to Rolf and Seth. He saw Rolf's
head stick out below and Malcolm screamed and
pointed over to the parallel slot and immediately Rolf
signaled that he understood the new threat. There was
further shrieking from below answered by the new
group opposite as Malcolm and Rahnuk started
scrambling again as fast as they could and moments
later Rolf and Seth crashed toward them panting madly.
The loose stones on the floor of the slot made the going
hard. Two steps up and one back and Malcolm's thighs
were feeling dead and his lungs ready to burst as he
pushed against Rahnuk's buttocks to help her make the
top where the steepness eased and they found
themselves moving through a deep groove which led out
onto a broad flat plain of small broken rocks where they
stopped, and while catching their breath Malcolm
looked around for some place of safety. There was
none.

In front lay the wreckage of old mountains, flat
stony ground, variegated with snow patches that sloped
gently up to where the way ahead was obscured by
dense rising pillars and curtains of steam issuing from
the ground, and shrouding everything beyond in cloud
except for the strange flat topped snow covered heights
in the distance. Malcolm turned and looked back down
valley, to the wooded gorge, and the escarpments
plunging down to meet the trees. No friendly trees up
here. Just open space. He turned and looked again at the
drifting banks of whitey grey fog in front. He guessed

they could cover the distance quickly enough but that depended on how far behind the Bitchfolk were. None were yet in sight but he could hear the ominous sound of stones being dislodged in the slot below. The next moment Spike joined them. He was holding up one front paw and his left ear was practically missing with blood pouring from the wound, and his formerly black and white coat was a mass of raw red slashes and cuts. Malcolm bent down and picked the little dog up, comforting him before putting him down again. He stood on three legs looking up at Malcolm and wagging his stumpy little tail.

"Mal. Mal. They're coming. Can you hear them? Can you?" Rasped Seth between deep breaths.

"Yes. Now shut up and follow." Malcolm led off clanking through the loose stones toward the steaming curtain.

"Where are we going?"

"Don't know. Can't stay here though."

They covered only a quarter of the distance when off to their right sounded an ugly chorus of shrieks as the five Bitchfolk coming up the other way broke out onto the top.

"Run, c'mon run for it." Urged Malcolm.

They broke into a tottering jog trying not to stumble on the loose cindery ground. The Bitchfolk were also slow to get going but then with a loud burst of laughter and screams the main bunch also broke out onto the top and started loping toward them. Malcolm motioned for

Seth to take the baby from Rahnuk. The screams and shrieks stopped as the Bitchfolk saved their breath for running. Malcolm kept looking behind him. The Bitchfolk were gaining but he saw they wouldn't catch them before the fog bank was reached. Malcolm thought it would be a good place to hide for a while – actually he thought it their only hope.

Having already passed some small drifts of foul smelling steam, Malcolm halted at the edge of the main bank of steam where it billowed out of the ground, surging and flowing, now toward them, now away. The Bitchfolk also halted, just beyond bow-shot and started talking among themselves. Rahnuk took the baby back from Seth and Malcolm ordered that no arrows be wasted. They kept peering into the steam and then back to look at the Bitchfolk who were now ranged out in front. Some screamed abuse at Rahnuk – her name being clearly called out. The hideous chanting started again and went on for a short time before stopping. A brief silence followed and then came the charge.

"Hold hands." Malcolm yelled as he turned and led the way into this different world. Rolf grabbed Rahnuk by the arm and dragged her into the stinking fog where little was visible beyond an arm's length. Dull hissing noises could be heard close at hand and then from behind came a renewed outburst of shrieking followed immediately by more chanting and all at once arrows began clattering against the surrounding rocky ground. The Bitchfolk had ceased their charge on the edge of the fog bank and stood there screaming and shooting arrows blindly into the steam. Still holding hands Malcolm lead the way further into the sanctuary of the dense foul smelling fog which all around poured with hissing and roaring sounds from small cracks and fissures in the ground and before long the screams and taunts behind them grew first faint and then could no longer be heard as the background roar of this new place took over.

They walked carefully for some time before stopping again. It was still steamy and damp but now they could see ahead for fifty yards or more to a flat area of yellow rock blotched with patches of snow. Overhead the steam cleared briefly and a weak sun broke through and, in the distance, reared those same flat topped mountains all white but streaked here and there with grey and black furrows narrow at the top and widening as they reached down.

The rotten egg stink worsened and their eyes smarted and watered, and Rahnuk opened her robe and carried the baby against her, sheltering it from the foul air. Seth with face screwed up complained of the stink while Rolf grumbled out loud about where to next. Malcolm answered that he didn't know and Rolf retorted that he was in charge and that they couldn't stay where they were. Malcolm with deep sarcasm thanked him for the reminder and asked for further suggestions – useful ones. Rolf said nothing.

"When can we go back?" Whined Seth.

Malcolm with a furious look turned and barked.

"What do you mean go back? Do ya wanna be killed? How can we go back? We're stuck. Stuck. Do ya hear? Like flies in a bottle. Just like you said. We're dead if we turn back and we'll die if we stay here. We've got to find a place for tonight. Okay? And then we've gotta find a way out of here."

Malcolm turned to start walking again and Seth waving his arm around said.

"But. But we can't go on. On into here."

Malcolm turned and silenced him with a look.

"It's her they want." Rolf nodded toward Rahnuk.

"Maybe. But can you promise me they'll leave us in peace if we hand her over?"

"We shouldn't have brought her. I told you that."

"Yeah. Okay. A lot happened this morning. And yesterday. And before that. Have you forgotten how this started?"

"Okay okay. But where to now?"

Malcolm looked away saying nothing.

Seth again asked. "Mal. Where are we going? Do you even know where we are?"

"Yes."

"Well. What next?"

"Do you think we should go back?"

"No."

"Well don't argue. Just do as I say."

Malcolm turned and started walking toward a flat patch of snow visible up ahead through the steam. Over his shoulder he called. "Well. What are you doing? Coming or staying?"

Rahnuk was the first to move. She walked off following Malcolm and then Seth looked at Rolf and the two stepped in and followed. Several small gurgling streams of water flowed toward them, straggling through the piles of soft brown rock and Malcolm thought they could be worth following up. He couldn't think why. In the absence of anything else it seemed about the only idea. At least the water was coming from somewhere so it should lead somewhere. Their feet made scrunching sounds in the brittle gravel. Most of the water flowed in a single stream but every so often it split into numerous narrow wandering braids which sometimes disappeared in the gravel and at others spread into thin glistening sheets when crossing areas of flat hard stone.

Rocks, each larger than the houses of Brakial heaved into sight through the steam and once behind them, faded from view. Shoals of small stones in shades of pink, orange, brown and even green paved the stream bed and small fields of soft snow came and went like the big rocks. Malcolm preferred the soft snow for walking on reasoning that there was a lessened chance of crashing through a fragile crust to be scalded by hot mud or steam. And all around was the noise.

The overriding memory of that part of their journey was the din, and the further they ventured the worse it got. Added to the background roar were the fumaroles that screeched and whistled out jets of steam. They looked like miniature volcanoes, only knee high with their pale yellow encrusted exit holes. Dull booms sounded regularly from unseen sources in the clammy steaminess. Occasionally they came across areas of firmer ground where there were pools of hot mud that plopped and gurgled.

While walking a light fall of ash started and now it coated their hair, faces and clothing giving a frosted aged look. Malcolm continued in the lead following up the little streams of water. Most of the time the surrounding noise ruled out speech and then at others it softened and faded as if somebody was eavesdropping. The water that needed to be waded was first tested by Malcolm putting his finger into it since some was icy, some pleasantly warm and some close to boiling. Although it was a good while since leaving the Bitchfolk behind, things happened so rapidly that it didn't seem long at all before Malcolm stopped and turned and asked who was hungry. Nobody said anything. Rahnuk crouched down and started to feed the baby while Rolf produced dried fruit from the pouch he carried, and each received a handful with Rahnuk eating hers as she crouched and fed. They sat and rested while sitting on a drift of dry sand and nothing was said until Malcolm stood and announced that it was time to get on and see if they could find a way out of this awful stinking place and that Christus willing they would soon.

The landscape ahead changed – the low hummocks of loose scoria and patches of soft snow giving way to a shallow valley bordered by low ridges of gravels and ash about two hundred yards apart and broadly confining the stream, and this they followed, and whenever there was a small lifting of the steam, either Rolf or Seth would walk to the summit of one of the gravel banks to look around, but swirling steam and higher gravel ridges always blocked the view and Malcolm thought it too risky to venture out of sight in such a place. As far as Malcolm was concerned, survival was the aim and waiting where they were or turning back were not options. Ahead lay complete uncertainty, perhaps death if they were unlucky enough to crash through the fragile ground crust or encounter a cloud of poisonous gas. Maybe the weather would change and the air cool rapidly and a fall of snow act as a covering blanket while they slept their way to death, or they might just become lost in this deafening stinking maze and die of starvation. All of these possibilities Malcolm kept to himself although he was sure they were running through the minds of both Rolf and Seth. What was in the woman's mind was beyond guessing. One hope he did cling to was that with a little help from Christus and his mother, they might find their way to some other valley that could lead back to Brakial.

Aimless their journey might appear but hope lived only with moving; the alternative being to stay where they were, a thought both horrible and hopeless. Malcolm not wanting to put on view to the others his sinking heart remained silent except for an occasional grunt or wave of his arm in the direction he thought they should walk.

During one short rest Malcolm talked about the dangers attached to travel in the Azmata. An old man from Dulce once told him that some fifty years earlier he and a companion were exploring the Western Azmata, prospecting for land suitable for grazing or maybe even settlement and had seen much of interest including one area with an abundance of flat grassland and plenty of good water but curiously deficient in deer. The area was dotted with many low old craters covered in lush grass and into one of these their dog chased one of the few deer they saw but while they watched both animals began leaping and trying to escape from the crater bottom before being overcome and dying in a layer of poisonous air. Rolf said he also knew the story and both he and Malcolm were aware that the Lams never went near the Azmata for probably similar reasons and most likely the Bitchfolk were also aware of how hazardous the place was and Malcolm added that it was just as well, or they might still have them hot on their heels.

# 12.

Mid afternoon found them still following the course
of the stream that was now hemmed by low ridges and
heaps of crumbling scoria and from all around the steam
loudly hissed as it burst from numerous fissures in the
ground making the air both warm and wet. Once
without any warning, a cool wind arrived and sucked
the steaming clouds upward and the sky cleared and
ahead could be seen the water course chafing its way
around the base of a large cone that glistened with
snow. Then while they stared at the scene ahead, the
wind lost its power allowing the steaming air to once
more close in, leaving only the silver stream prancing
and gurgling over its bed of stones: a smiling guide
running toward them out of the opaque unknown.

Several months later Rahnuk told Malcolm of what
was then going through her mind while she stumbled
along in this strange terrifying place, the baby wrapped
cocoon like and pressed against her chest her hand
supporting its back the way Arloht had shown her. She
kept wondering how she'd allowed herself to get into
this situation. She, Rahnuk, a high-ranking Zoel: a Zoel
who despised all Deeves now under the protection of
Deeves, and all the time she worried about the safety of
the baby. She couldn't resist snatching looks at his
small screwed up face with its tiny mouth sucking on
one tiny thumb. She had him wrapped in one of the thin
cloth rags given to her by Arloht and around that again

the small wool blanket.  Arloht also gave her a leather
bag with two compartments, one for dirty or wet rags
and the other for dry clean ones.  Without Arloht's help
she wouldn't have known what to do.  She wouldn't
have even known how to hold a baby, let alone how to
feed it or to keep it clean and warm.  The baby was now
nearly three weeks old.  Things moved swiftly since that
day.  And then yesterday, the escape from the tent.  She
thought her life was about to end when the Deeve stood
over her with his blood stained sword.  Instead of
plunging it into her he slashed through the ropes binding
her ankles and wrists.  She just grabbed up the baby and
ran.  Never mind that the ropes were so tight on her
ankles that she could barely feel her feet.  She had
darted through the slashed tent wall, through the smoke
and suddenly found herself among trees.  She stopped
and looked around before running again.  Without the
Deeve freeing her she would be dead by now.  Both she
and the baby.  Tortured first and then killed and both
impaled upright on sharpened posts as a lesson to
others.  A warning to all other Zoels or Verds who
might have similar ideas.  That's how things were done
in Latcho.

The baby was snuffling and making little cries.
Hungry or dirty or both Arloht would say.  If these
Deeves didn't stop soon, she would have to.  Her baby
needed caring for.  This baby that was all hers – to keep
and hold – to hold close to her – a warm snuffly baby
that needed her.  Yes, the baby needed her.  She didn't

understand it – she didn't understand her feelings for this helpless little thing – this helpless little thing controlled her now – this helpless little thing made her run away – from Latcho. And what about Ilgud? Yes, what would Ilgud be thinking now? But here she was; a warrior Zoel. Brought up and trained to renounce and reject all feelings of pity. Brought up to fight like all those born to be Zoels. To be hardened against the enemies of Latcho. And now this change was over her – like night becoming day in an instant. And she, Rahnuk; a warrior Zoel owned this boy baby; and she was on the run; with Deeves. Deeves she was always taught to despise. Because they were weak people, inferiors, enemies even. But these Deeves freed her and protected her. There was no going back now. Back there, behind her, on the other side of the foul stinking mist and steam of this place, Zoels were waiting; trying to catch and kill her and the baby, and Ilgud was certain to be with them.

Rahnuk was sure she heard her shrieking threats as she escaped up the cliff. That first night with the Deeves she dreamed of Ilgud. She dreamed of Ilgud's comforting arms around her, but then the baby woke demanding to be fed and Ilgud was forgotten. The Deeve who called himself Malcolm puzzled her. Malcolm has a hurt arm. It was Malcolm who stumbled into the tent and was attacked. Malcolm seems to be in charge and yet doesn't appear to know what's going on or where they are headed.

The deep voices of the Deeves; fascinated her. There was this funny feeling deep down inside of her – never had she felt anything like it. There was nothing like it in Latcho. No Zoels or Verds talked like that. But why did the Deeves come back for her yesterday? First, they paddled off in their boat and then they come back for her and the baby. Why? She needed help no mistake but in Latcho nobody ever asked for help, except maybe for children being raised by the Verds. Arloht was weak like that and Arloht and her friends were killed when the Zoels searched the camp and found her and the baby. She again found herself falling behind. She quickened her pace. She must keep up with the Deeves.

The stops for rest became more frequent. Seth was pleased by this and admitted out loud that he was tired and Malcolm and Rolf said they felt the same. The exertion, the lack of rest, the short rations and the fear, especially the fear, wearying and draining hope. Malcolm considered only Christus could be guarding them this far. So much could have easily gone wrong but the number of fluky actions, decisions that time and again proved right. But then why did Christus allow this mess to happen? But then why did he allow anything? Malcolm shook his head. Dangerous thinking this business of guessing the motives of the One Who Called. It's about trust isn't it? That's what old Dibius would say. Worrying was not trusting. How would you feel if you discovered somebody didn't trust you? Dibius was good value despite his crusty nature. Many times that morning Malcolm found himself muttering silent prayers to Christus and His mother and from the looks on the faces of Rolf and Seth he was sure they were doing the same. Probably striking bargains about how they'd change their lives for the better if they were led out of there to safety. Poor Spike was a mess. One side of his head was covered in dried black blood. His jaunty skip was gone; he limped and sometimes stopped and sat. Malcolm whistled to him and Spike looked up, wagged his stumpy tail, grinned and tried to stagger on.

At each stop Rahnuk would attempt to feed the baby but it was evident the toll of the last two days was drying her milk supply and now after a few attempts to suck; the baby would pull away and cry. It was hard to tell exactly what part of the day it was but judging by the angle of light slanting through the steam and his own hunger Malcolm guessed it was not far off sunset. He called to Rolf, and Seth came as well, and Malcolm said he thought it a good idea to look for some sheltered place to bed down for the night. He reckoned they were well into the Azmata and expressed surprise at how mild the air was. The wetting fog thinned a little as Malcolm led them across a flattish area through which the stream was again broken into wandering braids and on one side was a bank of ash and gravel with a slight overhang gouged by the water, but now dry and just large enough to provide some shelter from above, and its floor was soft and fluffy with pumice granules.

Within a stone's throw cool water rippled past and with thankful sighs they crawled in and sat down, their backs resting against the gravel bank.

The baby began to cry pitifully and Rahnuk did her best to feed it while the men pulled off their boots and massaged their feet. Spike lay on his side in front of Malcolm's outstretched legs. He was panting slowly and when Malcolm said his name, he responded with a pleading look.

Out in front unseen fumaroles roared and dinned in their ears, the sound waxing and waning in a soft breeze that carried a pungent load of stinking air. Rolf pulled one of the pouches toward him and passed it to Malcolm who inspected their meagre food reserves before measuring handfuls of dried meat and fruit leaving a small amount for the next day. They ate in silence and Malcolm put a prune down in front of Spike's nose but he just lay there ignoring it. Seth walked across to the stream and filled the canvas water bag and they took it in turns to drink. Malcolm said they should pray and Rolf and Seth joined in to thank Christus for their safety so far and to ask for guidance and help in returning to Brakial. In low tones Rolf talked with Malcolm on the chances of the baby surviving for much longer and both men expressed their pessimism. Their mournful discussion concluded that when the baby died, Rahnuk would give up and refuse to go on.

The light faded completely and in various attitudes they lay down and tried to sleep, Seth on his back, restless and sweating before sleep overcame him. Some time later he woke with a start. A faint glow made him step outside the shelter and turn to look where a huge arc of red flared into the night sky. He roused Malcolm and Rolf and they walked out further from the shelter to see better and looked back in wonder at the colossal crimson half halo of fierce light that surged into the night sky; its edge wavering and billowing and changing as clouds of steam continually built up only to vanish where the reach of the red glow failed and a short distance in front the jagged ridges of scoria stood up etched black against the red backcloth and the three men stood awestruck, their faces reflected red in the eerie light as they stared toward the distant fiery heart of the Azmata. For the rest of the night the swirling dampness, the undulating roar of the fumarole and the bursts of hungry crying from Rahnuk's baby made sleep impossible and from time to time the ground they lay on quivered. Just before dawn a thick wetting drizzle set in but by hugging close to the inside of the bank it was possible to avoid the worst of it.

As the morning light strengthened Rolf stood up and stretched and yawned and noted that the drizzle had ceased. Rahnuk sat up and her baby immediately began crying and she opened her robe to feed it. Overnight her milk supply was restored enough to make the baby seem satisfied and it soon lay back in Rahnuk's arms without complaint. Rahnuk was discovering what every mother knew and what Arloht told her to expect – the pleasure coming from feeding her own child – an indescribable thing that calmed and comforted her despite the fact of her being sure the Deeves were ignorant of where they were or were supposed to be going.

Seth asked about Malcolm's shoulder and Malcolm said it was stiff after not moving while lying down but was not as painful as the previous morning. Malcolm called to Spike but the little dog didn't move. Yesterday's fight was too much and Malcolm with tear filled eyes carried him away a short distance to bury him in a shallow grave he managed to scoop out with one hand. Malcolm remained silent as food was again shared around and after eating the men gathered to pray in low voices. Rolf asked about the day's plan and Malcolm said he thought they should continue following up the stream which when they looked up it showed in the distance as a white streak tumbling from under the roof of low cloud.

As they made ready to leave a single shaft of sunlight stabbed through and soon after a chill wind swept the steam and low cloud aside and they stood in sunshine. On one side behind the crazy stacks of rocks backing their shelter stood up the distant stuccoed domes of the Azmata. Opposite and closer reared steep snow covered slopes merging at the top into jagged craters whose rims turned butter yellow in the early sun. Rolf looked up and shivered. He said nothing but thought they reminded him of warriors swathed in white, laying in wait, armed and fickle. From some of the summits streamed plumes of steam that rapidly vanished but dashing toward them from the feet of that same threatening array, the little stream tumbled over bench after bench of rocks and having faith in it Malcolm with crunching footsteps led the way upstream and before long the din and steam of the fumaroles were left behind.

Where they spent the night was just inside the edge of the thermal field and once clear of it the only sounds were their footfalls in the loose scoria. The stream ahead gushed from the mouth of a narrow valley, which they climbed and entered and the near vertical mountain shoulders reached down forcing its water this way and that – making frequent crossings necessary. The climb continued steadily with occasional short rests and the water in the stream dwindled before ceasing where it issued from a steep bank of snow which extended down their valley like a stocking from a much larger snow field that sloped upward in smooth waves and hollows to a distant skyline. From now on they would be walking in snow and before stepping onto it Malcolm called a rest. Seth looked expectantly at Malcolm.

"What now?"

"We keep going."

"Up there?"

"Yes, up there."

"Where else is there to go?" Growled Rolf.

"But what's up there?"

"We're going to find out aren't we?" Continued Rolf.

"But it might lead nowhere."

"Right. You really wanna go back doncha?"

Seth shaded his eyes and looked up the sloping snow in front.

"It doesn't look that bad I suppose."

"That's not the top you're looking at." Said Malcolm.

"Oh."

"There'll be more skylines behind that one."

"You think so."

"That's for sure." Said Rolf. "So you better start praying that when we do reach the top, there's some place else to go."

Seth's face fell and Rolf grinned at him and Malcolm called to Rahnuk who was crouching further back feeding the baby. She quickly stood and gently patted the baby's back several times before putting the child in the back sling.

"Right. Let's go." And Malcolm turned and kicked steps in the face of the snow bank and waited at the top for the others to catch up.

Walking in soft snow was wearying, something they soon discovered when at times the crust gave way and legs would plunge in knee or thigh deep and before long all were breathing hard and their feet lost feeling from icy snow melt and calf muscles ached with the strain, but the walking staffs that Seth had cut proved their worth for Malcolm and Rahnuk.

For what seemed an age they kept plugging their way up the slope and Malcolm's prediction was proved as skyline after skyline dashed hopes that the top was near but at last the sky defined the broad summit ridge suspended saddle like in the stump of an ancient crater and climbing a narrow easy shoot of snow between a break in the vertical rock cap the men breathless and with legs aching, arrived on top. Rahnuk was well behind and Seth half slid down to where she was struggling and offered to take the baby which she accepted and then holding onto Seth's hand she allowed herself to be half dragged until she and Seth joined the other two resting on the wind hardened snow, and Rahnuk collapsed and lay on her side breathing hard.

Directly in front the snow sloped away into a large shallow basin the outer rock rim of which blocked the view into the floor of this new much larger valley and they were unable to tell if its draining stream flowed left or right. If right it could lead back to Terra Vivus; if left, it could end up in the wastes of Terra Defilia. A chaos of snow-plastered peaks and spilled mountain debris faced them from the valley's other side. Grim black cliffs capped with green jagged ice laddered in places down almost vertical rock faces to gather on broad white shelves. As they looked the long roar of collapsing ice cliffs reached them and a plume of white dust rose and the dying echoes gave way to a silence

155

that held its breath as if waiting for applause. Malcolm looked down again and pointing said.

"There's no gain for all of us to go down there if we can't get any further."

"I'll go look." Said Rolf. "The woman sure looks as if she could do with a rest. Can I use your stick?"

Malcolm handed it over and Rolf started down gingerly picking his way in the soft snow and then using the stick as a prop his confidence grew and he strode out pushing his heels into the slope.

"What's he doing?" Asked Seth.

"Looking to see if there's a way down."

"And if there isn't?"

"We might have to keep walking along this ridge until we can find a way to get down."

Seth looked worried but said nothing. They watched Rolf as he moved further away into the distance below. He could have been a small insect on a white background as he crossed the floor of the basin and climbed a rock outcrop to look over the edge. He jumped back down and walked further along before looking from another rock and then back again onto the snow, he walked much further this time before stopping to again look from the basin's rocky rim. They could see his black figure, his back to them, looking outward and down, and then turning around he jumped off the rocks and looking up he waved both arms slowly to say it was not good. It seemed an age for Rolf to trudge back up to where they waited. He said that directly below the basin rim the slope was almost vertical for about half its height before it eased all the way to a river a long way down.

"Which direction was the river flowing?" Asked Malcolm.

"Hard to say for sure but looking at the lay of the ground, probably heading out to the right."

"Good, good." Grunted Malcolm. "Could you see any other way to get down?"

"Maybe further along from here. I don't know. Couldn't see all of it but below over there; there's a big fan, might be an old scree, all snow covered"

"How steep?"

"I reckon we could use it to get down all right. That's if we can get onto the top of it."

"Right we'll eat first and then try it." Malcolm reached into the pouch and small handfuls of dried fruit and meat strap were given out. "There's enough for one more meal after this and then it's living off the land, if we can. I shouldn't have buried Spike." He stopped and laughed in a silly way but Rolf and Seth knew he was serious. They finished eating in silence and sucked on pieces of snow for water. Malcolm looked at the sun and reckoned it was just past noon.

"Let's go." And he led the way, prodding the hard snow with his stick. Seth came next then Rahnuk and Rolf came last. Their route lay along the ridge that now broadened into a hogs back studded with rocky stumps from the old crater rim. Malcolm warned that any slip would likely see them sliding at speed over the edge.

They kept on the side facing the new valley, Malcolm and Rolf constantly scanning for a way down. The hogs back began to narrow and slope away in front. They came to where a skinny spine of jagged rock angled away and down to join up with the fan. Malcolm paused to see if it could be used to get down but on one side it was sheer and the other was guarded by a menacing crevasse where the weight of the snow pack pulled away from the rock and the eerie gap it left twisted out of sight in shades of green. Malcolm shrugged and kept walking toward where the top of Rolf's fan joined their ridge just where it ended at the foot of a severe rock face that blocked all further progress.

They could now see almost to the bottom of the valley and soon afterward arrived at the foot of the cliff where a nasty surprise waited. The snow here was in shade; frozen, glazed and threatening. Malcolm looked at the others and said they'd have another look at the rock spine, and turning they retraced their steps and were soon standing and inspecting this option. Malcolm pointed to where a little way down part of the crevasse edge had fallen in and digging his staff into the compacted snow he began kicking deep steps down and gaining the edge he stamped his way on the softer loose snow down into the crevasse and toward a flat snow

ledge that ended at a place where the gap to the sloping rock of the far side was less than his own length. His voice floated up saying that if any of them slipped here they would never be seen again. Using his staff Malcolm leaped the break and gained the sloping rock where using his good arm he remained clinging before climbing out of the way and turning to watch as the others followed. Seth was next and then it was Rahnuk's turn. She looked down into the chasm. Malcolm called to her to not look but to follow in his steps. The green curving abyss terrified her. None of her training in Latcho equipped her to deal with this new dread – the dread of falling – the dread of losing her baby – of both being lost forever. Rahnuk froze. She felt unable to move – unable to stop herself from trying to see where the crevasse ended. Just in front of her and barely her own length away Seth beckoned but she refused to move. She seemed hardly aware when Rolf plucked the wrapped baby from her sling and gently as if in slow motion, tossed the little bundle across to Seth who effortlessly caught it and moved up to hand the child to Malcolm who now rested on the opposite rocky lip of the frightening gap. Rahnuk remained as if paralyzed, and again Seth pleaded with her to make the jump.
  Again her eyes swept down to where the gap twisted out of sight in an eerie green glow. She looked across at Seth and then up to where Malcolm crouched holding the baby. Malcolm called to her to extend the staff for Seth to grab. She appeared not to hear. Malcolm passed

his staff down to Seth who extended it toward her. She grabbed it with both hands allowing her own to drop and it rattled its way out of sight down the crevasse, and she now made a faltering attempt at jumping, and would have dragged both herself and Seth into the abyss had Rolf not caught her from behind and hauled her back to safety and Seth just managed to stop himself from toppling forward. Rahnuk stood still, breathing hard. Seth steadied himself and again extended the staff but Rahnuk could not bring herself to move. A mewing sound came from the bundle in Malcolm's arms and Rahnuk looked up. She put one foot back to brace herself, grasped the end of the staff and leaped, almost unaware of the mighty upward heave on her buttocks coming from Rolf. She landed beside Seth who grabbed her in his arms before pushing her up to where Malcolm sat in the sun. He handed the baby to her and she attempted to feed it. Now it was Rolf's turn and pushing one foot against the ice behind him he easily cleared the gap and then they were all up and over the edge and resting among the sun warmed splintered rock. Malcolm said they must keep moving and asked Seth to take the baby. Rahnuk silently agreed.

The route down the steep rocky spine was a scramble. Out in the sun, the rocks dropped steeply on that side. Rahnuk was afraid still but knew she needed both hands and feet free. Her fear centred not on herself but on the baby. Looking at the top of the fan where it was shaded by the cliffs she could see the hard bluish snow.  Looking further down she saw how the snow first sloped steeply with large rocks showing through but halfway down, the slope eased and the snow thinned and became patchy before ending completely just short of a glistening thread of water bending into view from the left. She watched nervously as Seth clambered down with the baby under one arm. The rock although shattered into large upright slabs, was solid and moving down it she began to feel more secure but always she kept glancing at Seth who almost casually and using one hand, kept on his way with the baby held in his other arm.

It didn't seem at all long before the rock spine ended in almost benign fashion.  It simply shortened in height and became submerged under the snow of the fan. At this point the fan was clear of the shade from the cliffs and the snow pleasantly softened and they could walk upright but Rahnuk again felt insecure without a staff and she looked bewildered and shuffled only a few steps until Malcolm seeing her difficulty handed his staff over and at each step she dug it into the snow slope in front and began walking with self assurance and a short time later she stopped and turned to Seth and by signs made it plain that she wanted to carry the baby herself in the sling.  Far below, the silvery river ran in a curve around the foot of the fan and vanished behind a spur intruding from the right – but best of all, Malcolm noted the water was definitely flowing left to right – toward Terra Vivus.  Piles of avalanched snow debris bridged the river in two places and along the water's edge several wisps of steam steepled into the cool still air.

Having left the rock spine behind the going seemed easier as they walked in a single file with Malcolm leading and the others placing their feet in his footsteps and the only sound was that of feet scrunching through the snow crust. In a little while the fan broadened and their pace quickened as weary legs were thrown forward ankle or knee deep in the now sun softened snow. Rahnuk's leg muscles were stiff and tired from the downhill effort but the slope become easier and the snow thinned and then there was nothing to walk on except a clutter of loose shale livened by drifts of stout fleshy white buttercups thrusting through. Closer to the river the flowers became abundant and formed large cheerful patches. The roar from the river was now plain and with numbed feet and shaking knees they tottered toward the water's edge where they stopped and sprawled among the rocks in the sun. Rahnuk put her baby down and kneeling caught water in her hands and drank deeply and then picking the infant up offered her breast but nothing came and the baby pulled back and cried in protest. She wrapped it again and rocked it; her eyes filled with fear. Malcolm allowed a lengthy rest and then urged Rahnuk to her feet and they started walking again. Now it was the water's edge they followed as it twisted and turned around the toe of spur and bluffs, and often the water cut in fast and deep against the steep rock, which meant a climb to make it past the difficulty, and always nearby the hurrying flow, milky with melted snow.

## 13.

Rahnuk was tired, so tired she felt close to giving up. For her the valley's broken stone pavement made the downstream trudge an unrelenting fatiguing drag. Her legs felt numb, her feet she could hardly lift, all she wanted was to stop and lie down, but these Deeves kept encouraging and cajoling her. The baby grizzled and whimpered with hunger. Rahnuk craved its welfare. She needed it. The baby was all she wanted. If the baby was to live, she must live and that was all that kept her going, but by mid afternoon her weariness came to a head. She stopped frequently, bent over the staff and gasping for breath. Malcolm called another halt and Rahnuk dragged herself to a flat rock and sat down, elbows on knees and head in her hands. Malcolm asked her if Seth could again carry the baby. She didn't even look up but just nodded and slowly standing she took the sling from her back and Seth took the infant from her. When they started walking again she felt a little stronger and now with nothing to carry and the stick for support she was able to stay close behind Seth and walked with greater purpose – like the true Zoel she was raised to be – well that was what she imagined.

The river continued to drop down its narrow valley and now scrawny ancient pines appeared standing defiant in sparse groves. The constant babble and rush of the river and the noise of tired feet kicking stones gave way at times to a distant rumbling noise as herds of house sized slabs tore loose from their mother snow packs and skidded and smashed their way down well worn gullies. Some made it as far as the river where the melting jumbles of snow slabs lay blocking their path, and Malcolm led the way through, kicking ahead, testing the piles of snow for strength in case thawing from beneath left only a thin treacherous crust to walk on.

Side streams also made the task of walking difficult, tearing down narrow gullies cluttered with large loose rocks. First a jarring clank down to the water, picking a safe place to cross and then a wearying climb up the other side, a short rest at the top and then on again. At one of these stops Rahnuk took the baby from Seth and attempted to feed it but no milk came and again the child cried and whimpered and Rahnuk despairingly returned the infant to the sling on Seth's back. The men frequently scanned the slopes above for deer but only in two places did they see sign. Some hoof prints in a muddy seep close to the river and several piles of droppings.

"Not even a hare." Muttered Malcolm. "You would think something worth catching would live here."

In fact, the only other living creatures they saw were sombre tail flicking rock pipits making the air lonely with their plaintive whistles.

By late afternoon the valley changed in character becoming wider and less steep. Pine trees were more common and the flow in the river slowed and widened and almost without noticing it low cloud pushed its way upriver and the air cooled as soon as the sun disappeared. Ahead the river turned and vanished behind the toe of a steep spur. The going was flatter now and the way led through numerous pine trees that met over their heads but arriving at where the river turned they were confronted with a chaos of huge boulders and Malcolm stopped and pulled from his pouch the last of the dried fruit and they stood there and chewed until it was gone. Rahnuk was sitting slumped over and only got to her feet to follow the others when she realized Seth was sloping off with the baby.

Getting through the boulders was less of a problem than Malcolm expected and once around the corner they found themselves close to the shore of a lake and again following the river to where it emptied into the breeze ruffled water, they looked about for some place to camp. To their left and barely visible through drifting mist, barren cinder and ash slopes reached up into the morbid roof of cloud. The mist barred the view down the lake but on their immediate right reared smooth cliffs of dark glassy rock curved down like water frozen in the act of sliding over a weir. A short distance away a stream raced out from under the cliffs and crossed a narrow beach to lose itself in the lake and a curtain of steam rose where the waters merged: a feeble reminder of the previous day's thermal violence.

Myrtle scrub spread up the slope leading to the cliff and on the other side of the stream, gulls scrambled into the air wheeling and yodeling annoyance at the intrusion. Close to the lake edge a leaning rock slab stood clear of the scrub and with the mist now turning into a wetting drizzle Malcolm led the way toward it. The ground beneath it was bare and dry and with the exception of Seth, the others sat down saying nothing. Seth handed the baby to Rahnuk turned and stepped into the scrub. Malcolm and Rolf with eyes closed lay on their backs and Rahnuk in desperation tried again to feed the baby. A short time later the screams of the gulls sounded and the commotion kept growing and swelling in volume and then subsiding only to reach a new crescendo before again dying away and then restarting.

"What's he up to?" Muttered Malcolm.

"Food – gulls maybe?"

Malcolm nodded. "Leave him to it eh?"

The anxious gulls continued screaming and Rolf said he would go and look for firewood.

Seth was gone for some time now and only the occasional complaint could still be heard from the birds. The next thing he stood in front of Malcolm grinning broadly and holding his jerkin. He crouched and opened it to reveal almost a dozen large gull eggs: lovely with their creamy green and brown blotches and speckles and already boiled hard. He said that the water in the little stream was so hot you couldn't put a hand in it and he'd been able to use it to cook the eggs using a stick to retrieve them. Rolf now turned up with wood and the four sat together and each shelled an egg and began eating after which Rolf set about starting a fire that at first filled their shelter with eye watering smoke until its increasing heat dispersed it and they sat close to the fire keeping warm and shelling and eating eggs.

Malcolm asked Seth to show him the gull colony and he followed Seth to the lake edge where the hot stream flowed in. Walking a short distance from the protesting gulls they stripped off and waded out over soft pumice and sat down and soaked in the warm water while the angry birds screamed abuse from the shore. A little later they were joined by Rolf. The light failed and their voices floated eerily in the darkness and as the air chilled, the steam became denser and through it waded Rahnuk carrying the baby, and she sat down at a small distance from the others; luxuriating in the soothing warm water with the dozing infant in her arms.

They continued to relax until Malcolm announced he was nearly asleep and one by one they waded ashore tired and relaxed and standing in the chilly air they used their clothes to dab themselves dry before dressing and making their way back to the rock and the fire where the last few eggs were finished off. The baby was now asleep in Rahnuk's arms. She seemed to have produced sufficient milk to satisfy its immediate needs. Before lying down to sleep Seth built up the fire although with the overhead cloud the night was not too cold.

Twice during the night Rahnuk woke to attend to the baby. The second time she discovered her breasts tight and swollen, her milk ready with a vengeance and spurting into the baby's mouth. Unaccustomed to this abundance the milk spilled out the corner of its mouth and then with a loud hiccup the infant threw almost all of it up again. Rahnuk felt a wave of pleasure and relief.

Toward morning the cloud roof drifted off and as the light strengthened Rolf revived the fire and then the sun's rim appeared and the shelter was flooded with slanting sunlight. For the first time since escaping Orlo's camp Rahnuk's milk supply was back at full strength and with it came peace of mind and the baby sucked away and made happy little snuffling and mewing sounds.

Seth muttered something about getting more eggs and bending low ducked out of the shelter. A short time later another bout of screaming erupted from the gull colony. Using a stick Rolf poked away at the fire and Malcolm standing with hands on hips announced he wanted to go further up the hill and see if he could get some idea of where they might be. He asked if Rolf wanted to come with him.

"You know what we talked about last night?"

"Where this lake water drains to?"

"Yes, most likely in the Deemah."

Rolf stood up from the fire and gave a low whistle. "Well it would make sense."

Rahnuk was sitting on the ground holding her knees with the baby wrapped and asleep beside her. Malcolm looked at her.

"We'll be back soon. We want to look around up there." He waved his good arm upward.

"Seth won't be long."

The band of scrub above the rock was dense and low with wrist thick twisting branches and the two men forced their way through with the bruised leaves and broken twigs giving off a powerful but pleasing fragrance. After a short distance the scrub grew thinner and lower before it ended, its edge a straight line extending to where the slope butted with the cliff. Above the scrub the ground was clad in short grasses and small rocks. Malcolm pointed higher up to the shoulder of their ridge, the toe of which they skirted yesterday before gaining their first glimpse of the lake.

"Up there." He grunted.

Malcolm led Rolf as they sidled this way and that up the steepening ridge until almost all of the lake came into view and then he stopped and breathing deeply, looked around. The sky was clear but the steep cliffs above shaded the sun and the air was cold. With yesterday's cloud gone the mountains hemming the lake's far shore could now be seen – beetling escarpments lording over a sequence of sloping snow shelves thinning to scree and yellow grass and isolated from each other by ribs of plunging strong rock. Malcolm turned and walked higher before again stopping. The sequence of scarp and snow shrank and faded into the distance but the far end of the lake could now be seen and further on the country was lower and wooded and a light misty haze confined the view except for where one fierce spike of bare rock reared up, isolated and high enough to be caught by the early sun. Then came the catch in Malcolm's breath as he realized that what they were looking at was a prominent landmark on the Riparian side of the Gullet that in fine weather was visible from much of Lamentasia. Again, he gazed across the lake. There was something familiar about that high variegated spine of rock and snow rising from the far shore – features suggestive of an old friend's fondly remembered face. The Comb – the northern end of The Comb – Malcolm was certain. The same Comb that paralleled the Deemah on its seaward journey and which further down-river would find Brakial clinging to its feet. The scent of home was in the air as Malcolm exitedly told Rolf what they were looking at and with a huge grin Rolf hugged Malcolm and began pounding him on the back.

"Somebody's looking after us?" Rolf looked upward and then shot a sideways glance at Malcolm.

"We're still not out of trouble though?"

Malcolm nodded solemnly. They turned and stumped down the ridge to the rock and Seth, who had returned, looked puzzled as they burst into the shelter, their faces wearing big grins. Malcolm and Rolf looked at each other and as Rolf told Seth what they had seen, a happy grin settled on the face of the younger man and Malcolm cut in to say they could be back in Brakial within a week and that the water of the lake almost certainly fed the river that joined the Deemah just downstream from The Gullet.

"We'll need to carry food. Can you get more eggs?"

"There's a heap."

"Fresh?"

"They've just started laying."

Malcolm turned and looked at Rahnuk whose face wore a sullen look.

"Coming with us?"

Rahnuk said nothing.

## 14.

Mid morning found them toiling around the lake-shore under a hot sun. On one side the cool lake water made little lapping sounds on the stony beach and a short distance on their right the sheer glassy cliff rose high to where small stunted trees leaned over the top as if peering down at them. Occasional creeks with scrub covered banks cut across the beach. Away from the water's edge they walked in soft sand and progress was slow. Rahnuk was in the middle, her baby asleep in the sling on her back. Before leaving, a last raid on the gulls netted more eggs, which they boiled hard in the little hot stream.

From time to time Malcolm called a rest, especially where small creeks crossed their path bringing the welcome shade of myrtles and it was at one of these stops that Rahnuk experienced something unique. They were sitting in light shade and Rahnuk was nearly finished giving the baby a quick feed. Cicadas were singing and Rahnuk became aware of one singing loud and close behind her. The large noisy insect was perched on her back and starting softly was now loudly clicking and zizzing. Rahnuk, with puzzled expression kept turning her head to discover the source of the noise. From where he sat Malcolm found the scene irresistibly funny and he started to laugh, a deep laugh and as Rahnuk's puzzlement grew Rolf and Seth also began laughing and Malcolm leaned across and deftly captured the singer and then opened his hand to release it in Rahnuk's face and she started in fright, and then for the first time since Orlo's camp she smiled with relief, and with the reason for the laughter now known, her shy giggles escaped to join the laughter of the men. With this laughter something happened, some impulse sparked an indescribable feeling of warmth that spread from inside of her: something became uprooted and freed and a pleasant weakness suddenly invaded her body – a new dimension of love and pleasure let loose. Laughter, yes laughter: yes even in Latcho there was

172

laughter, especially between the Verds and their children and sometimes the Kraaths would join in with their high pitched giggles. But this! This laughter was like nothing she had ever experienced. A rich, deep, melodious and happy sound. She heard snatches of it from the Deeves the first night of her escape as they compared their experiences of that chaotic day; but this was different: it both baffled and charmed her. This deep laughter from the Deeves was totally new. The Deeves had laughed with her bringing about a bloodless conquest; suspicion and unease dissolving right there and then, and all started by a cicada using her shoulder as its platform to sing from.

Rahnuk was to discover that Riparian humour was like that: often expressed in hearty laughter, its source earthy, stemming from minor humiliations and embarrassments, misunderstandings and miscalculations or deliberate practical jokes. Rahnuk was on the cusp of understanding that laughter was what marked the outward difference between the Riparian and Sessilite psyche - laughing with people, not jeering them.

In early afternoon the end of the lake was reached and the discovery made that its outlet ran underground. Forest proper began here, the trees low and close together in a narrow valley more like a chute with steep forested sides up to where the trees ended and bald rock escarpments marked the skyline but looking further into the distance they could see where the valley widened. Malcolm and Rahnuk now rested while Rolf and Seth scouted to find the best way down. They returned to report that a little further on, the stream rushed from a large rock fissure to begin flowing in a steep sided gorge and above the stream extended a flattish bench and it was on their side and looked a promising route down the valley. They started again, travelling now in the shade of the trees and hanging onto small bushes and exposed tree roots to get past the frequent steep pitches and always the river's dull roar their constant companion. Occasional bluffs forced them up and away from the river and then they could hear the liquid music of unseen thrushes and at regular intervals Malcolm would call a rest and chunks of gull egg were handed around and water drunk and Rahnuk would give the baby a quick feed, and at one stop she drew out of her bag some dirty looking dry cloths to change the child.

Late afternoon their valley bent to the left and the slope of it eased markedly and the noise of the river faded. The trees were taller and ferns grew plentifully on the forest floor. Deer droppings were frequent but only one animal was seen and it crashed out of sight before an arrow could be fitted. At one place a fallen tree provided a view straight down valley and climbing on its trunk and craning necks the men could see distant bluish mountains and Malcolm said he was sure they were the mountains bordering the far side of Lamentasia and that by nightfall they could be on the bank of the Deemah.

The gentle slope made walking easier, although for Rahnuk it was still a tiring trudge that she hoped would end soon on the bank of the river where they would be able to rest for the night. Their route now sidled to the crest of a ridge and gaps in the trees gave glimpses of the pale green Deemah and beyond the river the yellow rolling dales of Lamentasia, and now a new sound was heard – a dull roar growing louder all the time brought about by the full force of the Deemah being squeezed through The Gullet. Malcolm turned off the ridge and they went down steeply before finding the way blocked by a large area of fallen trees. At some time in the recent past a violent wind flattened the trees and scores lay all facing the same direction, and Malcolm and Rolf looked for some way to get through and reach the river now so close. The last of the sun was hitting the tops of those trees still standing as Malcolm began threading a path through the chaos of fallen tree crowns, ducking under some branches and clambering over others and Rahnuk often passed the baby to Seth so as to have two hands free to haul herself up and over the numerous crooked and broken limbs.

They were almost at the river when they encountered a massive fallen trunk barring the way. There was no way to get under it and both the tree's crown and roots spread in a tortuous tangled barrier that almost enclosed them. Malcolm looked at the man high log and turning to the others said that seeing that one arm was near useless the others could boost him up to where he could haul himself onto the top, and so Rolf and Seth each lifted him by the legs and feet and pushed him to where he was able to roll and stand up on top of the log. They next turned to do the same with Rahnuk but suddenly a babble of voices could be heard and Malcolm was talking to somebody on the ground on the other side. Next came a muffled burst of laughter and a deep voice was repeating Malcolm's name. Malcolm turned around grinning madly.

"It's Magnus and Hill. Magnus and Hill." He turned back the other way and said, "Rolf and Seth are here. Help us over this tree will you?"

Another man, large and with a full beard suddenly appeared beside Malcolm. "So they are." And he reached down to pull Rolf up. Now it was Rahnuk's turn and she handed the baby up to Rolf and with Seth boosting her from behind she made it up. Seth threw up the bows and pouches and then was hauled up himself. On the other side small broken branch stumps jutted out making it easier to clamber down.

Rolf started to bellow his pleasure at finding the two men here but Magnus quickly grabbed him and clapped his hand over his mouth.

"Quiet. Not so loud." He hissed. After the warning from Magnus the men all looked at each other wearing big grins and saying little but suddenly they all began embracing and slapping backs and shoulders and laughing deeply and softly.

"Good. So good to see you." Magnus kept repeating.

"What are you doing here anyway?" Asked Malcolm in a low murmur.

"Looking for you of course. Have you eaten?" Malcolm shook his head.

"Hill. The nosebag. Quick."

The other man with the ferociously red beard and head of hair walked out of sight behind a bush and returned immediately with a canvas pouch that he upended, and out tumbled an assortment of dried fruit and meat straps and cheese and bread and a full wine skin. Seth picked up some small loaves and handed them around. Rahnuk holding her baby firmly chewed on the end of one. Magnus looked over at her and said to Malcolm.

"So, who have we here?"

"This is Rahnuk; and her baby. They're fugitives from the Bitchfolk we think." Magnus and Hill looked at each other and then turned to meet Rahnuk, First Magnus and then Hill took Rahnuk's right hand in their own and looking into her eyes each repeated her name softly and laughed; they laughed in that same deep manner she had heard only since her rescue from the tent, and for the second time that day Rahnuk's anxiety was dissolved by this most tantalizing of sounds – men laughing– a new sound – thrilling and yet also frightening in all its novelty. The rigid Sessilite fanaticism binding Rahnuk now weakened and leaving her bemused and smiling as these Deeves laughing softly, rejoiced and slapped each other across the shoulders, and now they were laughing with her. These Deeves, with deep voices and faces covered in hair – all so different from the trilling Kraaths of Latcho.

"But how did you come to be here." Asked Malcolm.

"I'll tell you. Hill, back on watch. Wait. First the pigeons."

Hill grunted and walked behind a mound of dead branches. Magnus began to explain how they came to be there but was interrupted by Hill's reappearance with a pigeon in his hand.

"Is it green or yellow?" Hill asked.

"Green, green, green."

Hill squeezed a small green wooden ring onto the bird's left leg and passed it to Seth to hold while he again went behind the branches, returning almost immediately with another bird which he also ringed.

"Not too late to fly, is it?" He looked at Magnus who shook his head and Hill tossed first one and then the other pigeon lightly upward and they watched as the two birds clattered upward through the tree canopy.

"Hope the Bitchfolk didn't see that." Said Hill. "With any luck the folk at home will know you're all safe and sound before they go to bed."

"Luck's got nothing to do with it." Growled Magnus.

Again, Hill slipped into the thicket and was gone and Rolf asked. "You were saying." And Magnus returned to telling his story.

"The pigeons. Ah the pigeons. They came back didn't they? And without messages. Now that was a message. And then we heard rumour coming from the Lams. All mixed up. All over the place. So Edgar asked us to sail to The Gullet. To help if possible. So here we are."

"Thank Christus." Muttered Malcolm.

Magnus kept on with the story.

"Three days after you left two families crossed over, asking if they could camp a while. Lamentasia was suddenly a dangerous place with Bitchfolk swarming everywhere, hunting some runaway. There was a lot of random killing and taking of young folk and both these families had young boys. The Mentor Viat urged them to flee. Well Edgar got us together and said he was now very worried about you three and instead of using horses he asked us to sail as far as we could and try and find out what happened. Try and make contact with you although Christus alone knows how he thought we were going to do that. We took off the next day and stopped overnight with Kester, so he knows what's going on. Yesterday we talked to some Lam fisher folk on the other side. What they said was not good. They talked about the runaway and also about the two Mentor Viat at Orlo's being dead but nothing about you folk. That was puzzling. They said they'd meet us again at the

179

same place this morning and they would bring somebody who knew what had really happened. Of course we rewarded them and promised more to make sure they turned up. Anyway, we camped down river last night and early this morning put up the sail and drifted across to the meeting point. We could see nobody waiting and when we got to within about a good bow shot of the shore, I got this creepy feeling and put the boat about, really slowly, I mean there wasn't much wind and it was just as well because straight away four queer looking people stepped clear of the scrub and let fly. They were close enough for their arrows to hit the boat and the sail was barely filling but we managed to drift back out of range and all the time arrows kept coming so we stayed crouched down in the boat. If they'd come after us in a dugout, we wouldn't be here. We sailed down river for a bit and then headed up again and hid in this side river and we've been here all day. As soon as it's dark enough we're out of here – that means you folk as well."

"You know Mal, you wouldn't believe how folk have been praying for you lot."

"I can imagine." Murmured Malcolm.

Rahnuk moved away a little to feed the baby and Magnus pulled Malcolm aside and speaking in a low voice said.

"That woman." He nodded toward Rahnuk. "Bitchfolk?"

"Don't know. Could be."

180

"From what we've heard the Bitchfolk are dragging all Lamentasia for some runaway – she's probably the one – she must be high up. You walked straight into a hornet's nest. Many Lams are dead you know."

Malcolm looked at Magnus. "So you think she's the reason?"

Magnus nodded.

"But, but, we were attacked twice before she joined us. How come?"

Magnus shook his head. "Don't know. But I'd say she's the one they're after."

Malcolm wagged his head as Magnus continued.

"Edgar and Dibius are worried sick about the Mentor Viat at Orlo's. The rumours we've heard." He shook his head. "It's been a real shot in the dark meeting like this. We didn't think you stood a chance. What about her though? Will she want to come?" He jerked his thumb toward Rahnuk.

"What else can she do? Got room in the boat?"

"Just. But then what?"

"You mean what will happen to her?"

"Yes, well nah, forget it. Let Dibius sort it. Give 'im somethin' to do."

"But he won't be expecting anything like this."

"No, no he won't. But we won't be in Brakial tomorrow. We'll overnight at Kester's if we get a good following wind." Malcolm raised his eyebrows at Magnus.

"Kester keeps carriers. We could send a message from there."

"Don't see why not."

"Okay then, now where's the boat?"

"Hidden, it's well hidden. Look at the sun, it's nearly gone. I want to be ready to leave as soon as it's dark. So…" He extended his arm to signal to the others to hurry and finish eating.

"Magnus. Those Bitchfolk are very determined. They won't have given up that easy. They'll be watching the river."

"Yes yes I know. We were leaving tonight, but once on the water, the Bitchfolk won't catch us. Not in the dark."

Malcolm's worries were groundless. Waiting until the light was almost gone; they picked up the gear and walked silently through the trees to the edge of a scrub-lined backwater where the boat was tied up. The boat stank strongly of fish and Hill showed Rahnuk a space under the foredeck where she could recline on a spare sail and some ropes and holding the baby fast to her she lay down sheltered from the cold air. The rest of the gear was loaded and they waited a little longer until it was dark when Seth and Hill waded and pulled the boat into deeper water before leaping in, and Magnus and Rolf used paddles to move down the backwater to where it met the Deemah and they drifted in the gentle current while Magnus and Hill hauled up the sail which soon filled from the damp wind pushed downstream from The Gullet, and before long the dull roar of the fast moving water gave way to the quiet comforting rhythm of lapping sounds as the boat slipped its way downstream, and Rahnuk was lulled to sleep. Much later the baby woke her with hungry cries.

Sometime during the night the breeze dropped and the boat was enveloped in a thick fog. A pole was used to measure water depth and make sure they didn't drift too close inshore. At no time did the pole touch bottom and the boat merely drifted downstream in the leisurely current. In the morning when it became light enough to see, the breeze returned and swept the fog away and the sun arrived to bathe the river's surface and the little boat heeled in the increasing wind. In spite of reassuring words from Magnus, the boat's angle of heel alarmed Rahnuk and she refused to come out into the sun, feeling more secure in the cramped space under the foredeck and away from the sight of the water that looked to her as if at any moment it might flow over the side. From where she lay she caught occasional glimpses of land: sheer rock walls lifting straight from the water, or when the boat was gibed, she could see in the other direction to where a grass covered shore sloped upward to merge with low rolling swells of land covered in grass and distant trees. And then she slept fitfully and several times woke to feed the baby who was decidedly scratchy and restless. Since leaving the lake the previous day she was out of clean dry cloths to wrap him in. Those she had were well used and although she cleaned them as best she could, they were still damp and gave off an unpleasant smell, and now there was an angry rash spreading from the little man's buttocks around to the front of his thighs

.

## 15.

Rahnuk was asleep when near the day's end the boat grounded its bow with a sudden crunch on the sandy beach below where Kester's family lived and farmed. Rahnuk crawled out from her hidden place in the bow holding the baby and blinking in the bright light. She saw another Deeve standing there with eyes shaded by one hand against the sun and his other hand held the reins of a pony and nearby stood a panting black and white dog with slowly wagging tail. The Deeve was laughing and the first words she heard him say in a booming voice were.

"Ah. We expected you today."

Magnus stepped into the shallow water and sloshed ashore and embraced the man.

"Well we found them."

"Yes, thank Christus. We heard from Brakial." He continued laughing. "Mali made me come here with Jess and wait."

"Been here long?"

The man made a rocking motion with one hand. "No not really."

Hill was now being clasped by the laughing man and then it was the turn of Malcolm, Rolf and Seth.

"I should be chasing sheep. Four got out two days ago. But Mali" He shrugged. "Well I do as I'm told" He laughed some more.

Magnus and Hill now set about dropping and folding the loose footed sail and securing the boat with bow and stern lines that they attached to handy trees while the other four men on shore watched. Rahnuk holding her baby made to jump from the boat, but Seth stepped forward and she allowed him to take her hand so that she was able to step from the high side of the boat onto the little sandy beach. The Deeve holding the horse was introduced to Rahnuk as Kester. Malcolm told her he lived further up the hill with his woman and small child. Magnus and Hill now began to throw gear from the boat to the shore.

"I hear things have been grim for you eh?" Said Kester.

"They have indeed." Replied Malcolm quietly.

"And Rahnuk; she is the runaway from the Bitchfolk, right?"

"It looks that way."

"Would she like to ride on Jess? Up the hill?" He jerked his thumb over his shoulder.

Malcolm pointed to the horse and motioned for her to climb on its back. Rahnuk gave him a terrified look and Malcolm looked back at Kester, shrugged and said.

"No, she wouldn't. I don't think she rides."

"Well, anybody else?" Kester looked from face to face only to be met with smiles and shaking heads. Magnus and Hill now began gathering up the gear from the boat and tied it to the horse's empty pack saddle after which Kester announced.

"Well, it's walking then." And turning to where the path began under the trees he jerked the pony's reins and began leading the way up the hill. The pony clomped along, the dog trotted at Kester's heels and the others followed in single file with Rahnuk holding her baby and walking in the middle.

Rahnuk was still tired from the previous day and stopped frequently to rest. She flatly refused the continued offer of Kester to sit on the back of Jess and be carried and it was late afternoon before they emerged from the trees onto a broad well-grassed ridge and only a short distance from a simple house and immediately three large dogs raced toward them barking a welcome. Near the house a narrow clear stream gurgled past before sliding out of sight in the trees on its way to the little beach they landed on. Beyond the house were small fields with several cows and some sheep behind fences of stone and wood. A tethered goat in front of the house looked up and bleated and now the door of the house opened to reveal a woman who held in her arms a smiling boy of about three years. Kester unloaded the horse and holding Jess's rein led her to a little holding paddock behind the house while the others greeted the woman and stepped inside. They were still all standing around when Kester walked inside and in his deep voice boomed.

"You all know Mali don't you? Sit down, sit down, relax; you look dog-tired."

Mali pointed at Seth saying she knew him from long ago and Seth reddened as Mali reached with her free arm and hugged him and suddenly he remembered that Mali was Ailsa's older sister.

Kester was a large bearded man with a ruddy complexion. Mali was slight with olive skin and a halo of wavy black hair. Her face displayed a radiant and tranquil look. There was only one chair and two stools in the room but Kester stepped outside and returned with a chunky piece of firewood and Seth went and got another and the men made to sit down until Malcolm suddenly remembered Rahnuk who was standing apart and looking bewildered and standing again he said.

"Mali, this is Rahnuk. She and the baby need help and rest. She's the Bitchfolk runaway."

Mali took Rahnuk by an arm and ushered her behind a partition into the sleeping area. She returned almost immediately and picking up a wooden bucket from beside the doorway, went outside, filled it with water and coming back grabbed some cloth pieces from a pile on a shelf and went in to be with Rahnuk. The others listened to the baby's testy cries as Mali helped Rahnuk give the child its first good clean-up since leaving the lake two days ago. The men sat looking at each other, Kester the only tidy one, the others with unkempt hair and for those without beards, stubble clad faces.

"Let's celebrate." Said Kester. "I've got a full jar."

Mali put her head around the partition. "Not until you've fed them. I can't do everything."

Kester looked and muttered something and stood and going over to a rack he pulled from it a joint of dried meat and a loaf and grabbing a knife he began carving pieces off and handing them around.

"This house is small. I don't know where we'll all sleep tonight."

Malcolm said since they'd been sleeping rough for nearly a week another night wouldn't hurt them as long as they could be near a warm fire. Magnus walked outside to where the packs unloaded from Jess lay on the ground and returned with a large leather pouch from which he emptied food onto the table.

"Well now," said Kester. "Tell me what all the fuss is about."

"Wish we knew." Malcolm waved his hand toward the room where Mali and Rahnuk were. "We think she has something to do with it – probably a lot."

Magnus now spoke up. "From what we know there's been a lot of trouble among the Lams. Much killing by the Bitchfolk. The Mentor Viat up near the Vau are both dead, so we've heard."

Kester drew in his breath with a whistle and shook his head.

"Why? What's the trouble?"

Malcolm shook his head.

After the evening meal they talked at length.
Magnus said he wanted an early start in the morning to
make sure they reached Brakial in daylight. Kester said
the warm day and the sky with its streaky clouds all
signaled a change and he wouldn't be at all surprised if
an unfavourable wind blew up in the night. The light in
the small room steadily dimmed until Kester lit some
candles and then a little later he spread the floor with
skins and rugs and the men including Kester, who at
Mali's insistence gave up his bed for Rahnuk, lay there
trying to sleep through the resounding snores of Hill.
The baby woke twice in the night to be fed and again as
it was getting light.

Kester was right about the weather. In the middle of
the night an upstream wind began and it was still
blowing strongly at daybreak making travelling on to
Brakial out of the question. Kester released a pigeon
carrying news of the delay. With the bonus of extra fit
men in the house, Kester decided they would search the
scrub covered hillside to try and catch the four runaway
sheep.
"You'd wonder why they took off. There's no grass
where they've gone – nothing but tohmu – head high –
full of thorns. Something badly frightened them."
As soon as breakfast was over the men picked up
shoulder bags containing bread and cheese for a midday

189

meal and with two dogs on leashes, Kester led the way further up the ridge out of sight of the house to where he thought the missing sheep were likely to be.

## 16.

With the departure of the men, the house lapsed into quietness except for occasional snatches of song coming from Mali. Rahnuk was content to rest on the bed in the sleeping area, the baby beside her. Earlier, she had fed and cleaned the child and for breakfast Mali gave her a bowl of porridge sweetened with honey and a large mug of water. Rahnuk's feet were hurting. The walk from the cove up the hill yesterday was the final straw. Although it was the nature of all Zoels to scorn feelings of pain, the previous evening she showed her blistered heels to Mali who gasped at the sight of the reddened raw flesh and she got some soothing ointment from a jar and smeared it on the affected areas. Lying on the bed Rahnuk listened to Mali singing to her little boy as she went about her tasks - the singing puzzled her, it being so different from the deep chanting indulged in by the Zoels and Verds back in Latcho. She drifted off to sleep and woke later to find Mali sitting beside her and smiling.

"I have something for his bottom." And taking the baby she unwrapped him and together they inspected the urine inflamed skin at the top of his thin little legs. Mali held in her hand a cool damp pack of bruised leaves from some plant and she laid it on the reddened areas of skin before wrapping him again and all the while the baby grizzled and cried. There was a rocking cradle in the room and Mali persuaded Rahnuk to lay him in it to see if he would go off to sleep, and slowly his cries subsided after which Rahnuk followed Mali out into the main room of the house and watched while the other woman performed her chores. It didn't look right watching as this woman busied herself with tasks that in Latcho would be performed by others.

"Where are your Verds?" Rahnuk demanded to know.

Mali looked puzzled. "Verds! Verds?"

"You are doing work. Preparing food, cleaning. In Latcho I never did such things."

"Latcho? Where is Latcho?"

"Where Zoels live. I am a Zoel. I have been trained to fight. Work is done by the Verds."

"What about men? What do the men of Latcho do?"

"Men! We don't have men. Kraaths yes and the Dohma yes, but none like your men."

Rahnuk now pointed to a colourful clay wall plaque. "The Verd with the strange eyes, who is it?"

Mali looked up. "The Mother of Christus? Her eyes are not strange."

"We don't have such things. In Latcho the Verds are real – we talk to them – we tell them what to do. Mother of Christus! Mother of Christus? What is that?"

"The Mother of Christus." Mali repeated.

Rahnuk still looked puzzled.

"Christus: the man child of the one who calls."

"The One who Calls!"

"Do you know nothing of the one who calls? The Caller? The one who calls everything to life?"

"Ah, you mean Azrah. We have Azrah. Yes, Azrah is all powerful. He made everything, yes and he made Zoels especially; so we will be favoured by Azrah."

Rahnuk continued to look at the wall plaque.

"The mother of the one who calls. The mother of the one who calls."

"No Rahnuk. The mother of the Caller's son – the Caller's man child."

"This Caller has a man child? This Caller blew his seed into a woman?" She shook her head and burst out. "We have Azrah. Azrah has no children. Azrah has no need of children. Azrah has everything. Azrah made everything. Azrah is the strongest and when a strong Zoel dies she will have great pleasure with Azrah; forever and ever."

Mali recovered her composure. Her little boy who was playing outside came back in; he was carrying a puppy and holding his head back to stop the wriggling animal from licking his face. With his free hand he grabbed hold of the hem of Mali's robe.

"Rahnuk. Our Caller is yours as well."

Rahnuk looked away puzzled.

"But you say he has a man child?"

Rahnuk now pointed to a red clay crucifix on a small shelf on the opposite wall.

"What is that?"

Mali took a deep breath and bent down and told the child to take the pup outside. She looked up.

"That is Jesu Christus. The Caller's man child. He died to free us."

"Free you? Free you from what?"

"From ourselves."

"From yourselves?"

"Yes Rahnuk. He died to free us from ourselves – if we want him to."

"Why do you need to be freed from yourselves? We Zoels don't need to be freed. We are free to do anything."

"Rahnuk, please believe me – your Azrah is the same as our Caller. He came among us, walked and lived among us. That was a long time ago. He was killed."

"Ha. That is not Azrah. Azrah is all powerful – Nothing could kill Azrah."

Mali muttering under her breath sat down on a stool. Rahnuk also found a stool and sat down on the other side of the table. She was far from finished.

"Azrah would guard you. Azrah would protect you. You should forget your caller. In Latcho Azrah is strength. Everything weak is banished."

Mali looking confused reached out to take one of Rahnuk's hands in both hers. Rahnuk pulled her hand away and glared at Mali. Mali looked into Rahnuk's eyes, drew a deep breath and said.

"Rahnuk. This was told to our people. Many many lifetimes ago the Caller came amongst us, he joined us, and he was the Christus. It was always known that someday this would happen; it was a promise. The Christus taught people. He healed them of sickness. The leaders of those he healed hated him. They killed him. Christus was not who they were expecting, and they killed him."

"And this Christus is the Caller? Your Caller and Azrah are the same? What foolishness you talk."

"It's not foolishness Rahnuk. Christus and the one who calls – your Azrah – are one and the same."

"No, no, no, not possible. Azrah is invincible. This one you have, the one who calls is dead? He's useless. He's dead! What use would Azrah be if he was dead? Azrah would no longer be. It's impossible. Anyway, why was Christus killed?"

"The leaders feared him."

"Why?"

"Christus said he was the one who was promised. The leaders felt threatened. They mocked the Christus, they killed him. But he came back – he came back to life. He proved them wrong. And still they rejected him. But many became followers – I am one – Kester and I follow the Christus."

Rahnuk's face took on a sour look.

"In Latcho, Azrah is all powerful and when we die all Zoels will live with Azrah and if we die in battle Azrah treats us with special favour. Our other people, the Kraaths and the Verds: when they die they stay behind here, but unseen. There is no pleasure for them." Rahnuk stopped and looked away.

"Rahnuk, when we die, Paradise is our reward."

"Paradise! What is Paradise?"

"Happiness. Paradise is a place of unending happiness. The Christus promised us."

"Happiness?"

Mali took a deep breath.

"How can I say it? Happiness. Being without fear."

"Without fear? We Zoels have no fear."

Mali paused once more. She bit her top lip before replying.

"Happiness is everything we need to stop us wanting to wound others."

"How will that be? What will make this happiness?"

"I, I, we don't know. What we do while we're alive, alive here and now. If we have followed Christus as best we can, that will make us worthy of Paradise."

"So you don't know?" Rahnuk laughed. "We know. We know strong Zoels live with Azrah who pleases us all the time, forever and ever. Azrah is our afterlife. In

Latcho we don't have men. Men are forbidden, until we die. Then Azrah will be our man."

"But your baby. How, how, he is a man?" Mali was frowning.

"I don't know." Rahnuk stood and went and retrieved the sleeping baby from his cradle. She looked at him, lying in her arms. "I don't know. He is here now. He is safe, he's with me. In Latcho he would be dead." Rahnuk's voice now rose until she was shouting. "He would be killed because he is a man child."

Mali's hand flew to her mouth and Rahnuk continued, her voice once more softening.

"In Latcho, most men are killed at birth. Some others have their man parts removed – they are made Kraaths. A very small number are kept as they are born."

A horrified look came over Mali and she nodded for Rahnuk to keep going.

"Those men live in pits. They are guarded by Kraaths. The Kraaths do heavy work. The Kraaths help with fighting. Most men children born to Zoels and Verds are killed at birth. All female babies are treasured. Most become Verds, people who help and do the ordinary work. The others are trained to fight – Zoels – I am a Zoel."

Mali was speechless, the tears streaming from her eyes. Rahnuk put her cheek against the baby's head. "My baby was a man baby. There was no shortage of Kraaths and the thought of him being killed. I couldn't live with that. I ran away. I ran. I was alone when my time came. The Verds always guard Zoels and Verds nearing their time. Something happened and I was alone."

Rahnuk opened the front of her robe and the now awake baby fastened onto the nipple and began sucking.

"Having my baby with me for only a short time – I could not have lived without my baby. But Zoels came after me and caught me to take me back. Both of us were to be killed. Then your men came and freed me. When first I escaped across the river some Deeve women sheltered me. They hid me and protected me and warned I would be sold if others knew about me. I was with them fourteen days. When the Zoels caught me they killed my helpers, as punishment. Soon afterward, Deeves – your men came. There was a big fight. We all escaped."

She stopped talking and looked down at the baby and smiled. Mali was aware of gossip about life among the Bitchfolk – most of it was passed on by the Lams – but now the hideous truth about Sessilia was told her by one who so far had lived all her life there. Suddenly Mali cried out and flung her arms about Rahnuk and clasped her tightly and then as Rahnuk struggled to free herself Mali held her by the shoulders and staring straight into her eyes said.

"Have you named him?"

Rahnuk gave Mali a blank look.

197

"You must give him a name. You cannot leave him without a name!"

"In Latcho he would only have a name if he was a Kraath."

"But you can name him. He can have a name here."

Rahnuk looked puzzled.

"Do you want him to have a name?"

Mali released her grip and Rahnuk looked down at the baby in her arms.

"I want him to have a name. I want a name for him." Rahnuk looked at Mali. "Have you got a name for him? Mali, shall we name him Mali?"

"No. My name is a woman's name. We must give him a man's name."

"A man's name? Why?"

"But that's what he is. He will grow to be a man."

"I don't want that to happen."

"Do you not want him to be a man? Like my man? Like Malcolm or Rolf?"

"I'm a Zoel. Couldn't he be a Zoel? I could train him to fight."

"But you may not want to. Once you've lived here. Once you see how we do things."

"I want him to be safe. Safe here with me. Safe wherever I am. Is there a name that means safe?"

"Safe! A name that means safe?" Mali frowned and looked away as if gathering her thoughts.

"Yes. A name that means safe."

Mali brightened and turning again to face Rahnuk she said.

"He could be Titus. That is a very old name. Titus means to be safe I think, yes, I'm sure it does. Shall he be Titus?"

"Yes. Make him Titus."

"Give him to me." Rahnuk held the baby out to Mali who carried him to where a large pail stood near the fireplace. She picked up a dipping jug, filled it with water and began dribbling it over the little boy's forehead. Rahnuk rushed at Mali.

"What are you doing Verd? What are you doing? He's already been cleaned today; he's clean, clean. Do you hear?"

Smiling down at the baby Mali continued pouring water over the little boy's head and all the time murmuring words that made no sense to Rahnuk. Rahnuk tugged at Mali's arm and then yanked hard and the water in the jug sloshed all over the baby who now began to roar. Rahnuk pulled the child from Mali and with her free hand balled into a fist she punched her hard in the chest sending her flying onto her back on the floor. The baby was now holding his breath and Rahnuk hurried with him into the sleeping area where she sat on the edge of the bed and again offered her breast to the upset infant. Mali scrambled to her feet. She looked pale and scared and rubbed the back of head where it hit the floor. She could hear Titus struggling to breathe and she rushed after Rahnuk to help and managed to deliver several cuffs to the baby's back that restarted his breathing before Rahnuk again punched her into a sitting position on the floor. This time Mali sat there looking bewildered and Rahnuk glared at her before turning and attempting to soothe the upset child.

"I meant no harm. That is how we name children here in Riparia. We give our children to the Christus. We pour water on their heads. They are named at the same time."

Mali was still breathing heavily and her face was pale but she was trying to smile.

"He needed that. He couldn't breathe. Anyway, he has a name now. He is Titus. What does your name mean? Rahnuk, what does Rahnuk mean?"

Rahnuk at last managed to get Titus to begin sucking. She appeared not to be listening. Mali tried again.

"What does your name mean?"

Rahnuk did not look up.

"It means to be loyal. I am a loyal Zoel. In Latcho I am always Rahnuk."

"Who was the man you had Titus with?"

Rahnuk continued to feed Titus before standing and looking around for some clean dry clothing for the infant and Mali held out a large dry cloth which Rahnuk snatched from her outstretched hand.

"There was no man. I was seeded from the Dohma."

Rahnuk told of how she was one of a group of seven Zoels who were brought together and inducted in a ceremony and then afterward they were kept apart and tutored and fed a special diet extracted from a certain berry and this synchronized their body rhythms and after three months the seeding ceremony took place.

The seed was taken from the Dohma who were the men kept in pits. The Dohma were also fed a special diet and then for three days before milking, their hands were tied behind their backs and they were given a drink that kept them calm. After the third day the Kraaths milked the Dohma and the seed was carried still warm to where Rahnuk and her six Zoel companions waited, and they were served by the seed being blown through a straw into them. For ten consecutive days this was repeated and then after four weeks it began again. Two months after the first seeding they were tested to see who was carrying. In Rahnuk's group there was only one failure. Mali's face ran with tears all through the telling.

Later when Titus was asleep Rahnuk followed Mali around as she carried out more of her household chores. At noon Mali set out bread, cheese, dried fruit and water on the table and while they both ate and drank, Mali told her more about life in Riparia. Mali said that to live in Riparia was to work and that Rahnuk would not find Verds to do her bidding. Later Rahnuk watched while Mali worked outside hoeing a small patch of ground to ready it for a kitchen garden and afterward she stood by fascinated while Mali spun thread from a wool fleece, and then laid it aside so as to prepare food for the evening meal. Rahnuk asked what would happen tomorrow and Mali told her that assuming the wind was favourable the men would take her in the boat to Brakial. Rahnuk asked about Brakial.

"It is good. Very good. You will like it." Mali told her.

"How many live there?"

"About seven hundred."

"Do they live in a box like this?"

"You mean houses?"

"Yes."

"Brakial has more than one hundred houses."

"Why so many when there are only seven hundred? In Latcho we live forty to fifty in a house. The houses are long."

"In Riparia there is one house for each family."

Rahnuk wanted to know what a family was and then asked Mali if instead of going to Brakial the next day, could she stay on and live with her and Kester and the little boy.

"Kester could protect us and I could help fight enemies. I could share looking after Kester with you." Rahnuk's eyes sparkled at the thought.

Mali breathed out a long sigh.

"Oh Rahnuk. In Riparia, each man has one woman only and each woman has only one man. That is our custom. Kester would never think of having another woman and I would not want to have more than one man."

"Why not?"

"In Riparia, that is the law. To knowingly disobey that law would mean being banned from Paradise. What did you do?"

"In Latcho I had Ilgud. Ilgud was my Freyarch. We looked after each other. She was the only one allowed to pleasure me. I was the only one allowed to pleasure Ilgud. That is the law in Latcho. One Zoel for one Zoel. One Verd for one Verd." Suddenly Rahnuk again pleaded. "Can I live here with you? Can Titus and I stay here with you and Kester?"

"I don't know. I think it would be best for you to go on to Brakial." She tried to give Rahnuk a hug but the other woman pulled herself free. Malcolm and also Kester will decide on that if that's what you want. But I think it will be better for you to leave. I can still know you. I will still see you."

After pleading with Mali, Rahnuk became sulky and went into the sleeping area to rest with Titus.

The sun was still shining strongly when the men arrived back, their faces and hands marked with bloody scratches. Mali wanted to know how Kester managed to tear his shirt. Kester said one of the sheep was still missing. Mali asked if a wolf could have been responsible – she was frightened of wolves through hearing others speak in awe of their cunning and strength. Kester said it was most unlikely. Rolf asked why not and Kester said since he and Mali had moved to live there he had never heard a wolf's howl or even seen paw prints, and neither did he want to. Tomorrow, after the others were gone he would go back to look for the missing one – he was determined to find it.

The evening meal was set out on the table and Mali and her little boy ate first and then it was the turn of the men and they were already eating before Rahnuk with difficulty, was persuaded to come into the main room and join them. Afterward Mali pulled Malcolm and Kester aside and told of her talks with Rahnuk, of her life in Latcho, and her plea to remain behind instead of travelling on to Brakial.

"Would you be happy with that?" Malcolm asked.

"No. No I wouldn't. She has already struck me twice today."

"What over?"

"Nothing important. A misunderstanding."

"I think it is best she comes to Brakial. She must talk to Edgar about Sessilia."

"But where will she live?"

"We'll leave that for Dibius to sort out. He'll find somewhere suitable."

After the evening meal, Mali told Rahnuk of the decision and said for her to rest early since the next day would mean being ready to start as soon as the downstream breeze began to blow if they were to make Brakial in daylight.

# 17.

For Rahnuk, the lasting memory of her arrival in
Brakial was the stir that it caused. From the time the
boat's sail was first spotted in the distance, people
began gathering at the landing to welcome Malcolm and
Rolf and Seth back from what by then was well known
as a journey of great danger. Until the boat steered into
the Landing, the presence of Rahnuk was unknown.
Cheers and clapping broke from the crowd when the
boat was still two hundred yards away and increased in
volume until it bumped the landing and several men
grabbed the bow and secured it fore and aft with rope.
Now as Rahnuk stepped from the boat onto the
Landing's wood deck, the applause ceased and
everybody stepped back. They stared at her saying
nothing. Rahnuk holding Titus looked around. The
flimsy shawl that protected the infant from the sun hung
loose and now a gust of wind caught it and whisked it
into the crowd. Quick as a cat Rahnuk darted after it and
snatched it from the hand that offered it back. Rahnuk
looked around in wide-eyed wonder, her heart beating
wildly. Edgar shuffled forward to greet the men and
Dibius followed behind him. Malcolm took Rahnuk by
the arm and introduced her to Mentor Dibius and
explained in a few words how she came to be with
them. Dibius with his head inclined forward listened
and when Malcolm finished he raised his head, looked
around the crowd of fifty or so and singled out a woman

called Ursula and asked her to take Rahnuk into her home and care for her. Ursula had a pleasant round face and she smiled at Rahnuk and signaling her to follow she escorted her through the crowd and up the path toward the houses. It was to be the last time for four weeks that Rahnuk would see any of the men she had spent the last six days with.

Rahnuk's story or versions of it were not long in making the rounds and for the next week whenever she stepped outside, folk would stop and point to her. The smaller children approached, stared and sometimes laughed. Rahnuk felt uncomfortable being the butt of laughter. In Latcho it was unheard of to laugh at a Zoel and Rahnuk began to wonder what possessed her to follow those Deeves that day. She supposed it was because they were fleeing the same Zoels that wanted her dead. If they could be safe then so would she be.

# PART II

## 1.

At first Malcolm could not hear his name being called. He was working on a small slope up above the stone walled paddock where the Caveo horses were grazed, and was trying to improve the flow of the little spring that supplied their drinking water. If left unattended for more than ten days it would slowly clog and change course and the drinking troughs would dry up leaving the horses without water. Malcolm was sweating in the hot sun shoveling mud and sand out of the little stream bed and shoring up the banks with the spoil and batting it down with hard shovel smacks to make it stay in place. He vaguely heard a woman's voice calling in the distance but at first paid it no attention. But then he paused for a rest and realized it was his name being called and the voice was growing louder with each call. He turned to face the direction it was coming from and stood still, breathing heavily and with sweat pouring from his forehead and down his neck and then realizing it was some sort of emergency he dropped the shovel and started to run toward the voice.

A month had passed since Malcolm arrived back from the chaotic journey through Lamentasia and the Azmata Mountains and apart from two short day trips across the Deemah to find out the latest gossip from any Lams willing to talk, and most were still too fearful to say anything useful, he busied himself with work close to Brakial. He busied himself because the last thirty days were an absolute hell. Like a familiar blanket, loneliness fell again and covered him. While they were fleeing through the Azmata, life came to have meaning. He felt an attraction for this strange woman. He couldn't help himself. It was the old protection thing once more, the thing that made him want to protect Kamya all those years ago. Any excuse he found he would walk past where he knew Rahnuk and Titus were living. And gossip he would listen to while pretending to be indifferent, but inside him was turmoil. He feared losing again. Losing this strange woman Rahnuk, whom he had rescued. She couldn't possibly be happy inside that house. Sure Ursula was a good woman, she cooked well and was a talented seamstress and would make a good job of instructing Rahnuk about Riparian life. But Ursula's husband Gorgo was an oaf. He laughed at the mistakes of others. He taunted those responsible. There was no other like him. Why on earth Dibius placed Rahnuk in that house was beyond Malcolm. Later it came out that Brakial was rife with rumours. Rahnuk was attempting to fit in but Gorgo, whenever he saw her, would watch until she made a mistake and then mock her. Rahnuk began dreading the dawn of each day – a day waiting to be taunted. In Latcho each day was planned and organized, but here was nothing except laughter at her blunders. Finally, Rahnuk could take it no longer and even though at the time Gorgo was innocent of any wrong doing; Rahnuk burned with resentment and without warning and holding Titus in one arm, she snatched up the kitchen knife and slashed Gorgo's shoulder and then when he grabbed an axe to retaliate, she dashed from the house and hid in some bushes.

Now Ursula's middle daughter arrived breathless and stood in front of Malcolm to report that Rahnuk had fled with Titus and a dugout was missing as well. A child saw Rahnuk launch the craft and paddle across the river. The owner was furious. Rahnuk and Titus didn't matter, but dugouts were highly prized and the boat must be recovered and since Malcolm was a full time Caveo, he was expected to do something about it. Malcolm looked at the young woman while she poured out the story and when she finished he nodded and asked if she knew where Seth was.

"I, I don't know. I, I think he's around. Do you want me to find him?"

"Yes, as quick as you can. Tell him to come to the Landing. Tell him to be quick."

The young woman took off again running and a short time later Malcolm could hear her wailing calls as she summoned Seth. Malcolm hurried off in the direction of the Landing. As far as he was concerned the dugout was of no importance, but not Rahnuk. As he ran he kept looking out over the Deemah but could see no sign of any boat. He arrived at the Landing just ahead of Seth who immediately asked what all the fuss was. Malcolm was leaning into the prow of his own boat, trying to push it down slope through the long grass to the water's edge.

"Help me get this in the water and I'll tell you what's happened. We're going after Rahnuk. She's taken off."

A man with a worried look on his face approached and opened his mouth to speak.

"Yes, you'll get your boat back." Malcolm said between grunts as he and Seth continued pushing the boat.

Attracted by the commotion, a knot of curious children and mothers gathered at the Landing as Malcolm and Seth dragged the boat to the water's edge and launched it before each grabbed a paddle, got in and headed as fast as they could for the opposite bank where they commenced searching the shore by paddling upstream for several hundred yards. They then turned and searched downstream, drifting with a gentle current but occasionally paddling to stay close to the shore. Well downstream from where their search began Seth pointed to the abandoned dugout close to the bank and partly screened by reeds. They paddled toward it.

"Pull it ashore." Grunted Malcolm, "See if you can follow where she's gone. I'll go upstream again and try to head her off."

Seth got out and waded to where the dugout lay gently rocking, grabbed the short bow rope and towed it shoreward. Malcolm wished under his breath that Spike was with him. A dog would find her double quick. He wondered if she would try to hide. He dug the paddle deeply and steered upstream close to the bank, and when about eight hundred yards above where he dropped Seth off, he pulled into the shore, dragged the bow of the boat up onto the dried mud and walked up a short steep scrub covered rise. At the top the ground was sandy, sparsely grassed and dotted with low bushes. Malcolm quartered a wide strip looking to pick up Rahnuk's trail before satisfying himself that she was still downriver. In the sun it was hot, so looking for a place that commanded a wide view he sat down to wait in the shade of a low spreading bush. In the still air the only sounds were the sudden hums of passing flies.

A nearby pipit caught his attention. The bird was shuffling around collecting bugs. It flew a short distance to where Malcolm guessed its nest was and in what seemed no time at all, the bird returned for more supplies. Malcolm cupped his hand and with a swift movement captured one of the numerous flies. He held the buzzing struggling insect between forefinger and thumb and extended his arm toward the fossicking pipit. The bird paused and looked to where Malcolm was holding out an easily taken offering. It made little runs toward him, each run taking it closer to Malcolm's outstretched hand. It was about to dart in and take the insect when out of the corner of his eye Malcolm noticed a movement. Coming toward him across the sandy waste was a shambling dumpy figure. Malcolm stood up and the little bird flew off in fright. It seemed an age before Rahnuk arrived and then when she at last stood in front of him she sank to her knees, threw her arms around his waist and sobbing she buried her face in his stomach. Malcolm attempted to comfort her before helping her to a sitting position.

"I hate it here, I hate it." Rahnuk wailed. "I want to go back. Ilgud wants me. I need Ilgud. Ilgud told me everything would be all right. I want to go back. I want to go back to Latcho."

Malcolm looked puzzled. He wanted to put his arm around her shoulder and comfort her but instead he held her by the shoulders and looked into her eyes.

"Ilgud! Who is Ilgud?"

"My Freyarch."

"Freyarch?"

"The Zoel who is mine and I am Ilgud's Zoel."

"You've been talking to this Ilgud?"

"There are voices. They talk to me. Ilgud talks to me. Ilgud tells me to come back. I want to go back." She stopped sobbing enough to give Malcolm his chance.

"Rahnuk. That's a long trek to the Vau junction. You can't go back! Even a strong man would be walking four days."

"That's nothing for a Zoel. Nothing."

"Rahnuk, the Bitchfolk, after all the trouble you've caused, when they see you, you and the boy will be killed. You would have to go through Igen's land and Orlo's. You wouldn't stand a chance with the Lams."

"I would kill any Deeve who tried to stop me."

"But they are many. They would kill you."

"No matter how many, I would kill them. Next time I'm near Gorgo, I will kill him." Rahnuk drew her hand across her throat and made a gurgling sound.

"You could help me return to Latcho. What's to stop you?"

Their eyes met and Malcolm shook his head.

"But this Ilgud. Do you really think you would be protected? How did you hear from this this, this Freyarch of yours?"

Rahnuk's face took on a sulky look. She waved one hand upward.

"Up there, up there." She repeated. "I have heard from Ilgud. We are to be welcomed back. We will not be hurt." Rahnuk looked down as if embarrassed. Malcolm now noticed Seth striding his way and when a few paces away Malcolm put his finger to his lips and motioned for him to stop. Seth made a helpless gesture with his hands and turned and retreating a little crouched on the ground and picked up a grass straw and began to chew on it. Malcolm stood up and looked down at Rahnuk; he pitied this unhappy young woman. Rahnuk now looked up imploringly at the same time grabbing him, this time around the knees.

"Malcolm. Would you be my man? I would be useful to you. You haven't got a woman, I know. Everyone in Brakial has someone. I have only Titus. In Latcho there was Ilgud. I need someone. Could I be your woman Malcolm?" She looked up at him pleading. Malcolm's face reddened. He was stuck for words and began to stammer.

"I c-c-arn't su-su-su-ay."

"Why not? Don't you want me? Don't you want somebody? A woman? Gorgo has a woman." Rahnuk's face took on a petulant look.

"No, I mean yes. I mean I don't know. I'm not sure about these things. Th-th-ey t-t-t-ake t-t-t-ime."

Rahnuk's rush of naiveté startled Malcolm. He stepped back abruptly making her release his knees and recovering some composure said.

"Come back to the boat."

"I'll kill myself." She sobbed. "I'll kill Titus. I hate this place. Don't force me to go back to Gorgo's. Couldn't I go back to be with Mali? I could live there."

"Rahnuk. Come back to the boat. You can't stay here. You can't go back to this Ilgud. Come back with me across the river. Something will be sorted out." He called to Seth to go back in the other canoe.

Rahnuk stopped her pleading and giving a few snuffles she stood and sliding her sling around to the front she lifted Titus out of it and carrying him in her arms she walked behind Malcolm to where the dugout was beached.

Back at the Landing a small group of curious children waited and watched. Malcolm and Rahnuk also waited until Seth arrived who helped Malcolm haul his canoe through the long grass to its usual storage place, and the grumpy owner of the stolen dugout without so much as a 'thank you', grabbed the bow rope of his craft and stalked off towing it a short distance along from the Landing to where he strained to haul it ashore. All this time Rahnuk had stood holding Titus and watching and now she trailed behind Malcolm to his house where he laid bread and water on the little board that did duty as a table and they sat on the only two stools and ate, and afterward Rahnuk fed Titus and cleaned him, and using some dry rags of Malcolm's, she changed him and laid him on a bed of old clothing on the floor.

Malcolm busied himself with odd jobs about the single room house and then from a shelf in the room he lifted a large colourful sea shell and began polishing it with a coarse stone to reveal more of its iridescent blue and green hues. Rahnuk sat on the floor watching him. The day wore on and evening came. Outside was silence and nobody seemed to be about. Malcolm started a fire and lit some candles and put out more bread and some cheese. With complete darkness a light rain came on and then became heavier. Malcolm made a bed for Rahnuk with old clothing spread on the floor and a sheep skin for her to lie under. Rahnuk gathered Titus to herself before lying down. Malcolm's bed was a bench set against a wall with dry hay to soften it for sleeping on. He blew out the candles and lay down fully clothed and pulled over himself two heavy stag pelts. After some time Rahnuk stood up complaining that she was cold, and that the roof was leaking, because water was dripping on her face, and that even at Ursula's, she was warm and snug, and that in Latcho there was Ilgud to share a bed with and she would be kept warm with Ilgud's arms around her. She stopped talking, gathered up Titus, picked up her sheepskin and throwing it over the bed on which Malcolm lay, she first put Titus down under the cover and then got in beside Malcolm, lay down with her back to him and was soon sound asleep. Two adults in a bed intended only for one meant Malcolm slept poorly and from the time when Titus woke and demanded to be fed, he found it impossible to get back to sleep.

## 2.

Early next morning there was a hammering at the door. Malcolm opened it to find a stern faced Dibius standing there.

"I've come to talk. To you."

Malcolm's face reddened and he began swallowing. He guessed what was coming.

"Is that woman with you? The woman Rahnuk?" Malcolm looked flustered and he opened his mouth to reply but no words would come.

"You know – the one with the child? Is she with you? In your house?"

"Yes, yes, Mentor she is. She was unhappy, she knows no one else."

"Have you been…have you been … did you lie with her?" Malcolm didn't answer. His mouth kept opening and swallowing.

"Did you?" Yelled Dibius.

"Ye - hess." Malcolm finally got the word out but before he could add that nothing of importance happened; Dibius began nodding and talking as if to some unseen silent audience.

"Huh. I might have known. How did you let that happen?"

"She was cold."

"Cold!" Dibius pursed his lips and looked away trying to think what to say next.

"She's using you. You'll see. She's getting ready to do another bolt. She'll leave you. And that'll be a good thing."

"Mentor Dibius, I want us to be married."

"Married! Out of the question. You can't marry her."

"Wh wh why not,"

"You know nothing about her. You don't know where she's been, who she's been with. She's probably diseased."

"She's never been with a man."

Dibius laughed. "She has a child. A child Malcolm! Are you blind?"

"B-b-b- itch- f-f-f-olken are different. Totally d-d-d-if-f-f-erent to us. Ask Mali"

"Listen Malcolm. That creature - she's untamable. Ask Ursula. Her man has a stab wound. It needed stitching. You should have left her over there." He waved his arm in the direction of the Deemah. "It was a bad day the day you met. What possessed you to bring her here in the first place?" He began shaking his head again. "Well anyway, the woman knows nothing of the Christus, nothing. Nothing of marriage, what it means, the meaning of a vow. Nothing at all."

All this time Rahnuk was listening and now she stood and with Titus still clamped to her breast she appeared behind Malcolm and stared up at Dibius.

"We use vows. In Latcho we made vows." After which she turned and walked back inside.

Dibius stood with his mouth open.

"You heard that Mentor Dibius. The Bitchfolk use vows. Ask Mali."

"Malcolm, you know Mali lives a day's sail from here. Ask her? Ridiculous. Ah well there's nothing to be done now. But what if she has a child with you?"

218

Again Malcolm tried to explain but Dibius wouldn't wait.

"You could have found a woman in Brakial. Elspeth, what about Elspeth. She's available. She's a widow. I could have arranged it. Too late now. Wait 'til she hears about this. Won't touch you with a barge pole."

Malcolm didn't say what he was thinking. That he wouldn't touch the widow Elspeth with a bargepole either.

"She'll never work for you. She can't cook." Dibius turned and began walking away, shaking his head but muttering loud enough for Malcolm hear.

"Mad. Mad as a two headed snake. Just as poisonous to. May the Christus be with them both."

Malcolm looked back into the room at the same time as he shut the door and slid the wood bar across.

Just before noon Mentor Dibius returned with Ailsa's mother Mado.

"I want to know what Mali knows. What this Bitchfolk woman told Mali. I've brought Mado with me, as a witness."

"We're just about to eat. Will you eat with us?"

"No. We'll eat later. I'm here to find things out. You go ahead and eat."

Malcolm put bread and plates on the board as well as dried fruit and a large jug of water and mugs to drink from and while they sat and ate and drank, Dibius asked questions, such as who was in charge in Latcho, and Rahnuk told him the leader was the Theon who was the chief Zoel and who was advised by a council of twelve – all Zoels. Nigho was the name of the current Theon and the advisers were elected every three years. A big grin came over Rahnuk's face as she announced.

"But in Latcho, Azrah is supreme. Azrah takes care of all Zoels. All we have to be is a Zoel."

"Azrah? Who is Azrah?"

Rahnuk frowned before speaking.

"You don't know Azrah? Azrah who made everything?"

"Ah. You mean the Caller."

"The Caller? The one who was killed? No, no. In Latcho we have Azrah – we have no need for the one who calls."

Dibius looked stunned – he was silent for what seemed an age before again speaking.

"So when you die Rahnuk, what then?"

"Ah, after death Azrah comes to each Zoel and gives morgrah. Morgrah without stopping."

"What is morgrah?"

"Ah, morgrah. Morgrah is what Ilgud and I gave each other. With our hands, our fingers, our mouths, our words and when we are dead Azrah will give his special morgrah to every Zoel, without stopping. And the sun will shine and the air will be warm and perfumed – always without stopping. We are never allowed to give morgrah to ourselves."

"Who is Ilgud?"

"Ilgud is my Freyarch."

Dibius looked puzzled and Malcolm said.

"Rahnuk and Ilgud are both Zoels. Both Bitchfolk."
The mouth of Dibius dropped open.

"What happens when you die?" Asked Rahnuk
looking at Dibius. "Are you given morgrah?"

Dibius now began to stutter.

"No no no. "

"So when Deeves die, what happens? Is there
anything to look forward to?"

Dibius paused and then drew one of his famous
deep breaths.

"Something to look forward to? A reward? Why,
yes of course. The reward is the Caller – we are called
to be with him – sickness and injury and sadness are
ended. There is great happiness."

"Is that all you get? No morgrah?"

"That which you know as morgrah is no longer
important – nothing in this world is ever important
again. The Caller gives what he promised and for those
who put others first, what he gives is completely out of
this world. We don't know what it will be like but we
believe it to be better than anything here. Unthinkably
better. The One Who Calls has promised us."

"You're all wrong. Nothing is better than morgrah.
We Zoels keep strong and are ready to fight, so we can
keep on giving morgrah. Everything in Latcho is the
way Azrah wants it to be. Anyway, what is this, this

thing – putting others first? What does it mean – to put others first."

Dibius drew another deep breath. "To put others first is to be good! To be good Rahnuk is to obey the Caller. To care for others as he cared for us. To be ready to die for others if necessary. To put ourselves last. You were prepared to die for your baby, is that not why you fled your people and came here with Malcolm? To protect Titus?"

Rahnuk's face hardened and she remained silent. She looked across at Titus asleep in some clothing arranged on the floor. Titus asleep was telling her something. He was trusting her. Her reverie was interrupted by Dibius asking.

"Have you no cradle for the child?"

Malcolm shook his head and Dibius looked at Mado and asked if she knew where a spare cradle could be found. Mado said she would ask around and when one was found she would bring it– that day if possible. The meal was finished and Dibius and Mado stood and made ready to leave. Both were grim faced and silent as they left the house.

For the next few days, if Malcolm was absent from the house for even a short time, Rahnuk clutching Titus would come looking for him. On the third morning she even followed him to the barn. Other people were there doing various small jobs and they looked up and greeted Malcolm. Rahnuk was amazed at the huge long high wooden building, open on one side. Malcolm told her that each household is entitled to use a small part for storing things, tools mostly but Rahnuk noticed several small boats and many fishing nets. Malcolm said he kept some stores there as well as his spare saddle and some bridles and other horse riding gear. There were many swallows nesting under the roof and they swooped on Malcolm and Rahnuk, twittering and flicking close past their faces in an effort to frighten them into leaving. Malcolm laughed and carried on with counting Caveo's stock of spare horseshoes.


## 3.


Three days after first speaking with Rahnuk, Dibius returned again with Mado. There were things he wanted clarified and he seemed afraid of meeting Rahnuk alone. He told Rahnuk the story of how Riparia came to be, and after they went, Rahnuk thought about what Dibius told her. The record of the past in Latcho was completely different from Riparia's beginning. Zoels were taught their origin and memorized it so that everyone in Latcho could chant the stories in chorus. Other than that, discussion of things from hearsay was discouraged. In Latcho only the present and the future were important. But according to the Deeve Dibius, Riparia recorded everything – It was written down – it was studied and remembered. The origins of Latcho; well it was the way things always were – apart from that at some stage in the past, the Deeves wandered off on their own and twisted things out of shape. The Deeves did not have Azrah – that was a puzzle – Azrah who is the greatest you can think – Azrah who has always been – Azrah who made time – without time we could not be – none of us could be – Azrah who chose Zoels to be his favourites. Everything in Latcho was how Azrah wanted it to be. A Zoel she was. A Zoel she would always be. So who was right? The things they told in Latcho? Or the things she heard in Brakial? But now, first Mali and then Dibius told the same story – vastly different to what was believed in Latcho. So how could a dead man help she wondered. How could anyone dead be of any use apart from being buried within reach of a fruit tree's roots? When she told Dibius that everything in Latcho was how Azrah intended it and it should be the same in Riparia, he quietly asked if Azrah intended that she should have gathered up Titus and run away. Would Azrah have approved of her doing that? Her face reddened when she remembered that she could not answer that question. Here in Brakial Dibius told her men and women came together and exchanged vows. They vowed to stay together – no matter what. The vow shaped the couple. That's what vows did. In that respect, Brakial and Latcho were the same. But here, something different was in place. Listening to Dibius was an awakening. What brought a man and woman together here was not something organized. It was free; there was no force involved. Dibius likened it to a fire that warmed and kept warming, never destroying what it fed on. A fire that strengthened all who warmed themselves before it – a fire poured out on – running through everything. The Deeves called this fire love, and according to Dibius, this love formed everything. Men and women lived and loved and bore children and loved and cared for them. The face of Dibius looked horrified as Rahnuk described life in Latcho. There, Zoels controlled and ordered all life. Rahnuk bent and kissed the downy head of Titus who lay asleep in her arms. She looked across at Christus hanging from the cross on the wall above the fireplace. Her eyes filled with tears and she imagined she saw the man on the cross crying with her. A series of sobs involuntarily shuddered her frame and she shook herself to end the mastery of whatever she saw as attempting to control her.

The fifth day after Rahnuk came to live in Malcolm's house was Sunday. The evening was warm. It was nearly three months since Rahnuk last enjoyed morgrah with Ilgud and she longed for the caressing hands of her absent Freyarch. But there was no going back and now she wanted to reward this Deeve who helped both her and Titus to safety. She wanted to give herself to him and help him to give himself to her – to pleasure her. After all this man stood against Rolf who said they should abandon her. Malcolm refused to be pushed around and she and Titus owed their lives to him. Titus was asleep in her arms and first she laid him in the cradle before pulling the gown Ursula loaned her over her head and then pushing the shift down over her hips and stepping out of it she went and lay down beside Malcolm. She wanted his hands running over her body, she wanted to be caressed by him but he seemed almost frightened until Rahnuk turned and wrapped her arms and legs around him and pressed her mouth against his and guided his hands over her and then proceeded to remove his clothing until Malcolm's fear turned to desire and for both it became a drawn out time of sheer ecstasy that afterward neither wished to break the spell of and they lay together face to face until overtaken by sleep.

The next morning Malcolm turned up at church with Rahnuk and Titus. Malcolm had planned to go alone but when leaving the house Rahnuk made to follow. Once seated at the very back, the trio attracted many furtive glances. When it came time to distribute communion, Dibius carrying an ornately decorated silver goblet walked down the centre aisle and halting in front of Malcolm said,

"The body of the Christus is here. Until the matter of you and this … this woman is sorted out; I cannot give him to you. But I will bless you, and the woman and her child."

And with that Dibius raised his right hand and traced in the air a cross over Malcolm and then Rahnuk and finally Titus touching each on the head and all the while calling out the words that said each was specially loved by Christus. The little ceremony over, he turned about and with swishing vestments swiftly strode back to the altar.

It was this first experience of church going in Brakial that one month later was to lead Rahnuk to a misunderstanding that would test to the limit her resolve to persist living in Brakial. Irrespective of that there was still the matter of reconciling the strength of Azrah with this One Who Called, this man Christus, who according to the Deeves Mali and Dibius, allowed himself to be killed by the very people he caused to exist. But thinking about it later, Rahnuk saw herself as defiled. The law of Azrah she always obeyed without question and now it lay shattered by what she had done. She had given herself to the man Malcolm. A Deeve! She had given something of herself, without even knowing properly what she was doing. There could be no going back. The guilt and anger of the defilement brought a numbing despair. She found herself wanting to scream – snatch up a knife and kill everyone she could find – herself included. She had not waited for death to bring the special pleasuring that was reserved only for Azrah to give. But Titus, what about him? And then this man Dibius: the one who directed with authority turned up and yelled at Malcolm over what happened between them. Why? That first night in Malcolm's house, when in loneliness and cold she climbed into bed with him. And then days later when with that first embrace, security and comfort flooded her whole being, flooded her very root and centre. And now each night after accepting his embrace she would lie curled around him, giving gentle squeezes, nuzzling his shoulders, her knees in the back of his knees, and she silently being pleased, being grateful. To whom? And tears filled her eyes at the thought of Titus. Titus in the dark. Titus safe in the cradle the Deeve called Mado found for him. Was this Christus responsible, the Caller, the One Who Calls, the one she learned of first from Mali? Maybe she should thank him: without even knowing him, and an exquisite feeling of well-being and safety filled her and her fear and anger subsided. She, a skilled and feared Zoel now wanted only the loyalty of the Deeve Malcolm. He was her protector. She trusted him. She needed her Titus. And now as she lay curled around Malcolm's hard back, she was aware of something outside of her, something beyond her, and this something desired her allegiance.

Malcolm soon realized that having Rahnuk and Titus following him wherever he went was not going to work, so he shyly asked Mado and Ailsa if they could help Rahnuk overcome her fear of being left alone when each day he left to perform the routine tasks allocated by Caveo, and which often meant his riding out from Brakial early in the morning – and Ailsa or Mado agreed to help and sometimes one or both would come to show Rahnuk how to do the work needing to be done each day in a Riparian household, and that included helping her manage Titus with regular feeding and cleaning – getting him into good habits was how Mado described it, and you can never start too soon she advised.

Malcolm however still made the bread: making it the way often favoured by people living alone. First he thoroughly mixed the flour, salt, water and yeast and rolled it and shaped it before taking it to bed with him, but now with two sleeping together, their combined body heat made a better job of forcing the bread to rise and it needed less time in the iron pot near the fire to finish it off with a good brown crust. Made this way a single large loaf would last two days. Rahnuk's first attempt was good. The next was a failure – soft and gooey. She thought she must have kicked it away from her stomach during the night. She tried putting it in the sun and then beside the fire laid on a brick. It formed a crust on one side only but was still soft on the other. Ailsa said it must not be wasted so little by little Malcolm and Rahnuk ate it, breaking it up and putting it into bowls with goats milk and honey to soften it and it was edible – just. Rahnuk vowed to Malcolm she would not fail again in the matter of bread making.

Ailsa came around one morning before Malcolm left. She carried a small leather bag with inside it some green seedlings wrapped in damp moss. She showed Rahnuk how to prick out young plants when they were the right size and how to plant them in the ground. She came back later and giggled at how Rahnuk had done it. Rahnuk planted them all on top of small mounds and Ailsa using her little wood slat lifted them and leveling the soil replanted them lower, each with a slight raised rim of soil around it so that when watered, the water would stay and soak through the soil to the plant's roots without running to some lower place where it would be wasted. Ailsa said that tomorrow they would go to gather cow dung.

The next morning Ailsa arrived just as Rahnuk finished feeding and cleaning Titus. The child was to be left in the care of Mado while the two young women making use of a borrowed horse to tow a sled went out into the open common land behind the houses where they spread out with buckets to gather dry cow-pats and after loading up the sled they went back to the wood shed beside the house where Ailsa lived with her family and Rahnuk was shown how to break dried cow dung into small chunks and soak the pieces in water before spreading it around the plants. Ailsa said that if it was not wetted, the first wind would blow the manure away.

## 4.

After that first Sunday morning when Rahnuk
holding Titus accompanied Malcolm to the Church of
Christus Risen, she remained deeply puzzled and
curious by what took place there each morning, and a
month after moving into Malcolm's house her
determination to solve the riddle came to a head. The
Church was supposed to be the house of the Christus –
the Christus was supposed to live in the little cupboard
up the front. Well she would go there and open the
cupboard and look inside. Malcolm rode out at first
light and neither Mado nor Ailsa had so far put in an
appearance. She finished feeding Titus and he was now
asleep in her arms, so holding the infant close, Rahnuk
hurried to the Church. There was nobody around. She
lifted the wooden closing bar on the door and pushed it
open, jumping with fright at the loud creaking noise it
made. Rahnuk waited until her eyes adjusted to the
darkened interior. She could see nobody inside so with
purposeful step and pounding heart she walked up to the
front to where the little gilded wooden cupboard was
fixed and which people seemed so much in awe of – it
being the place they said in which Christus lived. She
stood in front of it breathing heavily and began to speak.

"Christus are you there? Show yourself. Let me see you - see how strong you are."

She repeated the words and then with a gesture of impatience slid back the wooden bolt, opened the little carved door and groped past the curtained front to see what was inside. Suddenly a woman came from behind and tried to drag her back, all the time screaming the word no. Rahnuk with her free arm flung the woman aside and reached inside the cupboard once more, and again the screaming woman tried to pull her away. Rahnuk now had her hand on a large shallow silver dish and the frenzied woman grabbed her arm causing Rahnuk to pull the dish out and drop it scattering the shining white breads all over the floor. Titus now fully awake added his cries to the screams of the woman who continued clawing at Rahnuk, and Rahnuk while protecting and holding Titus in her left arm now drew back her right arm and drove her clenched fist hard into the woman's face at which she fell back on the floor moaning and barely moving. By this time the commotion attracted Dibius who was working nearby in his vegetable patch, and cursing and throwing down the spade; he hurried around the corner and entered the Church. He stood there aghast. The woman lay inert on the floor. Rahnuk stood in front of the little cupboard with its door wide open. She was holding Titus who was crying and she was yelling, "Christus where are you? Show yourself. Let me see you – how strong you are." Dibius rushed to the front roaring.

"What do you think you're doing woman? Get away from there. Go go."

He rushed past her shouldering her aside as he bent and gathered up the scattered and broken rounds of flat bread and muttering.

"Jesu Christus, forgive this woman; she has no idea what she's done."

After putting the breads in the dish and replacing it in the cupboard and closing the little door and sliding its bolt across he turned and with purple face pointed to the door and ordered Rahnuk out. He then bent down to attend to the woman who with blood pouring from her nose was starting to come to. Dibius grabbed a napkin from a small side table and holding it to her face, helped her into a sitting position on a bench.

In the afternoon of that same day, Mentor Dibius stalked into Malcolm's house without knocking. Rahnuk stood as he entered, Ailsa was with her. Earlier when Ailsa heard what had happened, she hurried to the house and now she stood holding Rahnuk's arm as Dibius fixed a fierce gaze on her and barked out how awful was the thing she had done. Terrible he kept on repeating. All of Brakial knew what happened. They were outraged. If it wasn't for Malcolm she would be banished – right this moment.

"What were you thinking? Why did you do it? Why?"

Rahnuk quietly seethed. She said that all she wanted was to meet Christus. To see Christus.

"You actually wanted to see Christus?"

"Yes, why not? They say he lives in the little cupboard. Ailsa here told me it was so. If others can meet him, why cannot I?"

Dibius kept shaking his head and looking at Ailsa.

"It's not just a little cupboard. Anyway, you wanted to meet the Christus, is that what you wanted?"

"Yes."

Dibius asked if those in Latcho could see their Azrah. She told him no, that Azrah could not be seen but that everyone knew how he rewarded all strong Zoels after death. Dibius asked that if all Sessilites believe in Azrah who they cannot see, why was it so necessary for her to be able to see Christus? Rahnuk said it was because Malcolm and Mali and others told her that Christus was their guide and she looked at Ailsa. Rahnuk said she wanted to follow the Christus but was puzzled over following somebody who she could not see, which was why she opened the little cupboard to look inside. Dibius had now begun to calm down.

"Wanting to follow is the start. Everything comes from that want. The right path is there at your feet." He paused before again speaking.

"Rahnuk. The Caller came to us as the Christus. He told us each time we gather around his table, the bread is changed, the wine is changed, we eat, we drink, we are changed, changed to fit the role Christus has readied for us. He feeds us with himself – Christus is the food that makes us strong enough to ignore the fiend's empty promises."

"The fiend?"

Rahnuk looked puzzled. Dibius droned on.

"We have it written in the sacred texts – the people remembered the words Christus spoke and wrote them down. Christus said our belief need be only the size of a small seed to force a tree to be uprooted and planted in the middle of a lake – that sycamore out there – to be uprooted and set down growing in the middle of the Deemah."

"I couldn't believe that."

"No, very few of us do. But Christus said that to show us how frightened we are – frightened of believing him."

"But Christus is supposed to help. So far he's done nothing for me."

"I wouldn't say that. Are you and your child not safe here? Were you not led to safety here in Brakial?"

"That was Malcolm not Christus. It was Malcolm, and Seth and Rolf. They were the ones who brought Titus and me to safety."

"Rahnuk. Christus cannot help you or anyone unless you try to help him."

"Why should I help Christus?"

"Christus wanted you Rahnuk. Your running from Latcho was a cry for help. The hand of Christus reached down and you grasped it – you were pulled to safety."

"How could that be? I never heard of the Christus before I came here."

"No matter, you were wanted – the Caller has a task for you."

"A task? What sort of task?"

"Ask Christus. He always gives us exactly what we ask. If we want him we'll get him. If we want ourselves, Christus allows that also, but Rahnuk, I've never met anyone happy with getting only themselves."

"Well, I wanted Titus – I've got Titus. Is that all I get? Is there nothing else for me?"

"Rahnuk, the Caller placed us in command of ourselves. Without our agreement he's powerless to help."

"Azrah is not powerless. Azrah is all powerful. If we remain strong …."

"Forget Azrah. We're not here to move firewood from one place to another – to feel satisfied when we've finished. The work is never finished. We must never cease doing the work of Christus."

"Christus dead is useless."

Dibius's mouth dropped open but Rahnuk wasn't finished.

"Christus should have fought his killers – should have killed them. Wasn't he the Caller?"

"Don't say that again. Ever, do you hear?" Dibius was shouting now. "Christus didn't come to make warriors. Christus calls us to be good – always our hearts have ached for the good. Christus was killed yes – but he defeated death. Now, we walk with Christus and he walks with us. We help him to help us. I can help you know this. From the top of that tree out there much more can be seen than if you were to stand beneath it. You have to look a lot further than you've looked so far. Would you like to see further?"

"Yes."

"All right then." And Dibius told Rahnuk he would set aside some part of each day if necessary to come and tell the story of Christus. The story that was written down and that he knew by heart. He said that he would even bring the sacred texts with him but first she must learn to read and write the Riparian way.

"Would you like that?"

"Yes."

Dibius then wagged his finger at Rahnuk and made her agree never to go into the Church alone again. He said he couldn't take any more of this raiding the place where the Christus lived and hurling his sacred body all over the floor where ordinary folk walk with their mud-covered boots. He started toward the doorway but then paused and turned.

"And Miriam. Her nose is broken. Her face is a mess."

"Why was that Deeve hiding in the church anyway? She attacked me."

"Yes, she tried to stop you, that's all, she wasn't hiding. She was there visiting with Christus."

"She was what?"

"Wait; wait until I return with the texts. I'll answer nothing more until then."

Rahnuk stared back in stony silence and Dibius turned on his heel and walked out the door.

Late afternoon Malcolm arrived home and Ailsa who had stayed on with Rahnuk told him what had happened, and then first Ailsa turned her head to one side to hide her giggling and then she began to laugh and Malcolm began laughing and finally Rahnuk, and all three began laughing heartily at the absurdity of how Rahnuk's misunderstanding led to such an uproar.

That night after the day's excitement in the Church died down, Rahnuk nursed Titus in front of the fire and Malcolm sat there with her; the fire lighting their faces, the flames sending their shadows leaping and slumping against the walls and roof. For some reason Rahnuk decided to talk again of her escape from Latcho. With Titus now fed, Rahnuk sat there with the sleepy child in her arms. She told Malcolm that although she could not explain it, after she was seeded and knew she was pregnant, she nursed this secret longing to have a man child.

"I don't know why. I just wanted to know what he would be like. I knew what a woman child would be; what she would be trained to be; either a Zoel or a Verd. And I knew that a man child would have to die or at best be made a Kraath or perhaps reared by the Verds to be one of the Dohma. Whatever, he would be taken from me and I would never know his fate. All the other Zoels wanted female babies. I never let on. And then it happened all very quickly. My time came and I was away from the others. I was with my two Verds staying in a hut near the river. That morning the koraght visited."

"Koraght koraght? What is that?"

"The koraght, yes koraght. You know one of those," she flicked her thumb against her middle finger. "Those birds that come inside and catch flies."

"Ah, gnat-catcher, a gnat- catcher. A little squeaking bird with a tail that opens like a fan?"

"Yes, yes, that's the one. But the Koraght is white. White all over."

"A white gnat-catcher? I've never seen a white one."

"Ah, bad things happen when the koraght visits. Very bad things. My Verds were frightened. Very frightened. They fled. They left me. I was frightened, alone, and my baby was coming and he came fast and I saw he was a man and I didn't know what to do. Part of me said 'kill him' and another part said 'no keep him, keep him. He's yours.' So I cleaned him and my fear just seemed to vanish. I couldn't believe he was so beautiful and he was mine, mine, nobody else's and nobody was going to take him from me. I pulled the afterbirth from myself and cut the cord and wrapped him in a shawl. Then I saw Toru coming back..."

"Toru?"

"One of my Verds."

"Oh!"

"I carried my baby and bent over low; I sneaked out of the hut and hid in some bushes. Toru kept looking and calling my name but I went further into the trees and after a while she gave up and went away. But I couldn't stay near there. Others would come looking. I remembered the afterbirth was on the hut floor. All I wanted to do was lie down and sleep but I knew I'd be found. I was thirsty and hungry as well so I went back to the hut and ate and drank. I put food in a carry-sack and took off with Titus and hid among the trees where I could still see what was happening. I needed to be able to watch the riverbank. There were some dugouts beached not far away and I thought if I could use one to cross the river I would be safe. Later, Toru returned with more Verds and they formed a line and moved along looking for some sign of me and calling my name. They must have thought I had panicked. After a while they walked back the way they'd come."

"The sun was nearly gone but it was still light when I crept down to the water's edge. I lay Titus in one of the dugouts and managed to get it into the water and I paddled it over to the other side of the river. I was looking for some place to hide when two Deeve women who were returning from gathering clay saw me. They could tell I was hungry. They persuaded me to follow and I stayed in hiding with one of them until after dark when we slipped into their tent and I was given a safe place to sleep and rest. They hid me and dressed me in Deeve clothing and helped me look after the baby. There were another two women; one of them was Arloht. Arloht helped me the most. There were also two men and they all helped to keep me hidden and they bought food and helped me care for Titus. I was there fourteen days. Twice Zoels came into the camp searching but only my helpers knew where I was hidden. On the fourteenth day the Zoels returned with dogs and made a thorough search and I was discovered. Two of the Deeve women were killed on the spot while the other two and the men were taken aside and tortured. The male parts were cut off the Deeve men and then they were tied by their feet and hoisted upside down from a tree and left hanging for some time before being stabbed with poison tipped blades. They were cut down and the Zoels stood in a circle and chanted while they died writhing in agony. All this time I was tied up and made to watch and my baby was left beside me. I was to be dealt with next but Ilgud arrived with more Zoels and said I would be taken back to Latcho for special treatment. Another Zoel ran in with a message for Ilgud who gave fresh orders. The bodies were dragged away and I was pushed into a tent and left tied up, and then you men arrived and there was the fight and Rolf cut me free and I escaped with you and we crossed the river and walked through the mountains until we met the men with the boat and came on here to Brakial."

Two mornings later Dibius arrived with the writing materials. It was raining and under his cape he carried a leather folder with inside it some sheets of paper, some blank, and some with words in Riparian script and he also carried a little clay ink pot and some sharpened quills and a slate and pencil. Titus was asleep and Dibius made Rahnuk stop what she was doing so he could teach her. He got the wide table board that leaned against the wall and set it across two stools and laid out the paper on it with some stone weights to keep it uncurled and he made Rahnuk kneel with the slate on her knee and copy onto it from the written texts he had brought, and he looked over her shoulder and either nodded or wagged his head at what she wrote, and then he used a rag to wipe the slate clean before the copying started again. He also asked Rahnuk to write in Bitchfolken script on some unused paper familiar words like bread, water and wood and beside them he would write in Riparian script the words that meant the same, and he told her she must learn these new ways to write. Rahnuk found it not too different from what she was used to in Latcho. Dibius said she must try and find

242

some time each day to write. So for the next few weeks Rahnuk began learning this new writing and then quite suddenly she found herself able to form simple statements in Riparian and within several weeks she was keeping a daily record as well as writing in Riparian some of the ways things were done back in Latcho. Dibius said it would help her; that she would be able to read back and see how far she had come in fitting in with this new place and that she should also get Malcolm to help her. Mentor Dibius returned every few days and encouraged Rahnuk into writing about things she knew and experienced – things from her past, and what was happening to her now, and all of it was to help her learn quickly. And that is how it came about that Rahnuk learned to read and write in the Riparian manner.

## 5.

(1) I am here. Titus is here. Malcolm shelters us. What else can be said? Because Dibius said paper is hard to come by I must not waste it. I have to fill this sheet with what I know and then I must turn it sideways and write across what I've already written. I must put a number at the top and then turn it over and do the same on the other side. It has taken me some time to get the knack of sharpening the goose quills. Verds did it for me back in Latcho. I find writing on the slate easier –

the mistakes I make I can hide – just by rubbing them away with the rag.

*

(2) Today a woman with a soft round downy face, a woman I have never before seen stopped me in the middle of the lane. She was chanting softly and smiling and at first she held me by the shoulders and stroked my cheek and said my name twice. She stroked the little bald head of Titus and then leaned forward and gently kissed my forehead before continuing on her way still chanting. Malcolm is unable to tell me who it may have been but said her chanting could have been a lullaby - something folk here do to help their babies and children fall asleep. Titus has begun rolling around on the floor to reach things he wants.

*

(3) Malcolm's friend Lon came around last night. He bought with him a jar and poured some of what it held into a mug for me. I drank it quickly – as if it was water, and can remember little else. Malcolm told me I talked in a very odd way and then fell asleep and Malcolm lifted me on to the bed and Titus missed out on my feeding him and Malcolm was left holding and

comforting him for a good while. My head and my stomach felt really queer this morning.

*

(4) I never knew until now that Ailsa's older sister is Mali, the woman who belongs to Kester and who we stayed two nights with after I escaped from Latcho. Why didn't Ailsa tell me this earlier? Although I can remember now the fuss Mali made over Seth when she met him that first time after we escaped from the mountains.

*

(5) Edgar the head of Caveo has been to see me. Malcolm was here as well. I told Edgar much about Latcho and also that the Zoels knew exactly how to make the Deeves across the river obey their demands. It was sufficient to round up about twenty children as well as goats and sheep and the Zoels would get whatever they wanted. Male children, dugouts, cattle or whatever and the Deeves dared not refuse. All the time I was feeding Titus and he sucked away and looked up into my face and then his little hand would waver and wander upward and one finger would slowly explore my nose or the inside of my mouth and it made me smile and giggle and Edgar would have to stop his questions

245

because Titus would grin broadly and break off feeding, spilling milk out the side of his mouth and chuckling.

*

(6) Yesterday was Sunday. Ailsa was joined to Seth in marriage. Nearly all of Brakial tried to fit into the church. Those who couldn't stood outside and waited and when Ailsa and Seth walked out of the church door they clapped their hands together and cheered. Ailsa wore a white gown that covered her from her neck to her ankles. It was the same gown worn by her mother and grandmother when they married. Over her head and face Ailsa wore a white veil. After they exchanged their vows before Mentor Dibius the veil was folded back. They are to live in Mado's house until a small house is built for them. Ailsa said she wants lots of children.

*_

(7) I understand a little now of why Dibius was so against me after that first night in Malcolm's house. There is a story here from many years earlier of another runaway Zoel who lived a wretched existence alone near one of the upstream hamlets. She was dressed in rags when first noticed but was very frightened and always fled into the woods when anyone came near. Later she became bolder and the woman of the house

began leaving food out and she would come regularly at night and always the dogs barked and always she grabbed the food and ran. Once a warm garment was left outside for her and that was taken also. But about a year after she was first seen the runaway walked calmly inside and attacked the woman of the house with a knife. Her man who was working close by heard the screams. He ran to help and immediately was caught in a desperate struggle trying to avoid the slashing knife until he was able to grab a lump of firewood and kill his attacker with a single blow to the head. The wife received many stab wounds in the upper body and was bleeding profusely. Her man managed to halt the blood flow and get her into bed but a short time later she went unconscious and died just after sunset. From then on the word went out – have nothing to do with runaway Bitchfolk.

*

(8) It rained again all day yesterday. The rain was so heavy that nothing outside could be done. While Titus slept soundly, Malcolm and I spent much of the day lying together in each other's arms. I never want to be apart from him. Never. I hate it when he leaves me in the morning. I hate it even more when he leaves me and I know he'll be gone for more than a day. What if some harm should come to him? I cannot bear the thought. I

never want to see him sorrowful, to know he is sad; I never want to be the cause of that. Each evening I want only to be in his arms and to fall asleep like that.

*

(18) Titus is crawling now. Nothing on the floor is safe. The fire is something that fascinates him. When it is going well it is too hot for him to approach. It is most dangerous when low and the glowing heat hidden under grey ash. He crawls toward it and would put his hand in it if I did not stop him. Lon is letting us have a long wood bench we can lay on its side to block him. I need another one for the door. If I go outside and leave it open he is through it at once and grabbing small stones from the path to put in his mouth. Mado thinks it won't be long before he is standing, and then walking. When I lift him up in the mornings I get smiles – smiles like sunshine – and he laughs – often.

*

(31) For the last half year I have not touched the diary – I have been very angry. Once more I wanted to return with Titus to Latcho, to be back with Ilgud. Dibius has persuaded me to start writing again. For a long time I didn't want him near the house. I hated

seeing him, even in the distance. I haven't been near the church either and I refused to allow Malcolm to go. After the pouring of the water I was assured everything would be better. I even expected the weather to improve. I was thinking of the boat that Dibius talked of tied to the landing. No more would it need emptying out after a night of rain – I somehow thought the rain would no longer be a nuisance. And none of this happened. I felt terrible – empty, lonely and I loathed everyone – Malcolm, Dibius, Ailsa, Mado and even at times Titus. I dreamed – vivid dreams – of Ilgud and the Verds. There was much chanting, dancing and killing. And there were days, many days when I refused to prepare meals and Malcolm was left to do everything. He stayed close to the house, afraid of what I would do out of his sight. Several times each day anger would ripple through my body. One day in a rage I grabbed a knife and went for Malcolm. It was over something very small. I didn't think it important but he did. He was cross with me for throwing rubbish and leavings onto ground he had just readied for planting. Malcolm was angry: I was angry: our voices were raised and as I lunged at him with the knife he surprised me with how quick and strong he was – he caught my wrist and bent my arm behind my back and forced me to drop the knife. I was screaming with anger and pain and I managed to reach around and bite him hard on the shoulder and then little Titus lying alone in his cradle joined in crying bitter tears and my heart softened and I pulled free from Malcolm's grip and picked up my little man and held him and comforted him until he stopped crying. Malcolm also came and put his strong arms around both of us and without words we made up.

\*

(32) I crumpled up what I wrote yesterday. I intended to use it for fire lighting, but something happened and I've changed my mind. This morning as I went outside to toss leavings on the scrap heap, I stopped and stood and listened to a bird singing from the sycamore. Pure strokes of liquid music filled the air and there in the outer branches of the tree stood a thrush with chest puffed out, all cream with brown streaks and spots. I have often heard thrushes before but until now it never meant anything more than just the sound that birds make. I stood watching, listening and wondering. And then, a howl from Titus broke in on me and I hurried back inside to see to him. But I had to listen – it was so beautiful, and now I've decided what I wrote yesterday is worth keeping after all. So I've picked it up and tried to smooth the paper as best I can. I almost didn't bother – but I think it is still able to be read. I cannot see why I need to keep numbering these pages.

I'm sure Dibius won't mind if I stop.

# 6.

Dibius does not want me to fall backwards again so he has been visiting more frequently. He came this morning and while I spun wool and knitted and Titus rolled on the floor grabbing at things and trying to fit them into his mouth, Dibius talked. He wanted to know if there was anything still puzzling me.

"I'm here to help you know things – you know that don't you."

"Can I ask you anything?"

"Yes, yes, anything."

"All right then – there is something I want to know. Something I've wondered about since I first got to know you. I want to know why there is no woman in your life."

The face of Dibius reddened before he spoke.

"I've never told anybody this." He stuttered a little as he continued. "Nobody here in Brakial knows this – I don't know why I've never told anyone – it doesn't seem to matter now." Dibius paused and coughed to clear his throat. "Many years ago, before I came here to live, I was married. My wife died in childbirth – so did the child. Becoming a Mentor saved me. It's what I was meant to be."

"And the Christus did that to you? Doesn't he give us everything – everything we ask for – everything we need?"

"Yes Rahnuk, Christus gives us every thing – everything we need."

"But, but. You live now without a woman. How can you? All the other grown men here have a woman don't they? Why not you?"

"I'm not the only one. There's Sonnah and Lieftus and also Roklah. You've met Roklah haven't you?"

"Everyone knows Roklah – but he's a woman inside a man's body – he doesn't count. Don't know the other two. But you – how do you cope – living alone?"

"Rahnuk, the work of Christus is what I live for. My work is to allow Christus to speak to others – using me."

"So morgrah is not important to you?"

Dibius paused and smiled.

"Rahnuk, in all that is known from the past, there was never man or woman who sickened and died from not having morgrah as you call it. Legions have died of starvation and even more from being starved of love, but from not having morgrah – not one has died – ever – not ever in the whole world. As for me – without a woman – I'm free to help the people here follow Christus. That's my role – to be the mirror of Christus –

however dirty the mirror – that's what I live for – nothing else. And how much of my time has been given to you: to help you? Noticed that? How do you think you would have fared trying to make sense of life here if I wasn't free to spend time with you, helping you see what Christus is calling you to? Hmmm?"

"But the people here already know all they need to know. What more can you tell them?"

"Then why am I here now with you? Have you learned nothing from me? Have you not been listening? Do you not know that I must be here at all times? To bring Christus to the people of Brakial – every day – if that's what they want?"

"Yes and they all know of the Christus don't they?"

"Rahnuk, everyone is different. All who follow Christus have come in different ways – at different times. Some come angry and fighting all the way. Others follow like lambs after the ewe. None of us knows if a man is good or bad. Only the Christus knows that. See what I mean?"

"Yes, yes I do, but you, losing your woman – does Christus not want us to be happy?"

"Rahnuk, happiness and sadness are like summer and winter – they're part of what we are. Sadness comes and it goes. You of all people know that well, don't you? To forever weed sadness from our lives would be like trying to rid the seasons of winter."

"I know, I know. It's just that …, why can't I know things like you do?"

"Ah Rahnuk, always we want to see everything with a single glance, we want to run before we can walk – trying to do that leads to many a fall. For all who stop and listen to the One who Calls, both light and darkness is given – enough light to see some of the way and enough darkness to know a lamp is necessary to see further. That's where you and I stand right now – but if we don't keep moving forward we'll end up like those too lazy to bother looking. They are kept in the dark but with enough light to know they have no excuse for their laziness."

"Rahnuk, you must love this thing you're trying to know – love it – don't become angry – understanding always follows love."

Dibius stood to go but seemed to suddenly notice the shell on the board; the one Malcolm from time to time kept smoothing and polishing. He picked it up and turned it over to look at it – rubbing it with one finger.

"Beautiful, very beautiful, but it wasn't always like this." Dibius looked over at me and continued. "Malcolm has done a good job on this – to get rid of all the grey crust without cracking the shell beneath. And we must do the same – everything that stands between us and the beauty of Christus must be got rid of. The more we love Christus the more we know nothing else matters." Dibius replaced the shell on the board and walked out the door.

*

An axe has been borrowed and lost and its owner is very
angry. The one who borrowed it wanted to use it to clear
some sapling trees growing through a stone fence. On
his way to work the axe must have slipped out of his
saddle bag and for two days now, nearly half of
Brakial's children have been helping search for it.
Dibius heard about it and told them to ask the help of an
ancient holy man devoted to the Christus who always
helped folk find lost items.

*

Well the missing axe turned up – three days after
being lost it was found in a place repeatedly searched.
Nobody can understand why it was not seen before.
Some are saying it is as if somebody deliberately hid it
and then later placed it there to be found – a sort of joke.
Today Dibius has a smile on his face.

*

Titus is learning to walk. He stands and grins at me
and pushes first his left foot forward and then the other
and then falls over and cries pitifully and I take him in

my arms and comfort him but I know I cannot – I must not do this every time. I must encourage him to stand and not rely on me forever.

*

Dibius called in this evening. He said he wanted to talk to Malcolm. But Malcolm was still to come in from work. It was getting dark so I built up the fire and lit all the candles and he accepted my offer to prepare a meal for him. I think he just wanted to talk, so we ate while we talked. He mentioned the kept men back in Latcho – the Dohma. I reminded him of their purpose. Dibius was silent the whole time but now and then a tear would gather in the corner of his eye and run suddenly down his cheek and he would wipe it away with the heel of his hand and nod for me to continue. When I finished I asked what would happen to such people after death.

"Endless misery waits the cruel and the vengeful. The Dohma are victims of a horrible cruelty." Dibius kept looking into the fire, "I see them as blameless. Beasts of burden – oxen lashed into pulling the plough." He kept shaking his head and muttering, "Outside of what Christus calls us to do lies madness – madness and blood."

*

I have discovered I am once more pregnant. I am excited but at the same time I am frightened. When I told Ailsa she grinned and said she also was pregnant and so was her sister Mali.

*

Dibius has left some of the sacred Texts here for me to read. He does not want me to let anybody else know I have them – well Malcolm knows and so does Ailsa, but they won't tell anybody. Some of the stories are puzzling. There is one about a powerful leader – a Theon who plans to make war against another, thinking victory will be easy, but after setting out with a strong force, discovers the enemy advancing with three times as many warriors. Being so heavily outnumbered the Theon makes peace. In Latcho we sometimes fought with the Deeves living over the river and always we were heavily outnumbered and always we were victorious. When Dibius came by I told him I thought the Theon a coward, but he explained that this story was used by Christus to show how stupid people are who think they can defeat the fiend unaided. Dibius warned me to never take up the challenge to fight. The old father of lies likes nothing more than to entice us into a fight that by ourselves we have no hope of winning – he wants us to waste ourselves – to wear ourselves out fighting. Whereas if in our need we turn to Christus – the fiend is immediately beaten off.

Another story tells of a servant who because his master was going on a long journey, was entrusted with valuable goods that he was expected to use and present for inspection when the master returned. Because he was fearful of losing the goods he thought it best not to put them at risk and so he kept them where he thought they would be safe. When the master returned the servant was punished – punished not for handing the goods back in the same condition he received them – but punished for not using the goods at all – and they were taken from him and given to another. Dibius said that the good inside us grows when it is used, but if not used it dies and we end up like the fig tree in that other story. I must have looked puzzled because Dibius then found the place and read it to me. The tree was empty of fruit and Christus cursed it. The next day it was blackened and withered – dead. Dibius said that is the fate for those who cease giving. They became like the useless fig tree. That was what happened to the Technos. Love inside them died.

\*

My new baby was born three weeks ago. I have two men children now. All who have seen him say he looks like me. Three days after his birth Mentor Dibius poured the water on his head and asked what name he was to be known by. Leo we said together. After that Malcolm and I stood in front of Dibius and exchanged vows.

Ailsa and Seth and their small child were there as well as Mado. Malcolm and I are now like all the other couples here in Brakial. I am Malcolm's wife and he is my husband. Dibius got us to sign our names in the big book.

*

This Fall has seen a huge run of salmon in the Deemah. At times they seemed to be shoulder to shoulder as they made their way upriver. Every able bodied man and woman as well as many children have been trying to catch them – from the shore, from boats, even the barge was anchored in mid river and people took it in turns to go out and fish from it. You couldn't find a dry branch or piece of cord anywhere. Everything that could be used either for catching salmon or air-drying the split fish was pressed into service. All of Brakial stank of drying salmon. On Sunday the church was nearly empty. The face of Dibius displayed silent white rage.

*

Titus tries to be helpful. In the morning after the fire has been restarted and the porridge mixed he will stand stirring it with a long handled wood paddle that he moves from right hand to left as he tires and occasionally holds in both hands.

While stirring he leans away from the fire not wanting to get his face too hot from the flames. Within a short time he begins calling out.

"It's blubblin Mama, it's blubblin. Come and look, it's blubblin."

I ask him if the bubbles are popping.

"Yes Mama yes. Quick look."

I walk over and look and tell him it's ready to be served and that he's been a good boy. I need to use a thick rag to shield my hand while I lift the pot off its hook and away from the flames.

*

This morning Titus almost burned down the house. He rose very early. Malcolm and I were still soundly sleeping. He was so quiet and determined to light the lamps all by himself. One of them was out of fuel and in the poor light he refilled it and did not notice the oil he spilled over the fire wood and the floor. There were still hot embers in last night's fire and he lit a taper from them and succeeded not only in lighting the lamp but also in having the wood and floor mats dancing in flames. He began screaming and we woke to find the house filling with smoke. I scooped up Leo and grabbing Titus by the hand we ran outside. Malcolm without a stitch on grabbed the great pail in which the plates and mugs were soaking from the previous night and hurled them all at the flames. There was a great clatter and the fire instantly died but not before my screams brought neighbours running from all directions. After making sure the fire was really out we dressed and went to Mado's place to eat breakfast and wait for the smoke to clear. We dragged the wet and charred mats outside. Malcolm said they were ruined and when they were dry he would get rid of them by burning. When Dibius read my story he scolded me for wasting paper on something as trivial as a house fire.

After being growled at by Dibius for wasting paper a new lot has arrived from Dulce – bundles and bundles of it. Dibius said there was now more paper in Brakial than he can ever remember. From now on I won't have to write across what I have already written on the page.

*

I watched this morning. Malcolm and Titus together. Malcolm was filling a bucket with manure to be spread, and Titus was busy trying to help, using an old broken dugout paddle and when he managed to get some on the end of it as often as not when he went to empty it into a bucket he would miss altogether and Malcolm would look exasperated and help him pick it all up again.

*

Titus is unwell. He is off his food and frequently he becomes very hot and sweaty and lies on the bed tossing this way and that and mumbling strange things. The chief healer has called and brought some powder ground from a root which he is to take in water. This is the third day and there is still no change in him. Dibius has been and laid hands on him and marked his forehead with special oil from the church. I am so worried I cannot sleep. Malcolm also cannot sleep.

*

A week has passed and still Titus lies sick. He is losing weight and has a dry hacking cough. Yesterday I went into the trees behind the common land and looked for an herb we knew of in Latcho. I searched and searched and was on the point of giving up when on my way back I spotted a small patch. I brought a bunch of it back and chopped and ground the leaves and stems and boiled them in a pot and mixed cold water with it and managed to spoon feed some into Titus. He drank some more before nightfall and this morning seemed a little better.

*

The medicine I made up has worked. There has been a big improvement in Titus. He has even taken

some solid food but is still very weak but the heating
and sweating has gone.

*

Seth and Ailsa have sailed upstream to stay in
Kester's place and look after things while they come to
Brakial using the same boat. Kester and Mali cannot
keep a boat at their place for fear of it being stolen by
Lams. They want their little boy Nico examined by the
healers.

*

The word has been pronounced. Mali and Kester's
little boy is simple minded. Both are very tearful at the
verdict. They are leaving early tomorrow to return
home. In Latcho we would have killed the child. Mali
is pregnant – for the third time.

*

Last week the boys and I walked with Malcolm to
the top horse paddock. He wanted us to see the new
born foal. The paddock has dry stone walls and a wood
gate that swings on hinges. As we approached it
Malcolm grabbed my arm and pointed and we all
stopped and watched. A hawk and a hare were on the

ground on opposite sides of the gate. The hare sat on
one side, its ears flicking back and forth and on the
other side the hawk stood on the ground glaring through
the wood rails at the hare. Every so often the hawk
would launch itself furiously over the gate and come
down on the other side and at the same time the hare
would skip nimbly under the bottom rail of the gate to
the other side and look back through the bars at the
hawk, its ears still flicking back and forth and the hawk
glaring at the hare. This happened six times while we
were watching, the hawk and the hare exchanging
places. The hare was safe so long as the gate was
between it and the hawk, but if it tried to escape across
the open field, the hawk would catch it in a flash.
Eventually the stand-off ended when deaf old Ernest
arrived and drove his donkey and cart past the gate and
the hawk and the hare fled in opposite directions.
Malcolm asked if it reminded me of something. I told
him that what sprang to mind was my escape from
Orlo's when I was tied up in the tent.

\*

I have been having dreams again – unpleasant
dreams – dreams that wake me in a sweat – dreams
about things that happened in Latcho. I worried about
my friends who were Zoels, especially I worried about
Ilgud, even my Verd Toru, but I also fretted about my
life as a Zoel and the things I had done in Latcho.

Dibius told me I must stop worrying about what happened then. He told me that nothing we do is ever wasted. Forgiveness is rooted in asking for it. After that it's time to move on – constantly recalling the bad past is picking a scab – making it bleed again – nothing good comes of it. All should be seen for what it was and built on to help us move on to better things. He said the Bitchfolk way of doing things was in the past – the Bitchfolk loved power itself – so did the Technos – He said Christus replaced the love of power with the power of love – he brought the Caller to all peoples – the Caller is love. The Technos forgot that. The Technos mistook love for a thing like a horse that could be led or ridden. He told me he would listen to what bothered me most and decide if they really were offensive to Christus. If so he could act on behalf of Christus and pronounce me clean as long as I didn't return to doing them again which since they happened when I lived in Latcho, was highly unlikely. I told him as much as I could remember and Dibius didn't move an eyebrow but told me I could rest assured from then on knowing Christus had forgiven me, but that I must come back to see him if I was again troubled. He predicted my ugly dreams would cease.

*

To keep Titus happy I allowed him to play with some of Malcolm's spare arrow shafts. Some are now broken and the carefully feathered ends of others have been pulled out and the rest pushed into the ground to make a low fence. "To keep the goats out" he explained. Malcolm was not pleased.

*

Today Malcolm is joining with the small team who each year re-stack the rocks that dam the strong little creek so that water enters the flume and gets piped to every house in Brakial. A similar system existed in Latcho. Malcolm said if it isn't maintained regularly the dam can collapse and the houses would lose their water.

*

For some time now I have been complaining to Malcolm about how difficult it is for me to cook and work over the fire. Always stooping and leaning I am. Mado has a separate area for cooking and some washing and now Malcolm has at long last agreed to do the same in this little house. He's going to build on out the back. Just a small area and a roof that leans out over it but it will have a bench that will take three big bowls that I can prepare food in and do some soaking of clothes and some shelves that I can store things on, mugs, plates, knives but best of all it will have an enclosed stone part attached to the side of the fire and I will be able to raise the bread in it or keep meals hot. We won't have to take the bread in to our bed any more. Malcolm will also build the new roof further along to make two separate sleeping areas off the main room. I am so looking forward to these improvements. Malcolm said he will get Kester to help the next time he and Mali come to stay.

*

Edgar the Head of Caveo has gone missing. He got one of the bargemen to row him across the Deemah with his horse swimming behind on a tether. He said he would be back at the end of the day. The bargeman was grumpy at having to row the Deemah for just one man. Edgar never returned that evening. The next morning his horse could be seen grazing on the other side. It was still saddled. The bargeman rowed over to look. There was no sign of Edgar. He caught the horse and towed it back behind the boat. After noon Malcolm crossed over with a group of six others and began a search using dogs. They tracked Edgar's horse until they found where he dismounted. Soon afterward the dogs lost the scent. That was four days ago and Malcolm and the others have spent three days looking and shouting but with no sign of Edgar. They think he has become sick and wandered off somewhere. Dibius has asked people to pray for both Edgar and his wife Minoh.

*

Caveo has a new leader at last. A man called Felix has arrived with his wife and two children. They are from Dulce. Malcolm has spent much time with him to tell him how things are here.

*

At last Malcolm has stepped down from Caveo. At last I have my man to myself – without him being away from me for days on end. Malcolm's new job is to be in charge of the fish and meat drying and smoking. The first few days he has arrived home stinking of smoky meat. I have found some clothes for him to wear while he is at work and I make him take them off before coming inside. I would sooner have him stinking of meat and fish than him being away from home ten days out of every month. But Caveo still have the right to call on him if the matter is urgent.

*

The river is swarming with tiny shining salmon making their way downstream in huge shoals to feed in the sea and every bird that could catch fish from gulls to ducks, herons, kingfishers, wading and water birds of all sorts have gathered for the feast.

*

I have not written anything for some time now but yesterday something happened that I must tell about. I was outside weeding the small herb garden when I heard shrill cries coming from a child further down the hill. "Mama, Mama. Mama, Mama."

Leo was running up the path toward me his short legs pumping on the gravel. Behind him jogged Titus. I stopped weeding stood and shaded my eyes. I could see my two boys running up from down by the river. As I watched I saw Leo trip and he skidded on his tummy. I started toward him to help him to his feet. Leo's breath caught and he was unable to cry at first and then came the bellow, but before I could reach him Titus pulled him to his feet, brushed the dust off him and picked something off the ground and replaced it in his hand. Leo stopped crying and looked into his hand and then grinning through his tears took a few steps toward me.

"Mama, Mama," he said breathlessly, "I have a fright for you."

Titus leaned over and whispered into his ear and Leo began again, "Mama I have a surprise. Close your eyes. Close your eyes." I closed my eyes.

"Open your mouth."

I opened my mouth.

"You're too high. You're too high."

With eyes still closed and mouth open I crouched and waited while Leo stepped up and pushed a fat juicy strawberry into my open mouth.

"Hmmm. Hmmm." It was so juicy and sweet and opening my eyes I put an arm around both boys and hugged and kissed each in turn.

*

Malcolm has been teaching the boys to ride. Sometimes I watch but I hate the thought that either of them may be thrown or fall and get hurt. Titus is good at riding, his sense of balance is better than Leo's. Malcolm is making them learn using a lamb skin as a saddle – they don't have stirrups. For practice they use the last piece of flat common ground before the trail to Dulce enters a little gorge at the foot of The Comb.

*

We have just got back from staying upriver for a week with Kester and Mali. They have four children now. It was a very happy time for me being again with Mali. Malcolm was able to help Kester with jobs needing the combined strength of two men. When we arrived we tied up the boat in the cove downstream from where the track to Kester's place starts. We covered it partly with brushwood so it could not be seen from the other side of the Deemah although Malcolm did not think it likely that any Lams were about. We took with us a wicker cage of pigeons from Brakial and we brought some of Kester's back with us. Malcolm insists that any journey up river must not be purely for pleasure.

\*

   The boys have been helping a neighbour round up his nanny goats and kids on the common land. The neighbour needed help to separate his animals from others grazing there and the job took a long time. The boys came in after dark with frightened faces and breathing heavily. They said nothing at first but I could tell something was wrong so I asked what the matter was. Titus tried to pretend it was nothing. I looked at Leo and he said that as they were walking home something in the darkness screamed several times just above their heads and they ran home without stopping. Malcolm laughed when he heard their story. Titus and Leo stood looking puzzled. Malcolm finally managed to splutter out the words, "Snipe, snipe. That's what you were running from. They're trying to find wives. After dark they flutter up as high as a Sycamore and then glide down with their wings and tail spread and the noise you heard comes from their tail feathers. Harmless harmless. Yes they only do it after dark and if it happens right above your head you can get a bad fright."

*

Malcolm and the boys have just arrived home after four days away helping Rolf. They've been on the weaning muster of the free run cattle that graze further down the Deemah. At times some cattle make their way across the river to graze in Lamentasia. The eyes of the boys were shining with excitement. They have brought home a lot of fresh meat cut from a stag they helped kill. They've also brought home the animal's fine large pelt and its antlers. There is too much meat for us – some we will dry but we'll have to give away quite a lot. Titus is thrilled with the horns. I don't know where the boys want to keep them – they have an unpleasant smell – I don't want them inside. Both boys made me sit down and listen while they took it in turn telling how the stag was killed. They were on the Lam side of the Deemah looking for stray cattle and were about to recross the river when Rolf's dogs deserted them to chase after a deer they smelled hiding in the trees. There is a long shallow ford at this point and they were half way through it when the stag burst out of the riverbank trees and plunged into the river. Malcolm said because of the stag's large horns he could not run fast through the undergrowth so he jumped from the bank into the river where he could swim much faster than the dogs. The boys spoke of the bow wave the stag put up as he swam across just upstream from where they were crossing. Leo said he was as big as a horse – from the corner of my eye I could see Malcolm smiling. Leo said the stag's shoulders were enormous and they reared right out of the water as he swam fast with his head forward and the white tops of his antlers gleaming in the sun. The dogs were left well behind. Malcolm and Rolf and the boys kicked their mounts to go faster in the water and when they got out on dry land Malcolm and Rolf fitted arrows and waited to shoot. They each let fly three times as the stag ran out of the water but it kept cantering on and disappeared into the trees on their side of the river. They waited until the dogs made it across and putting them on the scent they soon found the animal lying dead a short distance into the trees. There were three arrows sticking in it – two of them Malcolm's. The boys also told of the way the dogs baited cows with calves and the cow would bawl in anger and charge the dogs trying to gore and crush them and all the time Rolf would be yelling, trying to get the dogs away and to leave the cow and her calf alone so they could return to the moving herd. The boys thought Rolf's dogs very disobedient unlike his horse – that was very well trained. The cows and calves are now on the common lands and tomorrow they and their well grown calves will be moved into the yards where the calves will be separated from their mothers.

Dibius is becoming forgetful. He has started to say things but then pauses as if forgetting what he was going to say. A week ago he greeted Malcolm in the lane near here and told him how sorry he was to learn of the deaths of his mother and father. Malcolm did not know what to say. And yet at other times although Dibius seems sleepy he will surprise you with a sharp answer. Just this morning, he was standing in the sun outside Mado's house. He seemed to be staring at their cat curled up asleep on the side of the path – it sleeps there most mornings unless it is raining. As I walked past I stopped and said.

"Don't you envy cats Mentor Dibius?" Dibius continued staring but then he turned with a smile and said.

"Ah, Rahnuk, you're teasing me. Yes, being a cat would be nice, very nice – imagine it – no worries. But no I think I would much rather live with the knowledge that ahead of me lies either Paradise or the Place of Hate. It is my decision. I like that."

*

Titus has come in to say he's just seen a white gnatcatcher – pure white all over. I asked where he saw it and he said it was flitting around in the sycamore. I told him I did not want to know about it. The one and only time I saw the koraght was when Titus was born. He wanted to know why my face was suddenly so pale. I waved him aside, and no I definitely did not want to go outside and see it.

*

The sycamore has been home to a colony of sparrows who for the last month have been busy, first carrying dried grass to build their homes and now after a period of quiet the first young have fledged and from the leafy tree's interior, the fat fledglings constant medley of begging chirrups issued all the day long, urging their overworked parents to keep up the supply of captured moths, caterpillars and other bugs.

*

It has been a very dry summer and the Deemah is abnormally low. The flat stone and mud wastes that are usually under water now look to be painted a pale blue as some abundant small plant hidden between the stones is now blooming. I went down and looked and I could see tiny fragile blossoms extending above the stones just enough to be noticed.

*

# 7.

I have just returned from Dulce – apart from
occasional visits to stay with Mali and Kester, this was
my first long journey from Brakial since coming here
when Titus was first born – that is nearly twenty years
ago. Malcolm went with me and we took Titus and Leo
and we stayed with Malcolm's cousin Lucy who is now
a grandmother with four grandsons. Malcolm and Lucy
haven't seen each other for a long time.

Nearly forty of us from Brakial made the journey
and we joined with people from all over Riparia who
were traveling to Dulce to see the image of the Mother
of Christus in the big church there. These festivals
happen every seventh year. I learned much. The image
is life size and nobody knows how it was made. The
Mentors say that it was known in the wider world before
the Technos took over and that even with their tools, the
Technos could not explain it. It is formed on some
ancient cloth, which the Technos said should have
rotted long ago. Going by old records the Mentors say
the image could be eight centuries old.
  The image is of a gentle young woman with
downcast eyes. She has her hands clasped together.
Her dress is pale with a blue veil covering the head and
shoulders and down to her feet and the veil is sprinkled
with gold stars. The woman is carrying a baby inside

her. The Mentors tell us that with their tools the Technos could see reflections in the woman's eyes of other people. The Mentors say that about three lifetimes ago, when Dulce was a much smaller place, a man minding sheep had his dog run away and soon afterward it started barking madly in the distance. The man followed and found his dog in a cave. Inside the cave was a pole wrapped in fabric. The man removed the fabric covering and discovered it was protecting the cloth image of the woman. Something made him nervous and he re-wrapped the image and left it where he had found it. Later, when back in Dulce, he told the Mentors of his find and they asked if he could retrieve it. Some months later he did. The image was briefly examined by two Mentors before being re-wrapped and then left leaning against a wall just inside the church entry doors.

About a week later a woman who suffered from one leg being shorter than the other, brushed against it as she walked past and a short time later she discovered that she could walk normally and that both her legs were now of the same length. The news that the image could cure people of various maladies bought many to the church, some curious and some seeking cures for themselves.

The Mentors began sorting through old records and after a couple of years were confident the image was the same Mother of the Caller image that many centuries ago was visited by huge crowds in an enormous city. We met a man now aged about thirty who as a ten year old was cured of blindness through touching the image. He was taken to touch it by his mother for that purpose only, and after she held him against it he walked outside the church holding on to her hand and then he told us he noticed something, first a lightness and then a broad streak falling against the light and he began to see, and the first thing he looked at was a small bird flying down to feed on the ground near him. He said it was the first thing he ever saw and to this day remains the most beautiful thing he has ever seen. He could not take his newly seeing eyes off it. He watched it hopping around. He told us he noticed the bird's beautiful brown and grey streaked back and tail and the brown cap of its head and the black bib at its throat and he couldn't stop looking at it until his mother began screaming to everyone that her boy could see.

Moerah was in our group from Brakial. She is old, blind and feeble. Her daughter Sarah travelled with her. Moerah was not worried that her eyes might not be healed. I asked her why if she couldn't see anything was she going to the Mother of Christus image. Moerah told me that she wanted The Mother to see her so that when she died and arrived at Paradise she would be known and admitted. I am envious of Moerah's belief. I cannot understand it. She was too unwell to return to Brakial with our group. She may never return.

On the central day of the festival hundreds of men women and children gathered. I have never seen such a large crowd. There was much singing and playing of musical instruments and banging of drums and the Mother of Christus image was mounted on a platform like a boat's sail and for a whole day was carried on the shoulders of teams of young men who carried it in turn and they carried her around and around the centre of the town for the whole day with everyone singing and throwing flowers at her.

Later the Keyholder came out and spoke to the crowd. He is a very old man but very gentle and people here in Dulce say he is closely in touch with the Caller. He said that ever since that ancient uprising, the Caller loaned his love at no cost to help us find our way back to him. We must put aside the things that block us from using that love – we must put aside envy, judgement, gloating. When our loved one tells us that we are loved most when we wear what pleases them: do we ignore them? Would we turn our back on that love? Be deaf to it? No, we must put on Christus, clothe ourselves with Christus and only then can we rest assured we will never be separated from Him. The Keyholder said that the role of the Mother of Christus was crucial to the Caller's plan. She spoke for all in saying yes to the Caller's messenger. She could have said no. If we refuse the offer of the Caller's love, we punish ourselves, and if we come to the end of our lives still saying no, we will have chosen to spend our afterlife with the Enticer – we will spend our afterlife in hate and fear and loathing of ourselves and everything else – what a terrible thing to say no to love – but that is what the Enticer wants us to do – with great slyness he disguises himself trying to convince us he no longer exists. The Keyholder said when we turn our back on the Caller we refuse to take part in his plan for us. We meet the beauty of the Caller at every turn, fragrant flowers, birdsong, smiles and laughter. But then for fruit to come the flower must wither, bird song give way to silence, smiles and laughter give way to sadness – this is life – this is the cross Christus carried for us. The Keyholder said one single act of kindness was greater by far than all the wealth the world could show us, because that kindness points always to the Caller – it is the sign of the Caller.

Before leaving to return home the group from Brakial met for a short visit with the Keyholder at his home. He stood with his assistant holding his arm to steady him and thanked us for coming from such a distance and then he prayed over us all and afterward I asked the assistant if it would be possible to have in writing what the Keyholder told the big crowd at the festival. The assistant whispered in the Keyholder's ear and he nodded and smiled and a little later the assistant handed me a roll of strong paper on which was written the main points from the Keyholder's speech.

*

    Since returning from Dulce I have been watching
things closely and wondering. The pigeon flock that in
fast flight hugs the cliff face above the Deemah and then
unexpectedly soars upward, rolls and comes tearing
back still in the same formation – what command is
given and obeyed? And when feeding on the ground,
what signal causes them all to spring as one into the air
and fly to some other place where they know they will
find food? And then I have noticed pigeons in flight and
frequently one will tremble and fall sideways before
straightening and others in the flock will mimic its
action. Malcolm tells me it is the pigeon's way of
confusing the hawk. The hawk loping through the air
behind the flock is bewildered and cannot decide which
bird to attack since experience has taught it that just as it
is about to strike, the bird it wants will tumble down and
sideways. 'To know is to have known' is how Dibius
explains it. Just like us, everything works toward its
proper end – of that I am convinced. The bee and the
flower are like husband and wife – each pleasing the
other. The fly entangled in the spider's web – the pigeon
that one day gets careless. Everything is in harmony,
everything works together, everything obeys some
hidden command – except for one thing – ourselves –
when we fight what we're called to be – how often we
do that.

# PART III

## 1.

Something happened yesterday that has me
worried. It was the first monthly trading day for nearly
a year. Trading was suspended after an outbreak of the
shaking disease among the Lams but with the outbreak
over, a large group from several different tribes turned
up, all eager to exchange their goods. It was unusual for
me to take any part in trading days but this time for
some reason I was curious to see what was on offer;
what sort of pelts and skins might be available. I was
wandering along looking at things when I noticed a
shortish woman with close-cropped hair and swarthy
skin staring at me. One glance was sufficient to know
what she was and I turned and started to leave but the
woman now hurried over and stood blocking my way.
A cunning smile spread over her face and she said,
"You. You were once a Zoel. You have the mark."
Before I could pull back she reached and touched the
tattoo on my forehead. "How long have you been here
with the Deeves?" I pushed her aside and tried to get
away but to my horror Ailsa called to me – using my
name – twice – wanting me to come and look at

something. The woman heard Ailsa's call and grabbed my arm to hold me. She looked pleased and said,

"Rahnuk eh! Rahnuk. I also am a Zoel."

The woman's eyes suddenly widened and she exclaimed,

"I've heard of Rahnuk. You ran away didn't you – many years ago?"

There was nothing to hide now so I turned to the woman and asked her name. She said she was known as Spilah and that she and another Zoel, who now came and stood at her shoulder, were there to gather news to take back to Latcho. I asked who the Theon was and her reply sent a shudder through me – the name she gave was Ilgud. Titus was also at the trade and he now came and stood with me. He could see my distress and asked what was bothering me and to make matters worse made it plain that I was his mother. I turned and hurried away without saying anything to him until we were both back home. I regret ever going near the Trade. Now I am very afraid. Revenge is the stock in trade for every Zoel. When that night Malcolm returned I told him what happened. He said I was worrying about nothing.

"How could the Bitchfolk hurt you?"

"Malcolm, apart from the little I've told you, you know nothing about Zoels."

"We managed to escape from them didn't we?"

"The One Who Calls took charge of us then."

"Yes, probably."

"You know nothing about the skills of Zoels when it comes to killing others. If they wanted, they could arrive here unseen. They could come down the Deemah by night and nobody would even know. And they could wipe out Brakial and you would know nothing until the moment your throat was being slit. And you know nothing about Ilgud, or the slightest bit about how the Bitchfolk think. And now Ilgud is Theon."

"What would they do, poison the water supply?"

"No, no. Zoels love hand to hand combat. They enjoy seeing blood run, that's all that satisfies them. Poison would only catch a few people here, and probably not the ones they would want dead – like me."

I slept poorly that night. The thought of Ilgud in Latcho knowing about me was like one of those small black clouds seen in the distance when you're trying to get dry hay gathered and stacked away.

*

A thrush has built its nest in the rose hedge near the house. As usual Malcolm noticed it first. He saw them carrying dried grass. That was three weeks ago and this morning I couldn't resist seeing how things were going so I carried a round of firewood to stand on and look. The mother raised herself up and I saw her lovely speckled throat before she slipped with a rattle through

284

the leaves. I reached my hand over the nest's rim and my fingers touched on the naked soft warmness of innocent baby birds and I withdrew my hand.

*

Outside the thrush is again screaming. Has to be the cat from next door. Leo has rushed outside to throw stones at it. First thing this morning he went outside and came straight back in with a thrush in his hand – it must have just left the nest – made its first flight and fetched up exhausted on the path. Leo took it back outside and placed it on the branch of a shrub. Turning to come back he discovered another two sitting on the ground. They must have all left home at once, so he picked up these two and found places for them to perch – hopefully out of harm's way. While this was going on the parent thrushes said nothing but now whenever Leo hears them screaming, he races straight outside picking up stones on the way to defend his babies from whatever threatens them. I asked him what would happen to our plum and current crops if every hatchling thrush survived. Would it be them or would it be them or us.

*

## 2.

Monthly trading days with the Lams were once more put on hold because of the Shaking Disease. News in the form of rumours began to filter back to Brakial. Rumours of Sessilite aggression against various Lam tribes and soon these rumours became so commonplace that the inhabitants of Brakial no longer talked or worried about them. There was so much that was supposed to happen and didn't that they were past worrying. Then one day, a Lamentasite man named Torok, paddled his dugout down the Deemah to Brakial and tying up at the Landing, insisted on talking to Edgar. On being informed Edgar was dead he asked who had taken his place and was told the new man was Felix. Torok said he carried important news but would not divulge it to anyone other than the man who had taken over from Edgar.

Torok was well known in Brakial from trading days and was regarded as one of the few reliable Lams. Felix was away but Torok insisted that what he carried was so important he would give it only to the chief of all the Riverfolken. He thought that Edgar was the chief and now it was Felix and he was not going to hand over his information to anyone less than the chief and he sat down at the barge landing and said he would wait.

Just before sunset Torok got tired and was about to paddle back across the river when Felix turned up. What Felix learned from Torok disturbed him. Torok told of coming across a party of Bitchfolk camped in Lamentasia just across the river from a Riverfolken hamlet. He did not know its name but knew it was away from the river and up the hillside. Two Zoels surprised him while he was collecting borith for drying and forced him to accompany them to their camp-site, where they relieved him of his precious borith and refused him any trade goods in return. He was kept prisoner for nearly half a day and feared for his life and while there he overheard two of the Bitchfolk discussing what they saw on a spying trip across the river and now that the layout was known, they planned to attack it some time in the next two days. Torok was annoyed with the Bitchfolk for stealing his borith but claimed that without that provocation he would still have come to warn the chief of the Riverfolken.

For Felix, this new rumour was more alarming than any of the others because Torok was not a party to any of the other unfounded rumours, and came of his own accord spending the best part of half a day paddling to Brakial to tell his story. Felix realized that the hamlet under threat was Kester's and to the question why he chose not to warn the Riverfolken of their danger Torok thought the risk too great. He said it was possible that there were still Bitchfolk in hiding on the other side and so he decided to come downstream and warn the Riverfolken here.

It was late in the day and much time was gone. Caveo was now down to two full time men and these two were away downriver helping on cattle matters and Malcolm was with them. Knowing of his friendship with Kester, Felix left a message at Malcolm's house to come and see him as soon as he returned. Malcolm was standing in for one of the cattle foremen who was unable to work after having a horse stand on his foot. The sun was close to dropping behind the comb before Malcolm returned and learned of the warning from Torok. In the meantime, Felix organized things including arranging for somebody to accompany Torok to Lon's workhouse to sort out a reward for him, and to send a runner with a message for Seth to ask if he could help Malcolm with an urgent journey upriver to warn Kester and Mali. Some of the smaller upstream hamlets were within hailing distance of each other but Kester was a good quarter day walk upriver from his nearest neighbour and none of his pigeons were currently caged at Brakial, which completely ruled out any rapid means of warning him.

Seth, with a worried looking Rahnuk was waiting for Malcolm to return. Weapons and clothing were already sorted and laid out in preparation. But Malcolm arrived home tired and in spite of having a sick feeling in his stomach at the threat posed to his friends, he said he would need a rest before starting on a grueling paddle and sail upriver. Titus and Leo were also away with a fishing crew at the river mouth and wouldn't be back for another day. As well as the clothing and weapons selected, Ailsa had packed food and drink for them both. Malcolm and Seth went to inspect the boat arranged by Felix. Speed of travel was essential and if the wind was wrong, it must be able to be paddled easily. The chosen boat was ideal, light with a folding mast and lateen sail. Malcolm came back and lay down to rest with Rahnuk beside him. She hugged him tight for some time and they prayed that Torok would be proved wrong and before long Malcolm's drowsiness turned into sleep.


### 3.


Near the middle of the night Seth arrived and woke Malcolm who felt refreshed. He dressed and hugged Rahnuk before stepping outside into the dark and with the aid of a lantern they walked down through the houses to where the boat was tied up. They stored their gear in it, got in, pushed off and started paddling rhythmically, keeping well off to one side of the main current and using as a course guide the faint dark outline where the Comb's crest sharply stopped the spread of the swarming stars against the inky sky. The air was still and cold and their breath steamed but it was not long before first Malcolm and then Seth stripped off their jackets as they warmed up from the paddling.

Quite some time after leaving, a large bird flew toward them unseen in the dark, calling with mournful, sobbing sounds that became louder and louder until it passed overhead and its calls then gradually faded to silence downriver leaving them once more with just the slop and plash sounds of their paddles dipping and digging into the dark water. They paddled on without stopping and after what seemed an age a patch of grey lit the sky in front and then turned vivid crimson, and high and directly overhead, small clouds showed as angry red weals. The painted display spread across the sky paling first to pink and then yellow until the hidden sun rose suddenly out of the river in front like an eager child waking and standing in its cot.

The light glared straight into their eyes and Malcolm and Seth ducked their heads forward to stop being blinded and the river all around was bathed in a wash of warm honeyed light that turned the surface of the water and the trees each side bronze. Rafts of diving ducks splattered out of the river in front and went skimming away into the middle or to the shallows on the other side. The sun stood higher and higher, the honey wash dissolved and the foliage on the riverside trees recovered its sombre green daytime cast. A light upstream breeze brushed the water and slowly gathered strength so that Malcolm and Seth stopped paddling and stepping the folding mast they set the sail and gratefully allowed themselves to be pushed along.

The breeze strengthened to a wind and dragged with it a mean mist that spread over the sky from behind and the young sun paled to a white disc before disappearing. With the sun now gone, a cold drizzle set in and made the men pull on extra clothing to keep out the chilling damp but at least the wind was strong enough to keep the sail filled and while Malcolm steered to take best advantage of any wandering gusts, Seth reached into their supplies and getting out the food and drink packed by Ailsa he handed to Malcolm one at a time, chunks of bread and meat, a couple of boiled eggs and some wine in a clay mug.

It was mid morning now and both men complained of how stiff they were from sitting still for so long, but in the distance in front the familiar shape of the lower part of the ridge that Kester farmed was now visible and it was not too long before Malcolm started to angle the boat toward the toe of the ridge that sheltered the small cove and beach where the track to Kester's house began.

Low cloud shrouded the higher land obscuring the house and farm. They were coming in fast and one end of the short beach was now in view when Malcolm drew in his breath sharply and cursed. From two hundred yards out could be seen at least three dugouts pulled up on the sand and suspecting they were probably guarded he gibed the little boat about, nearly knocking a startled

Seth overboard in the process and headed back the way they came until they were screened once more by the ridge, and now turning again Malcolm steered once more for the shore but this time several hundred yards downstream where a stand of willows wept down curtaining the water's edge.

Malcolm stood and dropped the mast allowing the sail to fall in a heap while Seth impatiently pushed the trailing willow stems aside and they both leaped into the shallows and dragged the boat half clear of the water leaving it heeled over on the head sized rocks. Reaching in under the untidy heap of sail they grabbed up swords and full quivers and strapped them on. Seth was already in the trees moving up the slope and buckling his gear on while walking before Malcolm started to follow. There was no path and drifts of pine needles made the footing uncertain. Their object was to cut through toward Kester's at an angle and arrive in time to warn the family and head off any possible attack. Malcolm thought it was just possible that the presence of the dugouts may mean only another look-see by the Bitchfolk to check things out. At least that was what he hoped. He called out to Seth to slow down a bit. He was feeling puffed already. He stopped bent over and breathing hard, his hand leaning on a rock and he looked back through the sparse tree trunks at the smooth dark river eddying slowly, its shot silk surface a changing mirror for the hillside trees and the dismal sky and his lips kept repeating a whispered prayer. "Christus and Maria help us to be in time."

Seth started off again and Malcolm struggled upright and forced himself to follow. Their route was still in the trees and continued that way for a good while longer until quite suddenly the broad steep hillside narrowed to a level ridge which Malcolm guessed would join the main spur near Kester's house. Using the track from the little cove to Kester's place was never just a short walk, but with no track and using a route that they hoped would take them straight to the house, they knew how critical it was not to get lost – no matter for how brief a time. Continually going through Malcolm's head was the whereabouts of the people from the dugouts and what their intentions were.

Malcolm reckoned they were close to Kester's before calling again for a rest. Dripping with sweat and head down and breathing heavily he leaned against a tree. They were now into the low clinging cloud. The air was still and drops of water beaded every twig and leaf. The river was out of sight. They waited only enough time for Malcolm to recover and were just heading off again when faintly at first and then more clearly, shrill voices and screams broke the misty silence. A groan escaped from Malcolm and the two men tried to jog up the slope. Then came a series of deep chants that abruptly ceased leaving only the noise of their heavy footfalls on the root bound ground.

It seemed like forever before the trees ended and open turf began. In the distance the shape of Kester's house showed faintly through the mist. Malcolm with aching legs and rapid pounding heart and urged on by the increasing distance between himself and Seth, broke into a half run when just off to his right and out of sight a commotion started. First a loud booming voice crying out and then shrill hideous laughter. Seth stopped and Malcolm caught up with him and both fitted arrows before creeping half crouched toward the source of the noise. Fifty yards away in a small hollow they found two Zoels in the act of pulling a tied-up Kester to his feet. Blood was streaming down Kester's cheek and neck from a wound above one ear. Malcolm who could see better let fly first and with a loud thwack the arrow struck the nearest Zoel who collapsed in a heap. The other Zoel leaped behind a bush and doubled over in a crouching run, disappeared into the woods giving Seth no opportunity to shoot. Kester groaning tottered on his feet; his arms bound and then fell down heavily.

Malcolm ran to his side and bending over cut the rope binding his arms. Kester was incoherent and Malcolm realized with horror that he was drugged, sedated, being readied for escort to the dugouts in the cove. Standing up Malcolm looked down at the helpless semi conscious Kester and then turned and kicked the body of the dead Zoel to one side. He tried to remove his arrow but it was too deeply embedded. He fitted another and signaling to Seth they cautiously moved the two hundred yards to the house. Two bodies lay outside near the entrance. The first was Kester's youngest son. There appeared to be nothing wrong with him until Malcolm rolled him over and saw the sickening wound in the back of his head. The other was one of the eighteen-year-old twins. The feathered end of an arrow shaft showed over his heart.

Signaling to Seth to cover him Malcolm moved doubled over to the door and stepped inside. What he saw caused him to instantly gag and vomit. In the main room four bodies lay close together in one corner. Mali and the twin girls were obscenely mutilated. The other twin boy lay with open bulging eyes and protruding swollen tongue showing that he died more slowly from a poisoned stab wound. He must have been trying to protect his mother and sisters.

Malcolm staggered back outside. Through tear filled eyes he gasped, "Don't go in there. Don't go in." Seth ignored him and darted past and inside the door only to almost instantly reappear. "Nico. Where's Nico? He's not here. He may have got away." And then without thinking he started to yell. "Nico. Nico. Where are you? Nico. Malcolm and Seth here." Malcolm grabbed him roughly by the arm. "Shut up. Shut up you fool. Let's have a quick look around. That other Zoel. The one that got away. The others will be on their toes by now. It took more than two to do all this." Seth with bow armed walked toward where the track to the river started in a grove of trees. His eyes swept the ground looking for signs. He called back softly. "Mal. Mal. Here quick." Malcolm joined him in looking to where he was pointing to a large patch of sand with the end of his bow. Overnight rain meant only the days footprints were visible – Bitchfolk sandals surrounding one set of typical Riparian footprints all leading down to the cove.

"Nico. They've got him. They've got Nico." Whispered Seth.

"No no they can't have him. If we hurry we can catch them."

Suddenly Malcolm seemed to notice only the tops of the trees and some sky, he grabbed at a bush missed it somehow swayed and then fell heavily. Seth jumped to his side.

"Are you okay?"

Malcolm blinked several times before sitting up.

"Christus. I thought you must have caught an arrow."

"No. I'll be all right. Just wait a bit. I'm feeling funny."

Seth handed over his leather shoulder bag of water and Malcolm squeezed some over his face before taking a few gulps and handing the bag back. He lurched heavily onto his feet, staggering a little as he did, looked at Seth and said.

"Let's go."

"What about Kester?"

"We'll come back for him. Now let's go."

Malcolm, spurred by the knowledge of what use the Bitchfolk put captured men to, grabbed his bow and followed Seth as he bounded off down the path under the trees. What they were going to do when they caught up with the raiding party neither of them thought about – being badly outnumbered was a certainty.

Malcolm in a hoarse low voice called out to Seth to wait but the younger man was soon out of sight and before long the noise of his footsteps was gone as well and Malcolm could only stumble along clutching his bow and moaning and praying to arrive at the cove in time. The odds against them he put out of his mind. He might halve the usual time it took if he was lucky and the Bitchfolk trying to guide a drugged captive down the path would be slowed. But what if they were already in their dugouts and paddling across the Deemah to Lamentasia. What if? It would be hard enough to stop them this side but if they made it across the river the situation would be hopeless. Malcolm staggered on, lungs near bursting and tears and sweat half blinding him, not caring if his noisy clumsy progress brought him suddenly and unprepared to face a flight of Bitchfolk arrows.

The ridge now narrowed and rose with bluffs each side and much as Malcolm would like to have taken a short cut down it was out of the question and he stayed on the now climbing track before it again dipped steeply down to the cove. The far side of the Deemah came into view. No dugouts in sight. Malcolm slowed to

297

catch his breath. He was blowing badly and annoyed with Seth. Annoyed with him for running off and leaving him. He thought of Seth rushing impetuously into a fight instead of waiting for him. He started again. Cautiously now and with an arrow fitted and no rushing footsteps. He was only two hundred yards from the cove. He moved quietly, stopping as the little sandy beach came into view. The dugouts were gone. He cursed and cried out and half slipped and fell down the slope with a small avalanche of stones leaves and twigs before landing in the creek bed. Regaining his feet, he strode to the water's edge. Frantic footprints seemed to be jostling in the blood streaked sand and in the shallow water of the river's edge lay two bodies. The first was a Zoel with one of Seth's arrows sticking through its neck. The other was Nico with only his legs on the dry sand and a small seep of blood coming from near his armpit where a feathered arrow shaft protruded and the escaping blood made a thin wriggling plume in the water. Malcolm cried as he grabbed hold of Nico's legs and dragged his still warm corpse from the water and then he rolled him over to look at his face. Nico seemed to be smiling with wide-open innocent eyes. Malcolm brushed his hand over and closed them. He lifted up the arm to extract the arrow if he could and then stood aghast. The arrow's feathered tail he recognized as one of Seth's. He pulled out his knife and cut it off and stood there inspecting the feathered shaft to see if he could be wrong before throwing it into the bushes and out of sight.

He looked back up toward the path on the rim of the little gorge. Somewhere up there he knew he would find Seth. He must have run past him. He walked up the little creek that watered the cove looking up its steep sides. Something caught his eye and he began to pull himself up the almost vertical slope, clutching at small stems of shrubs and grass. Seth was wedged against a small tree. Obscenely mutilated and face unrecognizable. A little further up was another dead Zoel trapped by the ankles in the fork of a small scrub bush and another of Seth's arrows sticking from it.

Malcolm pulled himself higher. A trail of thick blood splashes told of a badly wounded Zoel. Probably caught by Seth's short sword. He looked back at Seth. His sword was missing. Looking around he could see no more bodies. Malcolm moved back to where Seth lay and not heeding his bloody condition pulled the body of his friend over his shoulder and dragged himself up to the path and crying bitterly struggled down to the beach where he laid Seth down beside Nico. He covered both bodies with branches. He looked out over the river but could see no sign of the dugouts. They would be across by now and gone.

# 4.

Malcolm turned and trudged up the path to the house. He found Kester near where he had left him. He was lying with his eyes open and breathing heavily and uttering nonsense words. Malcolm cursed himself for arriving too late to prevent the massacre. He pulled Kester to his feet and supporting him helped him back to the house where he laid him on a bed in one of the smaller sleeping rooms and then went and looked around the house. Besides the killings, most things were thoroughly trashed especially crockery which lay in pieces all over the floor. Every chair was smashed and shelves randomly wrenched off walls. Strangely only one glass window was broken. In one corner of the main room a fire had been started but had died without doing any damage.

Malcolm went outside and dragged the two bodies inside and placed them beside the others in the main living area. He covered them with wool blankets from the room where Kester was recovering. This room although showing signs of Bitchfolk entry was undamaged. Malcolm worked as if in a trance, his mind numbed by the events of the day. These were his friends – Kester and Mali – friends for more than twenty years and their children too, and Rahnuk knew them and here they were all brutally butchered, bodies broken and almost unrecognizable. He tried to rub the blood off his hands on a corner of blanket and then went back into the room where Kester rested and sat down on the end of the bed.

Kester was staring at the roof and mumbling in low tones. As Malcolm sat down Kester's eyes rolled down and settled on Malcolm. A purple rage came over his face and he struggled to rise. Malcolm took him by the shoulders and gently forced him back down on the bed but Kester's hands suddenly grabbed for his neck and Malcolm found himself choking and fighting for breath as strong fingers tightened and closed his windpipe and Kester began yelling out for Mali. Malcolm fought to free himself and just as he thought he was about to black out, the throttling fingers relaxed and Kester fell back on the bed sobbing. Malcolm thought that the Bitchfolk poison might be wearing off. He got up found an unbroken mug on the floor and filled it from the water butt and returning inside offered it to Kester who took it in both hands. He drank half and then let go of the mug which slipped sideways emptying the rest over his chest.

Malcolm walked outside to the small pigeon house. There were four birds on the sending side and he stepped in and flushed them out and watched as they circled a couple of times before heading downriver. He went back inside to Kester. There was nothing to be done but wait until he was well enough to get in the boat and travel to Brakial. A short time later Kester drew up

301

his knees and sat there staring vacantly ahead with his arms clasped around his legs and his chin resting on his hands. Malcolm tried to talk to him but got no response. He sat there in the same attitude for what seemed an age and then looking at Malcolm he smiled and made to stand up. Malcolm helped him and he stood there a little unsteady at first but then stronger. Kester picked up Malcolm's right hand and looked at it. There were still splashes of blood showing on it.

"I want to see them."

Malcolm started to say that he didn't think it was a good idea but stopped when Kester again demanded.

"I want to see them Malcolm." And then he roared, "I'm going to see them. Get out of my way or I'll." He flailed blindly with one arm.

"Okay, okay."

Malcolm walked him into the sleeping room and watched as Kester bent over and slowly drew the blankets off the bodies. Kester looked down and suddenly convulsed in loud sobs, his whole frame shaking uncontrollably. He stopped and looked at Malcolm again.

"Nico. Nico. He's not here. Where is he? Where's Nico. Has he been? Have they taken him? Malcolm, have the Bitchfolk got Nico?" Kester was yelling now and shaking with rage.

Malcolm shook his head.

"No, no. Nico's dead. He's down at the beach with Seth. Seth's dead to. They're both dead."

Malcolm was sobbing now and Kester sank down on one knee and howled. Everything he valued most – gone. Wife and children dead – although he had no idea how Nico died. He stood and began cursing. Cursing The Caller for what seemed to him a punishment. Why did he deserve to be treated like this?

"Is this what life's all about? Is it? Is it Malcolm? Is this my reward for being faithful to the Christus, is it? Is this what I get? Is this all I'm left with? Dead bodies? Mali, my children, all dead?"

Kester stood for what seemed an age, howling and sobbing and railing against the name of the Caller. The Caller who protected. The Caller he worshipped. The Caller he loved. The Caller his all. The Caller repaid him with this. Death, destruction, the loss of everything worthwhile, everything he held dear.

"Why, why, why." He bellowed.

Kester's raging against the Caller ended as suddenly as it began as he remembered the terracotta crucifix behind him; the one specially blessed by the Keyholder in Dulce. The Bitchfolk must have missed seeing it and it still stood on the little shelf Kester built to display it, and now he lunged for it, intent on destroying it. He meant to hurl it to the floor and smash it. Smash this symbol, this effigy which for he and Mali and their children always embodied protection, mercy and love. Kester was a very strong man and yet as he grabbed the base of the crucifix his strength seemed to fail. Later he would describe what happened as if the little statue

increased its weight to be totally unmovable. He could
not lift with his two strong arms what any two-year-old
child could lift with one hand. He stood there impotent,
powerless to wrench it from the little shelf. Miracle or
not and Malcolm believed it to be a miracle, a surge of
relief overwhelmed him and his rage left as suddenly as
it came and he fell on his knees crying and sobbing for
forgiveness.

Early afternoon as Malcolm and Kester were
preparing to leave the house they were startled by a
shout and up the path toward them hurried four armed
men led by Hill. At first light two other boats set out
from Brakial, four men in one and two in the other.
They had already discovered the bodies of Seth and
Nico under their covering of foliage and leaving two of
their number to guard the boats they hurried up from the
beach not knowing what they would find but fearing the
worst. They were blowing heavily and drenched in
sweat. After a quick look around, a horror-stricken Hill
talked to Malcolm and agreed to delay returning to
Brakial.

The boat guards were sent for and told to bring the
pigeon cage. Malcolm sat down and wrote a short
message and when the men from the boat eventually
arrived it was pushed into a tiny hollow cane tube, tied
to one of the bird's legs and the carrier sent on its way.
Next a meal was set out and the eight men sat down and
silently ate. A roster of night watches was agreed upon,

although it was thought unlikely the Bitchfolk would return that day. Afterward Kester selected the place for the grave to be dug. Starting that evening and digging in relays a rectangular grave large enough for seven bodies was complete by the middle of the next morning. Seth would be taken back to Brakial for burial. The bodies were carried out and laid in the soil and brief prayers said and Kester took one more look at the remains of his family before squares of fabric were placed over their faces and all those present including Kester picked up tools and started shoveling the soil back in. Crosses were made by two of the men, each with a name rudely marked out with a pointed knife and the dates of their births and the date of the terrible day they died. A clean-up of the house was started. Bloodstains were swabbed away and broken items taken outside. The one broken window was boarded up and the main door hinges repaired so that the house could be left secure from the wind and animals.

While looking for a place to dig the grave they came upon another dead Zoel lying in some long grass – its head almost severed. Kester said he couldn't remember doing it – it must have been one of the boys. The other Bitchfolk body – the one killed by Malcolm was dragged to join this corpse and both were then rolled into a scrub filled gully. The two surviving working dogs were put on leashes so that they could be taken to Brakial. Kester said there were two other working dogs including one with three pups. The

305

mother with the pups was gone. The other dog lay
hacked to death where it was tethered.

Gates were now wedged open to allow Kester's
cattle easy access to grass and water, the chicken pen
walls taken down and Kester stroked the two cats before
the seven men and two dogs started on their way to the
river and the boats. A draught, the name the residents
of Brakial gave to the steady prevailing wind that
drained cool air from the upper reaches of Lamentasia
and Sessilia was now blowing so the men were spared
the arduous task of paddling and the three boats arrived
back at the Landing not long after dark. The Landing
was a hive of activity with people holding lanterns
milling around. The message sent by Malcolm the
previous evening resulted in warnings to the other four
upstream hamlets to evacuate and boats carrying these
people together with their hastily packed belongings
including kittens and puppies, were also arriving at the
same time, so that there was scarcely room to tie up and
many people were waiting to help and offer places to
stay for the evacuees.

## 5.

In Brakial the effect of the massacre was shattering.
Over the next few days small knots and groups of
people would gather and talk solemnly with much head

shaking. The Church was packed for Seth's funeral and the memorial Eucharist for Kester's family was held at the same time. The only people absent were those on watch. Felix organized a meeting the day after Malcolm's return. The meeting was to decide on plans for Brakial's defense in the event of an attack since it was now believed that the Bitchfolk would not be content with attacking only Kester's place. Felix asked Malcolm and Kester to give an account of events, and when it was written up a summary was made and sent off with a rider to Dulce. A much smaller version was written in four parts and carried by pigeon post which would arrive three days before the rider.

Kester moved in with Malcolm but it was a full week before he felt able to sit down and talk. Three days before the massacre, his youngest son walked to the cove to go fishing and there at one end of the little beach was a mark in the sand of a dugout bow and a partly brushed out footprint. The boy came straight back and told his father and Kester returned immediately to see what the boy had found. What Kester saw worried him. Whoever tried to remove the footprint had taken care to step from the sand to a rib of rock that led straight to the ridge carrying the path. Kester carried out a close inspection and found scuffed areas of leaf mould on the path and further along the ridge was a muddy patch that acted like a visitor's book for anybody passing and right on its edge he found another sandaled print.  It was not the first time he was aware of uninvited visitors snooping around but in the past he blamed curious Lams.  It happened on average once a year.  The worry this time was the lack of signs and the obvious care taken by the intruders to disguise their presence.  This and the rumours of Bitchfolk aggression coming from Brakial via the Lams made him feel uneasy.  Any time Lams came over to snoop, they never bothered about secrecy and left an abundance of footprint sign.

Kester told the others and for the next few days he decided to work close to the house and the boys and he got out bows and full quivers and placed them handy to the doorways, and Mali and the girls were told to go no further than the chicken house until Kester was satisfied things were back to normal.  Mali laughed at him and reminded him of the previous rumours which came to nothing and that this would turn out the same way.

On the morning of the attack Kester was inside when the tied up dogs started barking madly and going to the door and looking up the ridge he saw the two house cows out of their paddock and the gate open. Calling to Nico to help, they went to round up the cows, aided by the dog Jake.  The cows were put back and the gate hooked closed and they were walking back to the house when Jake stopped and stood still and began growling and the hair on his back rose like a comb as he stood looking into the scrub.  Sensing danger Kester and

Nico started running only to be confronted with two Zoels in full paint stripes and with their bows armed and aimed directly at them. Kester said he yelled a warning but then could remember little else. He was sure he was struck from behind and then drugged. They obviously dealt with Nico in the same way. And then the main attack must have hit the house with Mali and the others quickly being killed.

## 6.

I have written practically nothing since Spilah the Zoel talked with me at the Trading Day and that seems like months ago, but I feel the need to start writing again.

Ever since the killings I am frightened of going outside and I hate it when Titus and Leo are out of my sight. Each time the wind rustles the leaves of a bush I jump – expecting a Zoel to step clear of cover and kill me or my boys. And at night vivid dreams come to me, images moving across the inside of closed eyelids. Images of myself and others. Dense thickets of dark leaved branches shaking, arms pushing them aside, arms of Ilgud, struggling to get through, to stab, to strangle. Ilgud's voice piercing the darkness, shrieking threats and curses. I hear again the agonised screams of Arloht when she was being tortured and I dreamed I was cheering. I dreamed I was once more in the hot embrace of Ilgud as she pleasured me and then suddenly, I was in that bottomless break in the ice of the

Azmata, trying to jump across, frozen with fear, unable to move. I dreamed of Titus and Leo lying still; face down with arrow shafts sticking from them. I saw myself at the point of death, unable to breathe, watching my own blood draining from me, waking drenched in sweat and screaming, and Malcolm comforting me. These dreams torment me night after night even though it is six weeks since the massacre.

*

I know that what happened at Kesters was Ilgud's revenge for discovering I am alive and living with children among the Deeves. The killings were merely a trial run. Things won't stop there. I know Ilgud. I know in my heart she wants me dead. She wants all those who helped me dead. So do I go and tell Dibius that if I return to Latcho the Bitchfolk threat will die? But it won't. They will want Malcolm dead, and Titus. Especially Titus. And Leo.

*

I have been to see Mentor Dibius. Poor Dibius. He talked between long pauses while he gathered his thoughts, and I wanted to leave but didn't think it right that I should. He told me any thoughts of going back to Latcho as an exchange to keep Ilgud from attacking were ridiculous. He then got off the subject and I was made to sit and listen while he said much of the usual stuff such as, "Paradise is closed to all who cannot forgive – who cannot forgive everyone for everything." Then he said what he always says to end any talk, that he was busy and had much to do.

*

Malcolm, as a former member of Caveo was asked to attend a meeting called by Felix. The meeting agreed that an attack on Brakial was certain and we must prepare for it. The attack would most likely come from upriver and since it would be impossible to defend the whole town it was decided that each evening, the two rows of houses on the up river end of Brakial will be abandoned at sunset each day and their occupants made to sleep over at the church lodge, and men with dogs and lanterns will take it in turn to keep watch over the empty houses until sunrise when the people will be allowed to return. It has also been decided to make an ultra secure area centred on the Church and lodge and taking in two thirds of the town furthest away from where the last lane of houses ended at the upriver end. The houses facing the Comb, the Deemah and the downriver facing houses will also be part of this continuous defensive cordon. The Lodge is to be stocked with supplies of food, water and weapons. Already a makeshift platform is being built on the Church roof so that a daylight watch can be kept on the surrounding open ground and men with axes have been given the job of cutting and dragging away all scrub cover within a long bow-shot of any house. All livestock running loose; cows, pigs, goats and chickens, anything that could be useful to attacking Bitchfolk, is to be rounded up and enclosed in a special area near the Church, and if that is not possible animals are to be slaughtered and kept for food. Those in the watchtower will be keen eyed teenagers supervised by an older man. They will have a variety of hand bells and gongs to strike and of course they must be able to whistle through their teeth. The main problem is to persuade the people that this plan is necessary and that it will work. There are already those in the upriver houses who disagree and they have said they won't move even if the Bitchfolk do attack and why should it be assumed that an attack will necessarily hit the upriver houses first.

Others have been assigned to a night-watch of the ground one hundred yards out from the upriver end of the town. Those rostered for this task are to take their places after dark to prevent their presence being noted by Bitchfolk spies. A message from Dulce tells of a group of volunteers ready to set out immediately if Brakial is attacked. A dusk to dawn curfew has been imposed. Felix posted a warning that curfew breakers ran the risk of being skewered by an arrow from their own people. Malcolm and the full time members of Caveo are already on short patrols across the Deemah to see if the closest Lam encampments can provide early warning of Bitchfolk on the move. I told Malcolm that the Bitchfolk would kill any Lams they came across and so a warning from that source could not be relied upon.

I must stop writing. Malcolm and the boys have spent the last three days across the Deemah checking for any sign of Bitchfolk movements. I told Malcolm they were wasting their time but he said Felix is insistent. Now one of Ailsa's twin boys has just run in to say there are men and horses waiting on the other side of the river and the barge is on its way to them, so I'm sure my men will be here soon and hungry and ready to eat and I must have a meal on the table when they arrive. There are many gulls outside flying around and calling. I can't think why. There must be several hundred circling above the river and screaming. Usually at this time they are on their upriver roosting place. They roost on a sand bank, just upriver from where the water supply creek joins the Deemah, and that's another thing – the water – I've done a lot of washing today and now I've noticed that the butt is nearly empty and nothing is coming through the pipe to refill it. Usually by now it starts to flow through but for some queer reason it's not. I'm sure Malcolm will know the answer.

*

## 7.

The table setting was never used, the evening meal not eaten. No sooner did Rahnuk lay aside her writing than the church watch tower bell began ringing wildly and she gathered up her cloak and the special basket of emergency provisions and headed straight for the assembly point outside the Church. Out in the lanes it was confusion. People running everywhere. Men and boys clutching bows, spears and lanterns ran to take up positions in the perimeter houses and going the other way against the flow, mothers and children and old people.

The evacuation of the front two rows of houses went well, their occupants who formerly declared they would not vacate now joined the exodus. The word got around that something was wrong with the water supply including a rumour that members of three families closest to the upper flume, had suddenly collapsed and died. A short time later that rumour was strenuously denied – Felix did not want panic to spread. But Bitchfolk were immediately suspected of having sabotaged the water supply, and even though the story of poisoned water was rubbished, warnings were yelled that nobody was to drink from their water butts.

Because of darkness coming on Felix considered it too risky to send anyone to inspect the water intake.

For the people of Brakial it was a tense night and apart from some very young children, few slept well. Profound relief greeted the rising sun next morning. And the fervour of prayer was more intense than any day since the massacre. With the sun now up and no attack having occurred, a party of six armed men dropped into the gully to inspect the intake. One man stayed on the ridge-line in sight of the watchtower while he kept an eye on the others as they moved cautiously toward the dam. What they discovered was what they expected to find. A simple collapse of the stone cobbles comprising the coffer-dam, which backed up a small pond enabling the water to enter the wood flume. Water intake problems were unusual but not unheard of although they were invariably linked to violent rainstorms, which in some years might never occur. The dam was routinely rebuilt once each year. The information on the damage was shouted to the man on the ridge and he in turn using arm signals conveyed to those waiting that nothing seemed untoward. However to be on the safe side the man on the ridge and the five in the gully walked down abreast to check for signs of Bitchfolk activity. At the bottom the gully flattened out with no trees and scrub, just grass and some rocks and when the six men reached this point they relaxed, shouldered their bows and sauntered back to the town boundary.

Felix and the permanent Caveo men together with Malcolm and some of the other Elders waited at the line of the first houses to receive the report. They were puzzled as to why the dam should collapse in good weather. Malcolm was all for keeping the alert in place to give more time for a thorough investigation but finally agreed with Felix to allow people back into the upriver houses. The bell was tolled and the people began gathering up their children and possessions and casually wandering home talking and laughing. Titus was among them, helping the family of a widow named Paula to return home.

**8.**

At first nobody noticed the Bitchfolk irrupt from the mouth of the water supply creek. They were already halfway across the open ground before the lookout boys reached their position atop the church and even then did not realise that the running people they saw were armed Zoels. Roklah spotted the danger as soon as he stepped off the ladder but by the time he grabbed the bell rope and sounded the wild alarm jangle, the first Bitchfolk, hideous in their body and face paint, were already pouring down the second lane and attacking people in their houses. Brakial was caught relaxed and completely

316

off guard, eating breakfast and talking. Thirty four houses were captured as well as over half the number of people who usually lived in them, the only ones to escape being those in the top ten dwellings who spotted the approaching Zoels and screaming and dropping everything, had fled to the secure part of the town. The Bitchfolk controlled nearly one third of Brakial – but this was in accord with the town's defense strategy. The Riparian defenders moved immediately to occupy the houses designated as the defensive line. Only the twelve yard width of the lane separated them from the Bitchfolk hidden in the captured houses. Apart from a few chickens clucking and scratching in the dust at one end of the lane there was no sound except from the brief clatter of wings in the still air as six pigeons carrying identical news of the attack were released from near the lodge.

About mid morning came a horrifying act of brutality. Before the attack and as everyone was returning to their own homes, old Ernest left the town to search for his cow, which he was prevented from finding the previous evening. Ernest was deaf and from the watchtower he was observed leaving the edge of the pine forest at the foot of the Comb leading his cow on a rope with her calf running free alongside and headed toward the back of the Bitchfolk lines. There was no possibility of warning him and those in the tower watched helplessly as two Kraaths ran out and speared the old man. They then tried to grab the cow's rope but

317

the ornery animal wanted no part in their plans and tried to run away. One Kraath grabbed the rope and tried to hang on but the cow turned and butted him into the ground. Another Kraath ran out to help and the cow was speared and its calf easily captured and dragged back down to the Sessilite houses. Other Kraaths came out to help butcher the dead cow and carry the meat back. The body of Ernest was left where it lay.

About noon mothers and children began arriving from the Bitchfolk lines but within a short time began to show symptoms of poisoning. They arrived apparently healthy but unable to talk and not long afterward their throats began swelling and closing over preventing breathing and their eyes bulged and limbs began convulsing and by mid afternoon all were dead. The ruthless Bitchfolk disposed of all necessity to guard captives considered not useful, by poisoning and releasing the remainder.

Late afternoon saw the arrival of the monthly pigeon exchange from Dulce. As the horse drawn jogging cart with its cargo of thirty or so wicker cages emerged from the trees that marked the start of the trail to Dulce, the Bitchfolk were waiting and attacked it. The two unarmed drivers were killed instantly. The watchers on the Church roof saw the whole thing. The two horses were led away and the supplies on the cart plundered. The pigeons were a puzzle for the Bitchfolk and after pulling the heads off a few and laughing they ripped open all the remaining baskets and seemed to take pleasure in seeing the grateful birds escape and briefly circle overhead before departing for Dulce in a rushing flock.

The uneven split in the town, with the Bitchfolk occupying two rows of dwellings meant that the remainder held by Riparian defenders, were controlled in such a way that the Bitchfolk were prevented from occupying them. Every second house facing the Bitchfolk was guarded by at least two Riparians, a mixture of both men and women armed with bows who entered through rear facing doors and windows. Behind that line was a similar pattern of guarded houses. Those dwellings now vacant being overlooked by the guarded houses. Behind all stood the Church and Lodge and the four closest houses, which provided refuge for the mothers with young children and those folk too old or infirm for fighting. Everyone else numbering some two hundred irregulars and ranging in age from fifteen to their mid sixties was drafted into active defense. The Riparians were getting ready for things to heat up once darkness fell, and lanterns set up on staves were driven into the ground from where when lit they could throw light closest to the front line. Watch dogs were fed and watered and tied in similar strategic places. If the Riparians lost control of their current front line the next fall back position would see the Bitchfolk controlling nearly one fifth of all the dwellings since the layout was such that defense was possible only in lines of houses standing virtually shoulder to shoulder, and the further downriver the retreat might move, the shorter were the lanes which meant that the number of defensible dwellings also diminished. Felix and the Elders and Malcolm considered it vital to hold as much of the town as possible since if they were forced back to the Church, they would be overrun with everything abandoned and the people taking their chances in the open and the Bitchfolk having a field day killing at will and ending up in control of all of the land between the Deemah and the Comb. They could then withdraw in triumph having achieved their ends.

Late in the afternoon a solitary pigeon from Dulce arrived with a message that help would be coming with twenty fighting men starting for Brakial at first light the next day. A short time later Felix called a meeting with a selected group of advisers. They met in the house of Dibius and altogether twenty people crowded into the dwelling's main room and before long those gathered were perspiring freely from the heat. Malcolm was present. There was plenty to report but given the circumstances, everything appeared as secure as possible. Felix asked for an estimate of the numbers of Bitchfolk attackers. Talking to those who witnessed the first surprise rush and the number of houses captured, and the reports of others watching Bitchfolk raiding crops, a figure of between two and four hundred was arrived at. Following the turmoil of the attack and its aftermath the exact whereabouts of various members of families became confused. Leo was at his post in the defense. Titus was last seen helping the widow Paula and her five small children return to their home on the upriver lanes. A list was presented of all those known to be alive and where they currently were. The names of those confirmed dead were also announced as well as those unaccounted for. Malcolm's face turned white when he heard the name of Titus read out as being among those whose whereabouts was not known.

The list of the dead contained fifty-four names, mostly women and small children. For Brakial to have lost nearly one tenth of its population in the first wave attack was sickening but it made for determination among the defenders. Too determined in some cases and Felix found it difficult to restrain those bent on immediate retaliation and vengeance. He pleaded that such anger could result in impulsive acts that would not only further weaken their defenses but also endanger the lives of those presumed to be captive. Malcolm excused himself from the meeting to go to Rahnuk and relay the news about Titus.

Rahnuk met him at the door and one look at his face was enough to confirm her worst fears and she let out an agonizing scream and rushed inside to throw herself on their bed howling and punching the pillow. Malcolm followed her into the sleeping room saying he was not among the known dead. Rahnuk rolled over moaning that she wished he was. The thought that he could be in the hands of the Bitchfolk was too much. Images flooded in: torture and sexual mockery. Again she vented her anger on the pillow, sobbing and biting at it, a crushing pain seized her chest and she rolled over and grabbed Malcolm's shoulders demanding again to know if it was true. Was Titus definitely unaccounted for? Malcolm could only repeat what he already knew and that Titus was last seen helping the widow Paula carry her belongings and smaller children back to her house, which was among those now held by the Bitchfolk. At this additional piece of news Rahnuk again screamed and began to sob uncontrollably. She was horror stricken at the thought that Ilgud whom she was certain was behind the attack might discover his identity and use it for all it was worth to gain the revenge that was all she lived for.

Rahnuk now almost incoherent with grief turned and knelt on the bed, her forehead pressed into the pillow, eyes closed and sobbing. Malcolm was reminded of Kester's outburst at The Caller after the massacre and he scooped Rahnuk into his arms and lay beside her and the sobbing and wailing became muffled by the pillow of his strong shoulder until finally she laid still, her eyes fixed open as she breathed in short gasps. Outside the sun shone, the leaves of the poplars trembled in a light breeze and around the feet of the trees chickens raked the dust with their claws, pecked for food and contentedly clucked.

## 9.

As the sun dropped toward the crest of The Comb, an outsider might have wondered at the almost complete lack of activity among the inhabitants of Brakial; but as the shadows lengthened even further the defenders braced themselves knowing full well that after dark the Bitchfolk would try to strengthen their hold by capturing one or more additional rows of houses. From the church roof the lookout could see Zoels guarding the river both upriver and downstream of the town.

Fire was high on the list of Bitchfolk weapons to subdue Brakial but the usual prevailing downriver wind known as The Draft slowed and then stopped and a contrary upriver wind from the south now blew into the faces of the Bitchfolk, and their few attempts to start fires with flame arrows failed as they were caught by the wind and carried back behind the attacker's lines.

Before darkness closed in, lanterns were lit and fixed on poles extended from the defended houses and dogs were tethered outside some unoccupied dwellings. In the defended houses, wood battens were fixed over windows leaving slits through which both to observe and shoot arrows. The unguarded houses were still in the process of having their windows and doors boarded up from the inside. From the house assigned to them to guard, Magnus, Hill and Kester took it in turn to keep watch through the window slit. Everything seemed unnaturally quiet – there was no sign of life from either side of the lane except for two half grown kittens that for a short time carried on a game of ambushing each other and then tumbling together in a ball of biting and raking until the smaller animal broke free and pursued by the other, scampered off around the corner of a house on the Bitchfolk side.

Soon after dark the upstream wind tailed off enabling the Bitchfolk to flight flame arrows into the defended area. Many small fires started and the defenders were stretched in trying to extinguish them, and one of the few houses with a thatched roof caught fire and burned to nothing because Felix refused to allow drinking water to be used for fire fighting. And with the darkness came abusive and obscene taunts and chanting from the Bitchfolk and the known names of some captives were yelled out as well as what was being done to them and what was in store for the defenders. They were also taunted with the news that the road through to where the rest of the Deeves lived was guarded. The taunts then stopped to be replaced by a hideous moaning of a male captive being tortured. The moaning was punctuated by shrieks and would rise to a

crescendo and then briefly stop only to begin again with
a different voice, a different victim's cries of pain
splitting the night. The horrific chorus originated from
a house directly across the lane from where Magnus,
Hill and Kester waited on guard duty. In spite of
warnings being given that these tactics would be used
against them, Kester, still deeply affected by the
massacre of his family and unable to any longer bear the
agonized cries coming from across the lane, suddenly
grabbed his short sword and slid back the door bar.
Magnus tried to stop him and received a punch in the
mouth that sent him reeling and then the door was
opened and Kester vanished in the dark.

Magnus started to yell Kester's name then realized
the danger he was putting him in. The next thing a
commotion broke out: barking dogs, running feet, yells,
screams, thuds and then silence. A tense time followed
before Magnus and Hill heard what sounded like Kester
groaning. Hill unsheathed his sword. Immediately,
another outburst of shrill cries and running feet sounded
followed by another period of silence, and then a thud
against the door and another and the sound of some
heavy object collapsing on the ground. Hill waited
telling himself not to do anything foolish. He could
hear heavy breathing and gurgling. He knew it was
vital that no defended house be captured that might lead
to a Bitchfolk breakthrough. The sounds of torture from
across the lane stopped but the heavy breathing and
muffled groans continued from just outside mingled

with scrabbling sounds on an outside wall. Magnus peered through the window slit, aided by the dim light from a lantern. He could see nothing. He touched Hill on the shoulder and whispered he was going to take a look. With one swift movement Hill unbolted the door and swung it open and Magnus slipped out into the darkened lane and flattened himself against the wall of the house. He edged along to where the house front ended where it joined the side wall. He thought he could see what appeared to be a body lying on the ground. A sound made him stiffen and he flattened even further against the wall. He felt a light touch on the side of his neck; something was caressing or stroking him. He stood rigid with fear waiting for the knife to slash and his lifeblood to gush out. The caress came again stronger, harder, and more urgent with a small point of cold wetness and almost collapsing with relief, he reached up and lifted the kitten off the window ledge and carefully dropped it on the ground and immediately it bounded off into the darkness.

Magnus could still hear a slight gurgling sound. He crouched down and crept to where the body lay and grabbing it by the shoulders dragged it back to the door and grunted for Hill to open up. The door swung open and Magnus almost fell through the opening dragging Kester with him except that Hill attempted to force the door shut again with Kester's legs still outside. Magnus cursed under his breath and grabbed his old friend under the arms and hauled him fully inside before dropping him and Hill slammed the door and slid the bolt across. Hill lit a candle and held it close to Kester's face but one glance was enough. Their friend was already dead.

It was a long night for the non-combatants. Conditions in the Church and Lodge were crowded with nearly three hundred elderly, mothers and small children trying to rest. Sleep was impossible with continually crying babies and toddlers and as well the nearby enclosed livestock adding to the racket. The curtained off latrine area was at one end of the lodge and the vile stench of sewage and slops pervaded the building. A few lanterns provided just enough light to stop those attempting to rest or sleep from being stepped on by those going to relieve themselves. Some of the young mothers and elderly refused to use the inside latrine and insisted on stepping outside to squat.

Before first light the roosters of Brakial mixed their challenges with the tuneful repeat chords of thrushes and Magnus strained to peer through the window slit toward the furthest end of the lane. It seemed an age before the light was sufficient to make out what looked like three bodies sprawled on the ground at the end of the lane. One was further away than the other. The closer body was definitely Bitchfolk; beside it laid the naked body of a young Riparian woman. The furthest body he could not identify. A very poor exchange – one strong Riparian defender dead – a good friend – and only one of the Bitchfolk – possibly two. Later as the sun got up Magnus could see where a streak of blood showed the path crawled by Kester on his way back to the house. Sometime after that he noticed a little flock of small birds feeding from the now dried blood trail, and flies swarmed around the three corpses.

Two messengers made the rounds of the Riparian defenses to check on everybody and later food and water was passed to the front liners through back windows and doors and those not on duty were permitted to stretch their legs and relax in the sun or to join their wives and children at the Lodge where a simple meal was in the process of being served. The score after the first night was two dead defenders and one definite dead on the attacking side and one house gutted by fire. Shortly after breakfast Felix imposed severe restrictions on movement when a young mother was caught and killed by a concealed booby trapped arrow set during the night and a careful search revealed a further fifteen such nasty devices each armed with poisonous tips and carefully positioned and hidden to kill and maim the unwary. They ranged from arrows and spring-loaded darts to foot spikes. After the killing of Kester and the young mother, Felix sent a message that on no account were any defenders to leave their positions and engage in close quarter combat. The risk of being stabbed or pricked by the poison tipped Bitchfolk short lances was too great. Felix met with his advisers at noon and afterward issued another edict. To strengthen the perimeter and prevent Sessilite incursions at night he ordered a withdrawal to take place after dark of the next lane leaving the Bitchfolk with another eighteen houses. The withdrawal was carefully managed with only a smaller number of lanterns being set and the newly abandoned houses made to look as if they were still being defended.

## 10.

Mid afternoon Felix was alarmed to learn that three pigeons were perched on the roof of a house at the end of a row behind the Bitchfolk lines. The Bitchfolk appeared not to notice the birds or placed no significance on their presence but they must have been puzzled at the salvoes of small stones rattling down on the roof where the birds rested. Felix enlisted the aid of two young boys known for their ability to throw with accuracy. As the first stones rattled down the birds took flight and performed two circuits of Brakial before once more settling on the same roof. Again the stone throwers let fly and again the birds took flight making another two circuits before alighting this time on a house three away from their first resting place but still behind the enemy line. The pebbles rained down yet again and this time the tired birds flapped the eighty yards to the Brakial loft and entered where they were caught and their messages removed and read. The news was encouraging. Help was on its way; the first group, small mobile and fast moving had already left Dulce and behind them and leaving a half day later was a much larger force, well armed and bringing supplies but of necessity also slower moving. The brief message – the same on all three birds – concluded with the exhortation to remain calm and above all to hold their ground and that the people in Dulce were praying as never before.

From the Tower on the Church roof the watchers were able to monitor Sessilite activity to bring in food and water to their positions. By nightfall the cordon around the secure area was strengthened with the lesser number of dwellings being defended freeing extra men to guard the remaining houses and as well more help was recruited from among the non-combatants.

As on that first night the Bitchfolk began with their chanting and taunting and no matter how hard the defenders tried to block their ears nothing could shut out the blood curdling baiting and the screams of the tortured. The Riparian withdrawal caught the Bitchfolk by surprise and it was well after sunset that it was discovered. At first they acted with caution but then emboldened by the Riparian retreat they attempted to find the new defensive line. About midnight, a group of Bitchfolk attempted to slip through the cordon. The Riparians were ready and allowed the first of them to silently pad their way in before flaring carefully placed piles of oil soaked hay that lit the scene and six Zoels were cut down by a flock of Riparian arrows. This setback for the Bitchfolk settled things down somewhat and they made no further attempts to infiltrate that night, but the taunting and screaming and the threats reached a new high.

The next day the weather again dawned clear and warm and the southerly wind returned causing the Bitchfolk to abandon for the time being the use of flame arrows. From time to time however, screams could be heard coming from the Bitchfolk lines. The Watchers on the church roof reported the Bitchfolk raiding Riparian crops and gardens and catching and killing the last few chickens and pigs still running loose.

## 11.

The morning of the third day dawned and the first Riparian reinforcements arrived. Twenty armed men tired but still strong enough to force the siege with a surprise rush. Their arrival boosted the flagging spirits of the defenders and ensured the Bitchfolk noose could not tighten further. Food and water supplies were still a worry for the defenders but the word went around that not far behind the new arrivals was a force of two hundred mounted and armed men from Dulce complete with food rations.

The third evening of the siege commenced again with the same round of taunting and chanting mingled with the cries of captives being tortured. The wind now back to the north encouraged the Bitchfolk to again try setting fires among the defended houses. Salvo after salvo of flame arrows rained down and fires started in nearly a dozen dwellings and only the heroism of a large number of defenders, who were forced to leave cover, resulted in the fires being contained and eventually extinguished. In the confusion and smoke and darkness a group of Zoels made it beyond the cordon loosing their deadly poisoned arrows and four Riparians were killed. The downstream wind died soon after and the night settled down to isolated outbursts of chanting until dawn.

Mid morning the next day the tables were turned when the major relieving force from Dulce arrived. Together with the by now battle hardened fighting men of Brakial, the Bitchfolk were slightly outnumbered, and seeing the audacious manner in which the reinforced defenders now acted, they promptly withdrew into the original two lines of houses captured that first morning. Armed Riparians immediately moved into position behind the Bitchfolk lines to prevent any replenishment of food and water. Munnah who led the force from Dulce now held a conference with Felix and his advisers and a strategy was worked out to clear the Zoels out of Brakial and if possible foil their return to Latcho. It was agreed that the attackers must be destroyed – but not at the risk of severe casualties on the Riparian side. Looking at the scene Munnah said that they could make a start at one end of the lane and evict them house by house and cut them down in the open as they fled. The fate of the captives would lie in how quickly the operation proceeded.

A start was made early the next morning but the first attempt failed, the Riparian attackers losing four men in the assault. A halt was called and the strategy rethought. Wood shutters were nailed together to use as shields and to block windows while doors were broken in and burning hay forked inside. The defending Zoels were smoked out and killed as they emerged. By noon the technique was perfected with a team operating from each end of the lane closest to the defensive cordon and working toward the middle before moving on the lane behind. The Bitchfolk seeing the threat staged a planned withdrawal and the remaining Zoels and Kraaths assembled behind their occupied houses into orderly regimented blocks each of about fifty with shields and bows armed. The suddenness of their appearance surprised and alarmed Munnah as with captives in the middle the Bitchfolk forced their way beyond the houses and into open ground and while shadowed at a respectful distance the Bitchfolk and their hostages streamed into the reservoir gully and disappeared into the scrub. With close to four hundred Zoels and Kraaths and an unknown number of captives bottled up and hiding in the scrub-choked reservoir gully, Felix and Munnah faced the problem of trying to rescue the captives and destroy the Bitchfolk. Acting on an order from Munnah, the men from Dulce trotted into position and lined the two main ridges bounding the gully but being wary of approaching too close, they stood back somewhat and with arrows fitted they kept guard over the innocent looking greenery while waiting on Munnah to decide the next move.

Those not in the fight were back in the town helping search for missing loved ones. Rahnuk and Malcolm were among them, looking for Titus. While searching they heard their names being called and a runner carried a message telling them to immediately come to the reservoir creek. They headed off at once with Malcolm supporting Rahnuk's arm. In the distance stood a small group of men. As they got closer they could see Munnah standing in the middle. There seemed to be an argument going on with much arm waving, but it stopped when Rahnuk and Malcolm arrived and Munnah turned and held up his arm to signal them to go no further. In front and standing on the near bank of the stream where it issued from the gully, stood six figures. One was Titus. He looked dazed and his head wobbled as if he was unaware of his surroundings. Two Zoels, one each side of him appeared to be holding him upright to stop him falling over. In their free hands they held short throwing spears. Rahnuk recognized Ilgud among the group. Two other Zoels knelt menacingly with aimed bows at full stretch. Rahnuk let out a little cry and tried to pull loose from Malcolm but he continued to hold onto her arm. Munnah said the Bitchfolk wanted to talk with Rahnuk, to bargain something but that they must not move any closer or they would be within arrow range. Rahnuk looked and saw Ilgud's face crease in a grin as she looked across and began calling out. Through the noise from the stream, Rahnuk strained to listen.

"Rahnuk, Rahnuk; my Freyarch of old. All these years. So many years and we meet again. And we have here one of your man children. Is that right? They tell me he's known as Titus. A fine strong looking young man. In the prime of life to. He would be very useful to us back in Latcho. Very useful. We could use him. A line of many fine Zoels could come from him. Come over and join us. You come here Rahnuk. Over to us sweet Rahnuk. It would be like old times. Don't you remember? When we were pledged to each other? Remember what it was like? The pleasure we brought each other? Why, that must be, twenty years ago. Twenty years gone by Rahnuk! But we could take up again, where we were then. Come Rahnuk, come. Come to be with Titus. Your treasured Titus. What do you say Rahnuk? You come here and we say no harm will come to you or little Titus. And we must be allowed safe passage back to Latcho."

Rahnuk was crying now and shaking her head. She heard Malcolm say.

"No no, you must not. It's a trap. They're lying."

Another voice cut in. She recognized Leo. How did he get there?

"No mother, stay. I'll go across and get Titus, you stay. You stay. They won't harm him."

Munnah turned and growled.

"Don't be fools. Stay where you are. That lot isn't going anywhere."

Rahnuk again looked across the open space toward Titus. His head still lolled about. One of the Zoels grabbed him by the hair and steadied him and again Ilgud beckoned and called.

"Rahnuk, come. Come quickly. It's Ilgud. Come over here and be with little Titus. Come Rahnuk come. If you come here to help us and keep us safe, Titus will be safe and so will you be."

Munnah turned to one of his men and spoke behind his hand as if afraid the Bitchfolk might hear him.

"Do you think there's any chance of taking out those two holding him up? Do you think it's worth a try? Or too risky?"

The other looked and shrugged, looked again, shook his head and murmured. "Too far. Too far away."

Munnah nodded and turning to the others said to stay ready anyway. Any trouble and they were to shoot but to keep arrows unfitted unless he gave the word. Rahnuk seemed hardly aware of what was happening around her. She felt numb. The inside of her head rocked with a rhythmic crashing noise. Each crash seemed to choke her and in between the crashes came words. Munnah talking. Malcolm and Leo talking. Beginnings and ends of words like bits all chopped up. Nothing mattered now except Ilgud holding captive her first-born child. Her Titus. She listened as Ilgud called out again. Ilgud with Titus. Her baby she saved by escaping from Latcho.

Rahnuk's face fractured in a thousand crevices and tears burst from her eyes. Something primal, something beyond her control rose suddenly, tearing loose in her chest like a dam giving way. She gave an almighty heave and pulled free from Malcolm's grasp. He tried to grab her again but she struck out, scratching his face and snarling and he ducked and lost his grip and when he looked up she was gone, running toward Titus. Rahnuk could hear screams behind her. Malcolm and Leo screaming to come back and in front the screams of delight from Ilgud. Rahnuk, holding up the front of her robe ran with all her might, at times half tripping on the rough stone strewn turf, her eyes fixed on the vacant face of Titus. To one side Ilgud gleefully jumped up and down urging her on and from behind a distant male voice bellowing for no one to shoot. Arriving breathless Rahnuk immediately fell on Titus, hugging him and they both collapsed and fell to the ground. Screaming obscenities filled the air. Obscenities screamed at her. She laid on the ground her arms around Titus hugging him as she kissed him. She kissed his lips and eyes and she was certain he smiled, just a trace of a smile. She kept on kissing him and the obscenities kept raining down. Somebody was kicking her violently in the ribs. A rough voice ordered her to stand. She stayed clamped to Titus. Hands tried to drag them apart and now she felt a blow on her back and then another and all at once she coughed and a warm fluid filled her mouth and she coughed again and blood splashed over Titus's face. Everything was blurred and Titus's blood spattered face swung in and out of focus several times before it grew indistinct and disappeared. Rahnuk felt dizzy and faint as though her head was somewhere else. The coughing wouldn't stop and now she was being sucked toward the mouth of a cave in a swirling torrent of hot blood. She grabbed hold of a rock to stop herself but her arms were too weak and the current too strong and she couldn't hang on. She struggled to keep from sinking. From all around came screaming and moaning. Titus was calling her and she reached out. Their hands touched and she pulled him to her. They clung to each other as the cave mouth came rushing to meet them and then once inside, everything became suddenly dark and silent.

When Malcolm and Leo arrived, Ilgud and three of the Zoels had fled into the scrub. Rahnuk and Titus lay together on the rocky ground. Titus was on his back; his eyes wide open and rolled back into his head. Rahnuk lay on top of him half covering him. Both bodies were soaked in blood and a spear leaned at a crazy angle from Rahnuk's back. A short distance away one of the Zoels laid face down dead. Malcolm pulled the spear out of Rahnuk and threw himself on the two bodies crying and hugging them. Leo tried to comfort his father, putting his arms around him and with one hand caressing the bloodied faces of his mother and brother and all the while crying bitterly. Munnah's archers arrived and ordered Malcolm and Leo to go back but getting no response stepped past and took up kneeling positions with arrows fitted. Munnah was standing behind everyone, waving his arms and bellowing orders. More armed men arrived. Someone ran up with a bucket of fire. Oil soaked rags were wrapped around arrow heads and dipped into the flames and the arrows sent arching high and down into the dry scrub of the gully and in no time fires started where they landed and the light breeze became brisk and the flames fed on each other heating up and joining forces, making their own fire storm which engulfed the mouth of the gully before setting off to invade the rest of it: an army of crackling leaping flames with streaming brown smoke and hideous screams swarming into the scrub and up the gully spreading as it went. And on the ridge-line, the grim faced bowmen from Dulce maintained their cordon.

## 12.

There were few survivors from Ilgud's force. Most died in the fierce heat of the fire or suffocated trying to save themselves in the water of the creek, while the rest were cut down by Riparian arrows as they tried to break through the cordon. A small number did escape under the cover of the dense smoke pouring out of the gully head. Twenty- three of the men from Dulce died in the fight, as well as all of the hostages. On the evening of that same day, three pigeons arrived in Dulce carrying the good news that the siege was over.

In the following three days the Riparian dead were gathered up, prayed over and buried with Dibius officiating. The Bitchfolk bodies were tied together in bundles and dragged behind horses to a scrubby flat well away from Brakial where they were piled up and covered with dried brushwood and set alight. In spite of ill feeling, old Dibius creaked his way there and together with a few of the older women prayed over the heaped corpses before the fires were lit. With the dead dealt with, the clean up proper could begin, starting with the reservoir gully which was to be thoroughly searched to make sure nothing poisonous might have been placed in the creek. A goat was used to test the water. It remained healthy. Other groups of men started on repairing damage done to the houses occupied by the Bitchfolk. Several needed to be pulled down the damage and filth was so bad.

Munnah meanwhile was making plans for taking the fight back into Sessilia. In their weakened state he reasoned, the Bitchfolk would be easy meat and now was the time to deal to them, once and for all. Not everyone was in agreement however; especially Dibius and although Munnah ignored him he took the precaution of placing a guard on the pigeon house to prevent any complaints about his intentions reaching the Keyholder in Dulce. He was dead against any chance of the matter being put to a vote in Brakial. He wanted no dissent and was determined to provide no stage for it. He counted on his current popularity in routing the Bitchfolk for support to invade Sessilia and began working quickly and quietly behind the scenes, talking to key men both among his force and those who lived in Brakial, getting them on side and around to his way of thinking. Supplies and horses were his main concern but by the end of the second day, things were looking up and he was assured of having a force of about two hundred and fifty.

In spite of his grief, Malcolm got swept up in the prevailing mood of enthusiasm and revenge and agreed to act as a guide.  He told Munnah that once the raid commenced a good number of Lams would also be eager to join in and pay back some old hurts.  Leo also wanted to go but Malcolm taking into account the boy's sensitive nature and lack of weapon skills, barred him from taking part. By the end of the fourth day everything was coming together.  There were enough horses, men, arms and supplies to do what Munnah wanted.  Most of the food was to be provided by members of the force but he expected to be able to trade some from the Lams and plunder anything else he might need from the Bitchfolk.

Early on the fourth day the force began assembling at the landing, ready to cross the Deemah. The horses were to be swum across riderless and mustered on the other side.  All equipment, men and saddles would be carried on the barge, which would have to make numerous trips.  Munnah knew it was going to take most of the day and decided that the force would camp that night on the other bank and then head off in a body the next morning as soon as it was light.  Dibius was determined that this was not going to happen, at least not without him expressing his total opposition.  Dibius sought the help of a twelve year old boy and arranged to be rowed across the Deemah early the next morning to make his final appeal to Munnah.  A short distance upriver from Munnah's camp site the trail narrowed and led down to the nearest easy ford across a gorgy creek. The other bank of the creek opened to a small clearing

342

in some trees and it was in the middle of this that Dibius chose to wait. He stood shivering in his cloak, coughing and rubbing his watery eyes, the boy who rowed him across the river standing alongside him. From the other side of the creek beyond the trees floated the sounds of barking dogs and men's voices calling to each other as they packed bedrolls and saddled horses before setting off. Dibius, impatient, muttered and cursed to himself, but he didn't have long to wait. As soon as it became light enough to see, things happened. First came the dogs circling and swarming around to sniff him, and Dibius grumpily swiped at them with his staff. Then straight afterward came the clatter of horse hooves crossing the rough creek stones and splashing through water and the sound of voices and creaking saddles before Munnah lurched up onto the bank at the head of about a dozen riders. He held up his hand and halted his horse. The front horsemen crowded forward and also stopped and from behind sounded a ragged chorus of voices, grumbling and complaining about the hold up. Dibius staggered forward leaning on his staff. There was a sparkle in his tired old eyes.

Dibius and Munnah looked at each other. Dibius without turning motioned for the boy to go and stand under the trees before starting to speak in slow measured tones.

"So Munnah. I see the blood binge is to happen? You're all dressed for killing. Killing eh? Is that what it's to be?"

"Come on old fool. On with it. On with it and get out of our way."

"I want to tell you about life Munnah. Life is a gift. It's not for you to take. For yourself. You're not owed life. It's not your born right to take life from any man or woman. It's a gift. A gift. Do you hear?"

"I hear and I know what I'm going to do. Finish what you've come to say and stand aside."

"Munnah. Love is also a gift. It must be given, or it is not love. And death. Death is also a gift. It's not for you to decide. It's over to the Caller and his mercy"

"Fool. Old doddery gab-mouthed fool. Shut up. The best chance ever to rid the world of Bitchfolk and you're trying to stop us with drivel. The Caller's mercy. Huh." Munnah spat contemptuously. "Where was the Caller when the Bitchfolk attacked, eh? More than a hundred good Riparian folk we've buried these past few days and where was the Caller in all that? Out of the way old fool."

Munnah spurred his horse to go around Dibius but the elderly Mentor managed to totter in front and dropping his staff he grabbed the horse's bridle in both hands, forcing the animal to stop and looking fiercely up at Munnah he grated out in measured words.

"How dare you pass judgement on the Caller."

The two men remained glaring at each other, Munnah reluctant to kick his horse forward and Dibius grimly hanging onto the bridle with both hands. Dibius broke the silence.

"Malcolm is with you is he not?"

"Somewhere he is. What business is it of yours anyway? He's one of our guides."

Malcolm who was near the front now urged his horse forward.

"B-bah-ah-est if you go back D-ah-da-ibius. Bah-est if we get on with the job in front of us. There's a score to be settled."

"Score! Score to be settled. You've been listening to that idiot." Croaked Dibius pointing at Munnah. "What about the debt you owe? The debt we all owe, eh? Christus was hung on a tree. He died for you Malcolm. He died for every man here. And not just us. For the Bitchfolk as well. Is this what Rahnuk would want? You to join in the senseless killing of her kin, eh Malcolm? Do you think Rahnuk would want that? Would she?"

"Don't listen Malcolm. Three days ago we heard this old fool bang on. Remember what he said – at the burial? Remember? He told us the worst that could ever happen has already happened – long ago – when men killed Christus. Ha! He said it was worse than what happened here? Can you believe that? Can you?"

Munnah and those nearest him looked at each other and laughed.

"Well one thing's for sure, we're about to get even." Munnah, turning on his horse to address the mounted men began bellowing.

"By Christus we'll get even all right. We'll kill our enemies. We'll kill the enemies of Christus. We'll be rid of them. For good." Yells of approval greeted each threat.

"In darkness they walk." Shot back Dibius. "But you, you have the light, you kill in the light."

"Darkness! Light! What's the difference? Innocent people get killed. Now, out of our way old fool. Quick, before you get trampled."

Dibius stood in front, tears streaming down his creased face. He cried out in a loud croaking voice. "A blood binge is no answer. Can never be the answer. Christus lives in each and every one of us. Every one of us. Can't you see?" The only response came from Munnah who kicked his horse forward forcing Dibius to let go the bridle. Creaking saddles and the dull thuds of horse hooves on damp turf sounded as the rest of the company started to move and Malcolm rode around Dibius leaving him standing like a sad grey tree stump trying in vain to catch the eyes of anyone he might know.

Mid morning saw Malcolm peel off from the company and turn for Brakial. Those last words of Dibius haunted him. "Christus lives in each and every one of us. Christus lives. Lives." Yes, those words lived.

Not long after noon Malcolm was back at his house unsaddling a very wet horse. He was chilled and wet to the chest as well. At any time, swimming the Deemah on horseback was a hair-raising experience. Best to have a good reason for doing it. Leo was not home. Malcolm guessed he was out helping with house repairs. From various places came the sound of hammering and the voices of men and women.

Malcolm dropped his weapons and supplies on the floor of the porch and putting the saddle inside to dry out of the hot sun, he rode the horse bare-backed to the stone walled field where he turned it loose before pulling the two poles across to block the entrance. With the bridle draped over his shoulder he slowly walked down to the riverbank and finding a secluded spot took off his wet clothes and hung them over a bush to dry. He lay down and tried to rest but couldn't and ended up just sitting in the sun and thinking, and sometimes he pounded his fist into the ground and cursed. Late afternoon found him still there, wearing his now dry clothes and sitting in a shaded spot, hands clasped around his knees and forehead resting on them and staring at the ground between his legs. Every now and then he looked up and gazed out over the Deemah as if waiting some answer from it, but each time the river's smooth brooding skin looked the same. The water still slid away, escaping in oily swirls that continually vanished and reformed. Over the bare muddy shore a cloud of gnats danced slowly in the calm air. Sun-silvered specks in counterpoint; rising and falling, meeting and greeting, rising and falling, mating and dying, falling, falling.

The sun continued to glare down but at last Malcolm shook his head and took in a deep shuddering breath. Somewhere, in the distance, the ratchet song of a solitary cicada started. Malcolm heaved himself off the ground, picked up the bridle and turning away from the river, began plodding back up to his house. Once there, he paused outside, staring at the entrance and trying to see through eyes blurred with hot tears. Then he stepped inside and waited near the table, his gaze now fixed on the rough wood cross above the fireplace; the cross with its white bloodless clay Christ and the gaping spear wound in its side – the same wound that Malcolm's hands made all those years ago – the same wound that since the beginning of time the swelling sum of human pride had never ceased to inflict.

## FINIS.

## CHARACTER LIST

Ailsa – Wife of Seth.
Arloht – Rahnuk's helper after her escape
Dibius – Mentor of Brakial
Edgar – Head of Caveo
Ernest – elderly deaf man of Brakial.
Felix – Caveo leader replacement for Edgar.
Gorah – Lamentasite leader.
Igen – Lamentasite leader

Ilgud – Freyarch of Rahnuk and later Theon of Sessilia
Kamya – Young woman in Gorah's encampment.
Kester and Mali – Friends of Rahnuk and Malcolm who dwell upriver from Brakial
Lon – Friend of Malcolm
Leo – Child of Rahnuk and Malcolm
Mado – Mother of Ailsa
Malcolm – Husband of Rahnuk & member of Caveo
Nico - Backward eldest child of Kester & Mali
Nigho – Theon of Sessilia
Orlo – Lamentasite leader.
Pelto – Riparian recorder for Codex
Rahnuk – Escapee from Sessilia
Roklah – Transgendered inhabitant of Brakial
Rolf – Caveo assistant to Malcolm.
Seth – Caveo assistant to Malcolm
Spilah – Sessilite informer
Titus – First born of Rahnuk.
Torok – Lamentasite informant.


## WORD LIST

Azmata – Mountainous region bordering Riparia
Azrah – Sessilite (Bitchfolken) Supreme Deity
Bitchfolken – or Bitchfolk, inhabitants of Latcho.
Brakial – Riparian town on Deemah River.
Caveo – Riparian Defence
Comb – Mountain range behind Brakial
Deemah – River boundary between Riparia and Lamentasia and Sessilia and Lamentasia.

Deeve – Sessilite Name for Outsiders
Dohma – Sessilite Kept Men (entire)
Dulce – Main Town of Riparia
Freyarch – Sessilite Vowed partner
Gust – Riparian nickname for Lamentasite Shaman
Key Holder – Head of the Mentors in Riparia.
Koraght – Bird of ill omen for Sessilites.
Kraath – Sessilite Servant Class male eunuch
Lamentasia – Region inhabited by Lamentasites (Lams)
Latcho – Sessilite name for Sessilia.
Mentor Viat – Riparian Missionary.
Morgrah – Sessilite (Bitchfolken) sexual activity.
Riparia – Region inhabited by Riparians (Riverfolken)
Sessilia (Latcho) – Region inhabited by Sessilites
(Bitchfolken).
Techno – Technological Pre-Terra Vivus Culture.
Terra Defilia – The Defiled Land
Terra Vivus – The Living Land
Theon – Leader of Sessilia
Vau – River boundary between Sessilia and Azmata
Mountains.
Verd – Sessilite Servant Class female
Zoel – Sessilite Warrior Class

## amazon.com

Rahnuk © is available in both Paperback
& Kindle format.

Visit the Rahnuk Facebook page.